To Marry a Succubus

Chapter 1

It was just your average Friday night at Horn Publishing. Sitting off in his cubicle Lee West let out a long sigh as he shuffled the papers around. His eyes felt heavy. It had been a hell of a week, a long grueling one. Lee finally finished looking over the last manuscript. It had been a fine one, a little more erotic than the other ones. He'd have to deal with it during the month. It's about some guy inheriting a brothel and trying to stabilize the place. It was quite an exciting read in the first couple of chapters.

He was the only one in the building while his boss Grace Stone had taken off early today. However, Lee couldn't help but find it strange for her to take a day off. It wasn't like her to take one off, but whatever it was might have been vital since she left everything to her secretary to work on. The last time Lee had recalled, It's been a year since Grace took the day out; that was when Lee and Lucy stayed at her beach house. It had been a good time for the three of him.

Though what was strange was the fact Lucy wasn't here either. She had requested the day off along with Beth. For some reason, Lee wasn't able to figure out why as he continued working. The man chose to ignore it while returning to finishing his work. In some ways, he was thankful as he placed the manuscript over to the side. He is head-turning around, looking about.

I love that woman, but sometimes it's good to have to breathe time, though, on the other hand. His mind was lingering as he reached over to his drawer. He looked down at it, seeing a small black box. A light huff as he reached down there for a minute, pulling it out. His finger fumbled around as he opened it up, looking at what was in there, a small golden band with a diamond ring on top. It glistened gently under the fluorescent light.

It had taken him a while to build up the courage. But he did it. Lee had finally gotten the ring. Though he mumbled to himself,

"Tonight, I'll ask her. I'm sure of it." He grumbled some as he looked around when he finally bit his lips. He looked around, realizing it was getting late. He cracked his neck when he pulled up from his seat and gave his neck a hard pop.

"Well, I'm calling it a night." He flipped the box into the air before catching it and bounding it into the front pocket. He grabbed his bag and whatever he had and headed to clock out.

Lee bounded to his truck, got inside, and placed his seatbelt on. A good minute, as he sat back relaxing.

"I can't believe it's been over a year since Lucy came into my life. It feels like I bought that ring only yesterday and released her. What a hectic year it was, that's for sure."

It indeed had; since releasing her, his life hadn't been the same, though, of course, the constant sex, but Lee had managed to convince her to slow it down to four times a week instead of every day. Give him some time to recover. Since the succubus could go almost all night long getting her fill of. It was something he was thankful for. Even then, when they did have sex, it was beyond words—the passion the two held in the bedroom. There was nothing that could stop them.

Lee smiled, reminiscing on the past, thinking about more events throughout the year. Just them hanging out. It was the small things that mattered; the traffic roaring as he drove down the road, a bit fast, sure. But he honestly wanted to get home all the more. The truck belched in response as he went down the road.

I swear I've got to get this checked out. Lee grumbled under his breath. It was hard to bring stuff like that done. Life always seemed to get in the way of life. In some ways, Lee wondered what was in store for the future. He took a glance looking down at the bulge in his pocket. He was pretty sure he had an idea of what could be stored in the future if this night went to plan.

Soon Lee turned into the Apartment complex. He parked away and began heading to his place. He fumbled over, grabbing his keys. He moved through, found the right key, and slid it into the door. Lee walked on inside.

"Lucy! I'm Home!" He called out, laughing at the joke, shaking his head as he stepped inside. It was dark inside the apartment. It was pretty strange. There was no response as he reached over, turning the light on. At that exact moment, Lee turned the light on. People began jumping out of nowhere, screaming.

"Surprise!" Lee's only response was him jumping out of his skin with the utmost surprise. Lucy appeared behind the couch- Beth and Sharron appeared out of the closet. (That amused Lee, the Lesbian couple bouncing out of the closet.) Even Grace was emerging from the kitchen. Sure, there were other people as they popped from different parts of the house with a smirk.

"Holy- how when?" Lee asked as Lucy came over, kissing

him. Lee returned the public display of affection for a good minute. They could hear the whooping in the background. A slight laugh as they pulled back.

"Yesh, thanks, guys though you honestly didn't have to do this. I forgot it was my birthday today." Lee laughed hard as he rubbed the back of his head. Sharron looked over toward Beth and said.

"You got to be kidding me; okay, everyone! Party cancels; I'm taking the cake home!" She ran to the kitchen though Beth reached over, grabbing Sharron's collar and leaving her in place.

"Oh, fine, I'm staying. But I'm getting the cake." She snarked and gave Lee a thumbs up. A slight laugh as Lee chuckled.

"I swear some things never change." Lee rolled his eyes as they moved inside, shutting the door behind him. Lee looked back towards Lucy for a second, merely asking, "So, where's Dawn? Wasn't she able to come?" a simple question though Lucy shook her head,

"Sadly not; she's busy with other things, hanging with Alice, and learning to control her powers."

-000-

Dawn was looking down from the top of the Brooklyn Bridge. At this point, she looked as though she was about to piss herself,

"No- This is fucking insane!" She wanted to climb down; she felt Alice grab her by the arm with a smirk;

"Relax, it's only a two-hundred and seventy-eight feet drop into rapid waters during the middle of the night; it'll be okay," Alice said as if it was nothing, though Dawn just looked at her stun

4

when she found herself thinking,

I'm going to die; I'm going to die because of this psychotic Succubus that is supposed to train me to seduce men! I should have stayed in the nunnery!

"I said relax, and you've got to learn how to use those wings; they're not just for show. I've been letting you run on training wheels for a while, and now it's time to see what you've got."

"Yeah, but shouldn't we do something that won't result in me ahhhhh!"

Without warning, Dawn felt herself being pushed off the edge as Alice looked down at her for a minute and called out,

"Flap your wing!" while watching her fall.

"Bitch!" Dawn screamed as she fell in the air.

"She'll do fine." The smug look on Alice's face as she clicked a pen she happened to have in her notebook down writing notes for her next book. One ,she called *The nun and the succubus.*

-000-

"I'm sure she'll be fine. Hell, she might come to visit in a few days," Lucy said, and Lee nodded,

"Sounds good. Though again, I worry about her." Soon Grace reached over, handing them each a beer.

"Well, where ever your one friend is, I'm sure she'll want you to be happy, so have a drink, relax, and enjoy your party." She a slight smirk as she patted his back.

"Sure thing Ms.- I mean Grace, Might as well." Lee took a

drink from the bottle and took a quick swig. A light smirk as he began walking into the party, basically forgetting about the ring, at least for now. The music was playing onwards as they got nice and comfortable.

The party would continue for a few hours; Lee was enjoying himself—no funny business. Lucy wasn't using her abilities then; just some beer spread out some of the cake. Lee had a piece of Lucy also. But boy, did Sharron take the cake, Literally, as she nearly took out the cake, Beth had to pull her away from the thing so others could have some. Sharron acted like she hadn't eaten in the last two days when she scarfed it down.

Grace raised a bottle and called out.

"A toast to another year, for Lee, may he have another one, and another one- and another one." Grace's voice was slurring as she was tipsy as she looked towards Lee. He could see a lust in her eyes as like she was ready to strip naked before everyone and ride him like a horse. Though she eventually shuddered at the idea, A hiccup was escaping her lips. She looked at Lee, almost while everyone else raised their glass, joining her.

"To another year of life." The cheering was getting louder as they enjoyed themselves. Such passion- for a short time. They took another drink, and Lucy pounced on Lee, giving him another passionate kiss, with the group cheering for them. It was quite the time, quiet the passion as they held on. Lee couldn't help but skip a beat at this point as he embraced her.

Eventually, The Party guest began heading out late in the evening while Lee smirked. Grace was passed out on the couch, a slew of Beer bottles all around. Beth sneaked over with a sharpie and wrote on her face, figuring to have a bit of fun fucking with her boss, writing on it. *'I love cock!'* And *'I'm a super Bitch!'* A

'Penis' was drawn under her nose like a mustache. With a slight giggle, having a few too many herself, Sharron had practically carried her out over her shoulders while giggling like a drunken madwoman.

"She'll be fine, though hopefully, she doesn't get into one of her frisky moods. That happens when she has tequila." Sharron had told Lee, though, when she said that, Beth slurred out.

"Aahmm, always frisky! Come over here and give me a lisbian kiss!" Beth slapped her lover right on the ass with a string of more giggling, Sharron's face getting redder in response as she looked at Lee.

"We better go; I'm taking another slice. Though now come on you Lisbian." Sneaking over and taking another plate. Sharron pulled Beth over her shoulder while she spoke up with a snort.

"I love my lisbian girl!" Sharron shook her head, amused by the drunk woman, before heading out. Lee was closing the door when he heard what sounded like hurling; Sharron's screaming came right behind him. Lee snorted hard as he knew he wouldn't be cleaning that up and slammed the door behind him.

The living room was a mess, seeing Grace lying on the couch. Lee wasn't sure if he should call her a cab or let her lay on the sofa for the night and get some rest. It wouldn't be the first time she stayed the night.

"yeah, think we went a little overboard?" Lee asked the Succubus; though he found she was gone, Lee just chuckled, rolling his eyes as he picked up a few things, tossing them off into the garbage.

"Lee…" Lucy called out from their bedroom. Lee looked over, seeing the door partially open. He raised his eyebrow for a minute.

"Lee, come back here. I've got a present just for you, baby." Her voice was soft and somewhat seductive. Lee shuddered, smiling as he had an idea as he walked to the bedroom. The bedroom had changed since Lucy had moved in. Adding her flair, sure, some of Lee's stuff got moved to another room. But the property he enjoyed remained. A couple of pictures on the walls, Though the bed was made a little bit bigger from a queen size bed-towards a king, giving them more room. Of course, it was a bit bigger, especially for the room. However, it was a fun time, mostly when there were more than just those two.

Lucy had added pillows to the bed, so many- Lee honestly didn't understand why as they mostly got in the way. Lee looked around, finding that he was all alone. He stood in the room for a good second when he heard Lucy calling from the closet.

"Lee, sit down and close your eyes for me." He sat back, tapping his foot for a minute. Her voice was getting a bit louder, probably wanting to make sure he heard her, and Lee did so, complying with her will.

That was when the door began opening. Music began playing; it was soft-seductive. The beat was moving gently. Lee could almost imagine it was coming from a song from the nineteen-twenties. The kind showgirls would play. A leg appeared as the door swung open slowly. Lucy started walking out.

When she did that, Lee found his jaw dropped, hitting the floor. Lucy was wearing a long red dress that moved down to her knee. In Who Framed Rodger Rabbit, a strapless top reminded Lee of Jessica Rabbit's clothes. Her hair was long, silvery-white, styled up as it moved down her shoulders, her lips ruby red.

"Hmm, do you like your present, Honey Buns?" She

whispered in her hush voice, causing Lee to moan as he was lost in her beauty. Her fingers were caressing his chin. Lucy's fingers were soft to the touch. Sex emulated from her very being as she made her way toward the edge of the bed.

"Yes, I do," Lee muttered, almost hypnotized as Lucy giggled, "Good, cause while you normally care for my desires and urges. Tonight. It's all about you." She gently muttered, kissing his neck. Her hips were swaying back and forth, showing off her glowing hips. Lucy's scent was entirely overwhelming for him.

"Such a tempting Vixen," Lee Mumbled as he reached over, giving her ass a firm smack.

"Oh, wanna have a little Furry action." Lucy winked as she suddenly morphed her face to look more foxlike. As she flashed, Though Lee shook his head,

"No- No, I don't think so Though maybe some other time." He chuckled while Lucy rolled her eyes.

"Fine Spoil-sport." She snorted and snapped her finger, turning back to normal. A tail was wagging for a minute before it retracted back into her body.

"Heh, I know I'm such a horrible person," Lee muttered, his hand reaching over, rubbing his head almost overdramatic. Lucy Laughed in response.

"Hmm, maybe I should give you some birthday spankings." She winked as Lee bit his lips at the thought. He moved his fingers against the soft fabric as Lucy pushed him back and shook her fingers. His fingers wiggled and massaged her fine ass.

"Now relax, birthday boy, 'cause before you get your spankings, I'm gonna give you a bit of a show." She moved to sway her hips as she began to dance slowly. Lee's eyes focused on her. She began raising her dress, revealing a pair of long stockings-Stock white as she raised her foot on the bed, pulling them off slowly. Lee saw flashes of her panties that were as red as rubies, sparkling gently, with a light groan under his breath.

She pulled them off and whipped them off to the other side of the room as Lucy stripped away more clothes. Her fingers were reaching over toward the top. She pulled them down slowly, revealing her luscious breasts large and round, They sagged down slightly Lee couldn't help but enjoy the view.

"Hmm, you've always been such a boob boy." Lucy giggled when she was spinning around. Before stopping, her ass pointed towards him. Giving him an incredible tease as she bent over. Her ass was bouncing as she wiggled it. Her body was shaking. Lucy's clothes were moving down, exposing her back off to Lee.

"Well, what can I say? I've got great taste, but your ass looks delicious from where I'm sitting." Lee teased as Lucy blushed more.

"Hmm, you've always got the right words for me." She began pushing the rest of her dress off. The music seemed to move with her beat. Lucy eventually stood before him, wearing only panties and a garter belt.

"Fuck me," Lee grunted, his pants feeling much tighter as his cock was erected. Lucy was driving him wild, and they hadn't done anything yet.

"Not yet, big boy." She giggled as she moved over, Her fingers pointing toward his pants. A slight glow in her eyes as those jeans began tearing themselves apart. To the point Lee was sitting there naked, His cock throbbing hard.

"Heh, my favorite toy," Lucy moaned as she reached down, her fingers wrapping around that pleasing cock of his as she rolled her thumb around his head in small circles. Lee sighed as he leaned back. Her hands were soft as she began pumping her hand up and down. She a long grunt as Lucy leaned in, her breast pressed against his face as she pushed a nipple into his mouth.

"Please, Lee, suck on my fat titties." Lucy moaned hard. The music was fading behind them, starting another song. It matched Lee's mood as he moved in, his lips wrapped around her nipple, sucking on them rather greedily. His tongue flicked against it as Lucy moaned, gently jerking him faster.

Lucy moaned; she loved how he sucked on her nipples, how his tongue flicked her hard nubs, even how he nipped the tiny bits of pain against her sensitive breast. She felt Lee's hand grabbing her other breast. His fingers sank into her while massaging them, letting out another moan. Her fingers were only going faster as she took long deep breaths.

"Hmm, Lee," she moaned, pushing her breast deeper into his face. Lee closed his eyes, sucking on them harder as he played with the other. Lee's dick was twitching in response to Lucy's actions. His breathing was getting heavy. Lucy pulled back with a sly smile.

"Now, what would you like now?" she growled, clearly looking hungry, as Lee had a smile.

"Hmm, well, I guess you could blow my candle," Lee responded, nudging his head down, indicating what he meant. Lucy didn't need to be told. Her body was sliding down to her knees. She pulled her face close to his cock, her tongue slowly licking it. Lee grunted. The way her tongue swirled around was driving him up the wall.

No matter how often she did that, Lee loved how Lucy sucked his cock. She was the best- and it was clear she knew that. No one could beat her as she wrapped her mouth around him— such a warm feeling as she bobbed her head up and down.

Lee felt his eyes closed. His mind shot away as he let pleasure roll around him, as he took a deep breath. Her head was moving up and down faster as he took deep breaths. "Oh yeah, just like that." He muttered, his hand reaching down, brushing through her hair.

"Like this?" Lucy muffled at least that's what Lee, thought she said it was almost impossible to understand, especially with his cock between her lips. Lee only nodded as he laid back. His mind spins. His heart was pounding as the Succubus was driving him insane. Then, without warning, his balls tightened, and Lee felt the words slipping right out of his mouth.

"Will you Marry me, Lucy!?" He suddenly felt himself about to blow when Lucy suddenly stopped.

"What?" Lee looked down at her for a second, a shocked look on her face. It was then Lee realized what he had said, "Oh, shit- I – I mean!" but before he could find the right words. Lucy suddenly jumped on him, a squeal of excitement as she was practically on top of him.

"Did you ask me to Marry you?" Her eyes on him glowing brightly. Lee tried to find the right words but his mouth was dry as the desert so he could only nod. Lucy looked as though she was about to explode, the excitement running through her as she howled to the moon, screaming out.

"YES, yes! Oh YES!" She seemed as if she had a hundred orgasms all at once. Lee was kind of scared for her but smiled as she kissed him.

The rest of the night was pleasant. Though Lee had passed out, Lucy had gone on after saying yes. Fucking his brains out. Lee wasn't even sure he was going to walk right in the morning with his sore thighs.'

-000-

It was a couple of days since Lee had Purposed and grunted hard. Lee's thighs were bruised beyond belief. His hips darkened from how Lucy had ridden him that night. He could barely get out of bed the day after his birthday. Lucy had to ensure Grace was taken home while he had an ice pack on his crotch. Heck Lee was tempted to ask if he could work from home. Lucy had gone overboard. Though Lee knew this wasn't the first time it happened and would not be the last time.

"I swear it hurts like Hell… But fuck was it worth it." He muttered under his breath. He sat back comfortably for a minute, watching one of his favorite films, Star Wars- Specifically, the Empire strikes back. Lee rested back as he let the ice back numb him. Lee got comfortable as he watched Han Solo, stuff Luke into a tauntaun. That was when a goat walked right past Lee. It walked in front of the tv. It stopped staring at Lee for a minute, just watching him. Lee stared right back for what seemed like a long time.

"Um… How did you get in here?" Lee found himself asking the goat. All the goat did was turned away and make a huffing sound as it walked away from him. Lee couldn't describe his confusion as he looked over his shoulder and called out.

"Lucy! Why is there a goat in the house!" He was met with a moment of silence before footsteps moved in. Lucy suddenly appeared. She called out

"What?"

"Lucy, Why is there a goat in the house? I mean- why?" Lee was confused, not even able to believe the words he was saying as he watched the goat running around the house and just looking utterly bored.

"Oh, Nothing much, Just planning to talk to my parents, especially Dad; I wanna see the look on his face when he knows we're getting married." She smiled in excitement. Lucy's eyes glanced over the ring. At the time, it was probably one of her most precious belongings for the time,

"I mean, we've got a phone. We could call them," Lee muttered as he looked over to the goat, having a slight idea of what would happen.

"Not really; you can't get reception down in Hell. I really wanna tell Daddy about the wedding.." There was a light in her eyes as she imagined telling her parents.

"I also want them to meet you. So wanna join me?" Lucy asked with a smile as she turned around and grabbed the goat by the horn, practically dragging it off. Lee rolled his eyes and mumbled under his breath.

"Some animals were harmed in the making of this wedding…." He paused for a minute as he came to a realization.

"Wait a minute, where did you get the goat from anyway?!" He practically bounced off the couch. Lee ran towards Lucy as she pulled the goat into the bathroom. He stepped in, where he saw the room covered with plastic bags. He looked around as Lucy looked back.

"Heh, Let's say I found it, running around." She looked guilty, But Lee shook his head,

"Fine, but we'll need to discuss your goat Borrowing later."

Lee sighed more.

"Sure, though, after we visit my parents."

"Wait. What?"

"Lee, we have to work on your hearing problem, But I'm about to open a portal and see my parents." She laughed as she lifted the goat without a problem, placing it in the bathtub.

"Well, while you do that, I must get something on." Lee turned around quickly, ran to their room, and took a deep breath, wondering what the Hell he might've been thinking of doing this. Going to Hell, apparently, what could he even wear? Lee figured he'd grab some T-shirts and Jeans. All that could come to mind. He wasn't even sure what would happen next. Lee just figured he could go with the flow. What's the worst that could happen?

I'm about to meet Lucy's Parents, relax Lee- We're just going to Hell! Lee's mind spouted off more. She found the place a complete mess when he returned to the bathroom. Blood dripped off the side of the bathtub. The goat lay there dead. Lucy was looking over for a second as she whipped some of the red liquid off her face.

"Shit, I went a little too far." She looked embarrassed as she dipped her fingers into the goat's blood. Her finger moved over the plastic walls as she began drawing symbols- Symbols Lee couldn't understand. They wrapped around the room as Lucy started to speak in a language not known by Lee.

"G a dooain c Ascha, unlock oi door!"

For all he knew, it was one far since dead. The room shooked, and the symbols began glowing brightly. It seemed they were popping from the wall as they began spinning around in a circle and shining brighter. They began turning around, wrapping around the two as they continued moving. Lee's eyes widened, watching as the restroom began melting around them.

"Hold on." Lucy smiled, offering a hand, and Lee instantly grabbed it. Holding it tighter,

"You know, I think we should change internet providers next time. I hear ATT&T has a Hellish reception." He laughed nervously. Without warning, the light Blew out. They were surrounded by pure darkness.

CHAPTER 2

Lee stood in the darkroom for the longest time. A slight chill ran down his spine as there was a dreadful silence. It was not like before, where he could hear the traffic from outside as he looked about. He eventually found himself calling out.

"Lucy… Are you there?" There was a moment of silence, his eyes dilating as he continued looking more profound in the silence. He could practically see the silhouette of a woman. Though as he looked on, she began changing, twisting, and forming.

"I'm here, Lee, Don't worry." The figure moved in, kissing his cheek, reassuring Lee for a minute as Lucy brushed passed him for a second. The sound of her grabbing the door handle and jiggling it. Lee quickly turned around while Lucy smiled. He couldn't see her smiling. But he sure felt it as she muttered in a calming voice.

"Lee, Welcome to Hell." She opened the door. The room was immediately filled with Red lights. Lucy stood there in her Succubus form as she gave that devilish smirk. He looked onward, and the only thing he could exclaim was.

"Oh, Toto, we're not in Kansas anymore."

"Huh, that's a new one!" Lucy was momentarily excited while Lee was lost walking outside his bathroom, stepping into Hell. The most he could do was make a note to show Lucy the Wizard of Oz. Lee shook his thoughts off while looking around. He was standing in Hell. The literal location of Hell, Lee found the place disturbing in a way he couldn't describe in words. Lee tried to find the words to describe the very essence of Hell. It shifted, changing whenever he blinked.

Hell was Red. That was the first he could describe. Looking towards the sky- seeing how the sky flowed, clouds running off blocking the sky. Though every second. He watched as what looked like a meteor falling from the sky down. Off in the distance, he could hear what sounded like light screaming. Every ounce of instinct was telling him to run. Run fast and run far. His body was trembling. At the same time, Lee felt the hands of Lucy on his shoulder. A calm feeling was rolling over him. He felt safe with her- Felt relaxed as she was there.

"It'll be fine, your with me, Babe." She giggled and reached down, taking his hand and pulling him off. Lee looked back towards his bathroom door, which began closing. It vanished from sight. While lee turned around, looking off into the deep recess of Hell.

Lee looked around in total amazement as he looked over the very City. The streets were quiet. Not a soul in sight as He was stunned by everything. The screams off in the distance seemed to fade away.

"So Hell seems kind of Empty."

"Well, this is where Demons normally live at. Most are probably working down in the nine circles," Lucy said as she took

Lee's hand and pulled him in close.

"Whatever you do, don't tell a demon you're human, they might try Dragging you down to the circles, and you might get lost forever." Her voice was soft as she whispered it, and Lee felt a chill running down his spine. A sense of danger popped through his head as he wondered what would soon come in store for the man.

"Why didn't we just teleport into your house? Why so far away?" Lee asked, rather curiously, as they turned off down an alley.

"Well, I probably would, but Dad's place is kind of guarded." Lucy seemed to be dodging the question as they moved off, entering a subway station.

"Who the Hells your father, Satan?" Lee asked, joking some as Lucy looked back.

"No, my father isn't Satan, don't be ridiculous." Lucy laughed as they pushed on and got into a train cart. Lee sat at one of the leather seats next to Lucy as the subway began heading off.

For the longest time, Lee sat there, looking back and forth, just thinking about the situation. If you had told him a few years ago, he would get married and suddenly ended up in Hell's literal plains. Lee might've called you a nut case before walking away. But now that he saw it himself. He was shocked.

Lee sat back, taking a deep breath. Somehow with everything going on, Lee felt exhausted. The warm air was pretty calming- Hell Lee had imagined Hell would be much more generous. Like walking in the sun, but it seemed more like a room with the heat on a little higher.

Suddenly there was a stop when The subway doors began

sliding open. Soon crowds began running in- as Lee was shocked to see, Demons. Actual demons were roaming in each various shapes and sizes. She looked human with horns upon their heads, others that seemed to change with each glance. His mind was trying to protect him by not revealing what they were.

Soon a massive creature, the type of Demon that might've come from a horror film- Long boney arms, a skull for a face, deep black eyes. Its skin is tightly wrapped around, making it look unnatural. Lee felt himself shaking, looking towards this skeleton figure. It eventually looked over to Lee, twisting its head, the lips moving wider for a minute as Lee was sure it would try killing him. He was about to scoot closer to Lucy when suddenly.

"Hey man, how's it going!" Its voice was overly friendly, with a slight chuckle as it smiled wider. Lee was lost for words.

"I'm doing fine," Lee said as he wasn't sure what to say,

"Awesome- you know you look familiar. Do you work in the fifth circle? Or First?"

"Um, First." Lee lied with a slight smirk as the boney being nodded,

"Noice, I work over in the third. I swear, just dealing with those guy's insane, always wanting to eat, wanting more. I mean, they are just greedy as Hell. I swear I had to go and construct a room for a few future arrivals." The skeleton looked exhausted, hunching down. He just seemed worn out.

"Wow, that sucks- Sounds like you had a rough day."

"Like you wouldn't believe, Dude. I mean, I swear, what are those Mortals doing? Dick heads, and they call us the Demons! By the way, what's your name?" the skeleton smiled as he watched him.

"Uh oh yeah, I'm Lester." Lee shuddered using his actual name, but he was close to saying Fester at that moment though the skeleton nodded.

"Nice to meet you, Lester. Yeah, it sounds like a name for the second circle, But I'm Balaam. So what are you up to?" He chuckled some as he popped his neck.

"Meeting future In-laws," Lee answered truthfully as He looked at Lucy.

"Oh, that's rough, buddy; I remember when I met Karren's parents; I think I was ready to take on Heaven's arm at that point, but congrats, who's the lucky lady?"

"Oh, that would be me." Lucy interrupted with a light smile as she wrapped her arm around Lee,

"Noice mate- got a Succubus. I don't see them around here often. Well, I should let you two be." Balaam moved back, minding his own business. Lee just seemed confused while Lucy looked back.

"Now, Lester, I told you to be careful; just try not to talk too much." There was a hint of teasing as she used his real name while she scolded Lee.

"I'm sorry it just happened. I didn't want to be rude. Also please don't call me Lester. I hate that." He muttered while eyeing around.

"It's okay. It would help if you didn't get in too much trouble. Our next stop should be coming up soon." It was almost like clockwork. As the subway stopped and Lucy reached over to take Lee's hand, Balaam waved off as Lee gave him a thumbs up.

"So, long Lester, good luck with the in-laws. If it goes bad,

I'll visit the funeral."

Lee nodded as they headed out of the subway. They stood there for a second as the subway began rolling away. Lucy sighed slightly while turning back to Lee, annoyed as she grabbed his shoulder.

"Please don't do that; I know it was something simple. But Demons are normally smart- If they figure out you're human, It might not end well for anyone."

"Don't worry, I won't get into trouble. Besides, we'll meet your parents and leave here as soon as possible."

"Alright, though, please, when you meet Daddy, don't freak out. I know how humans aren't his biggest fan." She reassured him, though Lee couldn't help raising an eyebrow.

"Again, is your father Satan?"

"He's not Satan! He and daddy are two different people!" Lucy sighed as she gave Lee a light Punch. Lee just gasped and muttered,

"You monster! This marriage is over with!" his expression exaggerated as he returned the light punch to her arm, responding in a massive fit of giggling as she wrapped her arm around his neck, leading him off into the abyss. They moved down deeper, following through the City of Judea. Lee felt himself getting colder. He reached over, rubbing his hands, trying to get them warmer.

"Jesus Christ, it's cold as Hell here." Lee stammered, shivering profusely. Lucy snickered more while looking at him. She seemed perfectly fine. Lee suspected that she was warming her body up Hell. Her arm around him was beginning to warm him up.

"Was that Pun intended?" Lucy asked as she led him along. Lee only shook his head but felt a chuckle pass his lips. "Not really, it just slipped out."

"So, how far are we till we get to your parent's place?"

"Almost there, just be patient. When we get in there, I'll turn up the heat, maybe show you where my room was." She whispered, some of her hand reaching down, giving his butt a firm squeeze.

"Well, if you insist on it." Lee responded, his thighs feeling better. He was sure he could make it another round or two with the Succubus. Lee just imagined what her home was like. As he moved on, thinking it might not have been that wild. Though what could he expect from a house in Hell? But soon, Lucy muttered,

"Oh, look, we're here." Lucy pointed off in that direction. Lee's eyes shifted as he looked toward where Lucy was pointing. His jaws dropped right there as he exclaimed.

"Holy sweet baby Jesus…" Random demons eyed him with annoyance for his wording while they passed them.

Lee was looking forward as he saw what looked like a castle going miles into the air. One of them vanished off into the blood color sky. Spikes were forming on the sides of it. The place reminded him of something a villain in a fantasy novel might possess. Gargoyles were hanging over the edge. However, they seemed to fly off and walk around, guarding the location. Lee could practically see bats flying from them.

Lee couldn't find the right words. Nothing came out when he opened his mouth, so he eventually closed his mouth as if he wanted to fall over. His legs were feeling like Jelly.

Lucy, though, just smiled and turned back to her fiancé

with a light smile.

"It's so good to be home; come on." She grabbed him by the arms dragging him off past the iron gates and into the dark lord's Castle.

They headed inside the Castle. Lee's heart was pounding as he felt as if he was regretting everything he's done, mainly coming here.

No- No, stop thinking that way. We're here to meet Lucy's parents. I have to make a good impression. Lee started pumping his chest up, trying to look confident. Lucy giggled as Lee tried to look bigger, smiling as she shook her head. It was one thing she could consider him to be quite cute.

The stone doors began pulling opening. The loud creak as they opened widely for The two. Bat's flying out with a screech. Lee couldn't help admiring the sight as they pulled in and headed inside. Indeed the place was a palace. Walls aligned with portraits of finely lit torches. It was a sight Lee had never thought he would see. Nothing about it was familiar. This was the home of a king. Lee looked down at what he was wearing and realized he was underdressed.

Lucy leads Lee as she passes down the halls, Lee looking over the vast wonders of the place as they soon reach a set of doors. That was quite impressive. Black stone, lined with gold, etched the doors. It depicted imagery of what looked to be angels falling from clouds.

Lee watched as Lucy pushed the door over there. Lee was more shocked, looking in the room. The place was more extensive than any home Lee had lived in. Hell, it was more significant than a school. It was empty for the most part except for a group of guards, Rather demonic-looking beings- massive bulking beasts that seemed to eye him, and Lucy for a second. However, it was on the other side of the room.

There was a throne of fire that emanated heat in this frozen room. A figure sat there; the model was male, Tall, and slender. Lee was mesmerized by the man as he was truly handsome. He was drop-dead gorgeous, even for Lee, a straight man. Even Lee would admit he would've been attracted to him. He stood there wearing a white suit with a red rose on the side hanging over it. His tie was pure red, like blood clashing. His smile was growing wide as he watched him.

Then there were those eyes. Those eyes were quiet mesmerizing deep Black- like looking off into comforting darkness with stars that twinkled in them. His eyes seemed to be on Lee and Lucy as He popped his neck.

Lee soon noticed he wasn't alone. Sitting by him on a thrown of fire herself was a woman- She was gorgeous, looking practically like Lucy though a crown of thorns and fire upon her head, wearing a black dress. That revealed her bosom; Black bat-like wings were spreading out. She was practically staring at Lee. As if she was examining him- planning something- something Lee wasn't sure about. The handsome figure pulled himself from the throne.

When he stood up, the throne vanished as if it hadn't been there before. He walked down those ebony stairs as the guards began falling to their knees. They held their weaponry close as if to strike at a moment's notice. This being-this man, Who Lee suspected, was none other than Lucy's father—soon walked towards them. His broad smile reminded him of a cat, and Lee noticed he had what looked to be a monocle in his right eye. The more Lee looked at him. He couldn't help but imagine he looked quite like Ryan Reynolds.

"If he starts spouting off pop culture references, I'm running." Lee whispered to Lucy, who gave him a quick nudge.

He turned, looking towards Lucy, and that smile grew wider as he watched her. Lucy stood there almost stoic, her head held up, eye her back straight and shoulders broad. Though as she kept herself looking stern, she suddenly found herself giggling laughing almost as she suddenly muttered.

"Hi, Daddy," she laughed more as this handsome beastly man suddenly laughed too. It was practically infectious. From laughing, Lee had to do everything he could, but a smile began spreading. Soon The one Lucy called daddy opened his arms up and screamed.

"My little Cheftzi-Ba, It's been so long." He reached over, pulling her in for a tight hug. He lifted her practical feet off the ground as he held her dearly. He was almost swinging around. Lucy's only response was giggling, like a child who hadn't seen her father for the longest time.

"It has what A hundred years." She thought about it more, "Very, What happened? I know you hung around with mortals for fifty years, but you normally called us when something happened?" He chuckled and even laughed more as he patted her head.

"I kind of got locked inside a ring." She sighed, remembering her past and how she had allowed herself to be locked up and trapped in that old ring. Her father sighed.

"Well, you're free, that's all that matters, but you worried us." He caressed her cheek, clearly a kindness on his face, but soon, he turned to overlook Lee.

"So, who are you? Why have you come to see the great Lucifer? Are you here to bargain for fame? Fortune, a chance to fuck A supermodel or have a super sexy wife with all the stops? Yada yada- I don't have all day; I gotta spend time with my baby girl!" He was utterly excited for a moment. Lee just looked at him, blinking, not sure what to say.

"Uhh no, I came with Lucy…" Lee muttered as it sank in. He was looking towards the Ruler of Hell, The Fallen Angel Lucifer. He was practically shocked as he was looking at an angel. Who seemed to look at him unamused.

"Cheftzi, is this true? Did you come with him?" He looked towards her for a second, a simple smile on her face. Lucy nodded with a smile.

"Yes, Dad- and I'm currently going by Lucy- but He came with me; in fact, he's the one who freed me from the ring." She smiled, looking towards Lee; Lucifer looked towards him for a second as he heard those words. A smile grew on his face as he suddenly, without warning, grabbed Lee by the shoulders and hugged him.

"Thank you, my good man! Whatever you desire, if it's in my power, it shall be done, no matter what it is, ask me!" there was a goofy smile on his face, which seemed purely sincere.

Lee felt weird as the Angel practically shoved him when suddenly, The woman dropped by him.

"Darling, please let the young man breathe; otherwise, he might be unable to breathe."

"Oh, fine, Lilith, But I must thank him somehow for freeing our daughter from the ring. I am glad you brought him here, Lucy." He smiled, looking back towards her, Lucy giggling at her father being such a dorky man as she bounced some.

"Well, I have some good news." She muttered as she hugged Lilith. The calmer woman smiled some as she looked back towards her daughter.

"What would that be, my dear?" Lilith asked Lucifer dropping Lee at this point, who grunted slightly as he landed back on his feet, staggering for a second.

"Well, Daddy has gotten to know Lee. we've been seeing each other since he freed me from the ring… Also." Lucy raised her finger as she showed the engagement ring. Lucifer and Lilith looked at them blankly. A long pause went by as the realization came over them.

Lilith responded first as she squealed in excitement, "Oi Vey, My baby is getting married!" she suddenly hugged Lucy for a second, as she was fluttering her wings, excitement in her voice as Lucy laughed. Lilith pulled back and grabbed Lee, Practically examining him.

"So, you will be my future son-in-law. Him Lucifer, my darling, he is quite a cutie." Lee felt her squeezing his chin as she turned his head around.

Lucifer just stood there, his eyes twitching as he looked back from Lucy towards Lee for a minute as if a million things were running through his head. He looked around and forth, towards Lucy and then towards Lee. Simultaneously, the realization came to mind—a choice of how he would react for a second.

"Really," He positioned his arms, presenting Lee; it was clear Lucifer's guard dropped as he looked towards. Lucy nodded while she looked over at Lee for a hot second. The room seeming to get warmer. At least by Lee's perspective.

"Yes, he proposed a few days ago," She looked to Lee, as the young man just didn't know what to say- Lucifer just looked over to him for a minute, saying.

"I mean- for a mortal, he seems okay- But Honey, I could've introduced you to all sorts of mortals. Some offense." He looked back At Lee- Not sure of what to say.

"Don't you mean no offense?"

"No…" Lucifer responded as he rolled his shoulders. A pitchfork appeared in his hand as he leaned against it. His hand was gripping the handle tightly.

"Well, I don't want any old Mortal. Lee is an amazing guy. I wouldn't trade him for all the gold in the world. I wouldn't even trade him to marry a God."

"You know I could have that arranged. I know Donn, and he owes me a favor. The Irish Bastard." Lucifer chimed in a small laugh under his breath, But Lucy gave him a look that made the Devil himself shudder in front of Lee. It brought Lee a second of amusement.

"Okay, okay, never mind. So what do you do… Lee?" Lucifer asked, his white smile practically glowing for a moment. Lee quickly responded- his voice shaking, somewhat intimidated by all around him.

"Well, I work for a Publishing company; I mainly help look over some of the manuscripts to see what might be worth publishing," Lee said- Lucifer didn't look impressed.

"Damnit, Dad! You are not giving me much to work with."

He mumbled through; eventually, he clapped his hands and exclaimed.

"Alright- well, How about I show you guy's your rooms and then get dinner started- I know I'm starving to death." He gave a smile and looked toward Lucy.

"Could you get the chiefs to make something special for Lucy and her fiancé? Make sure they can make something edible for a mortal." He smiled some as Lilith nodded,

"As you wish, my Princes of Darkness."

"Anytime, My Forbidden Apple.." Lucifer smiled. Lucy only groaned, embarrassed by her parent's actions. Still, Lee snickered, never seeing Lucy so frustrated as the Devil began leading them off.

"Lucy, my dear, you know where your room is. I'll Lead Lee to his. I wanna talk to him in private." He glanced toward Lee for a second as Lee shuddered at the idea.

"Dad, he can sleep in my room with me. I'm not a child," Lucy responded though Lucifer just grunted.

"Darling, it is my reality I make the rules," Lucifer responded with a light laugh.

"We're not going to do this?" Lucy responded while Lucifer gave a hard laugh.

"Yeah, We are pumpkins But don't worry, dear. It's until I get to know him, and he earns my trust." He patted Lee on the shoulder as he took him off. Lee looked back and looked surprised.

Lucy had an expression with a slight smile reassuring him that he was in good hands.

Yeah right! Lee thought as he started being dragged off. Not sure what might happen. He just hoped it ended well. Lee and Lucifer walked down the corridors of the Castle, passing various paintings. Each depicted an angel, sometimes a demon- both horrifying and stunning simultaneously.

Lee recognized that Chronos was eating his children, which brought a question to mind from something Lucifer had said.

"So, who's Donn?" Lee asked, more curious

"He's the Irish God of death, Kind of like Hades."

"So Hades… So he's real?"

"Yes, Hades is real, and so are Kali, Allah, Kami, and Thor. Every God you have ever heard of exists."

Lee was shocked by this, nearly stunned as he didn't know what more to say as he followed the Fallen Angel. He soon leads Lee off towards the side as they pass a corridor of rooms. Going down what appeared to be an endless Hallway. Lee couldn't even see the other side of the room. It only went on.

"So, I guess if every god is real- It must be difficult to get souls." Lee's voice echoed beyond the room as it bounced into the abyss.

"Not exactly, so many souls come down here, and each God who rules the underworld owns a part of Hell. I own the largest part, containing the nine circles. Hades Rules Limbo- Hel Rules the fifth circle anger if you're unfamiliar. But I am the ruler of Hell." He muttered, knowing what he was saying.

Lee listened to most of it but was distracted as he looked towards one of the doors. He was getting a good look at it When Lucifer appeared by him.

31

"This section holds certain souls I like too. Let's say personally punish." A Cheshire grin was rolling on his face. Lee wasn't sure what that could've entailed- In some ways, he might not have wanted to know. The idea of torturing someone was wrong, at least for him. Though Lucifer, that Devilish man, smirked more and leaned in.

"Wanna try? Or you know what fuck it, we're nearly family gets over here." He reached over, grabbing Lee by the wrist. Lee didn't have time before he's dragged off. They jogged almost ten- No, twenty feet. Lee wasn't sure as they appeared before a door. This door had a Pair of Letters reading A. H. Lucifer stopped before Lee and gave a chuckle.

"Not sure what your stance is in the world. But I'm sure you'll like this."

He grabbed the doorknob and swung the door open. Lee took a second to see the room and stood there. He was practically older, wearing a pinkish suit: short black hair, and a small mustache under his nose. Lee didn't need Lucifer to explain who this was. He realized he was none other than Adolph Hitler.

"Is that…" Lee pointed over, still shocked as Lucifer nodded.

"Very much that is none other Than the Nazi Bastard." He walked into the room, Lee Following him as the door slammed shut. Hitler looked towards him as if reawakening from a trance, and once he saw Lucifer, he screamed. He screamed like a child as he tried pushing himself back deeper into the bed.

"Oh, Adolph, It's Pine O'clock!" He laughed as Hitler looked more shocked, his hand reaching over and grabbing his buttocks.

"Bitte! Nein! Nicht die, Ananas!" Hitler pushed back as he watched Lucifer laughing as he suddenly raised his finger, forcing Hitler onto his stomach. His pants ripped off; Lee couldn't look at this turning away- He always imagined kicking Hitler's ass, but whatever was happening. Lee didn't have a stomach. Soon Lucifer screamed out.

"Oh, Ho, Mr. Hitler. I don't think so!" Soon Lee heard Hitler scream out.

"NEIN, NEIN!" Before it went, Silent Lucifer walked off, and Lee followed, not daring to look back.

Lucifer closed the door, and everything went on to complete silence. Lucifer popped his neck as Lee looked toward him,

"Um, well, that was…."

"Interesting, exciting- Maddening," Lucifer said with a broad smile as he growled some of his iris slittings.

"It feels like you ripped Adam Sandler off…" Lee said as he just imagined it though Lucifer looked annoyed, calling out,

"Who do you think gave him the idea? I watched him write the script and said, 'Shove pineapples up his ass!'" Lee suddenly began bursting out, laughing at the idea as he snorted. But a second later, he thought of something,

"You said it was pine o'clock. Was that you were making a pun?"

"Yes, why?"

"You truly are evil," Lee responded. Lucifer only laughed at the idea as he patted his back and led him from the room. Lee just wondered what else might be hiding in this place.

"Now let it be a lesson for you, Lee- I love my Sons and daughters more than creation itself. So if you hurt her or make my little Cheftzi cry or upset, I will do far worst to you than Pine O'clock." He looked towards him, reminding Lee of a serpent as he moved closer. That expression truly made Lee look into the face of Evil.

He paused momentarily, steeled his nerves looking towards the Devil himself, and uttered these words.

"If I ever hurt Lucy, I wouldn't fight it. Though Honestly, I think she'd be able to care for herself." He watched him, never blinking, even if he was metaphorically freaking out.

"Very well. But you have to earn my trust, but we'll deal with that later. Come on. I'll show you your actual room." He turned around, heading north as they continued down the hallway, as they appeared by a door with no name. As Lucifer opened it, Lee wasn't sure what could be behind this door.

"Here's where you will be staying." He reached over and pulled the door open. Lee looked inside, discovering there was already someone in there. A sizeable demonic beast looked like a hound, a bipedal wolf with bulging muscles and wings springing from his back with long shaggy hair and lying on the bed, with a woman on top of him.

A short-stack woman with quite the bosom, bouncing on the giant cock. Cold sweat ran from her face like they had been at it for several hours. The woman was screaming, getting louder as the Wolf demon growled more as Lee watched him releasing the money shot. Though it seemed for the Demon, his semen wasn't pure white but oozed black.

"God damn it, Cerberus! Will you quit fucking earth girls in my house? I thought we agreed you could do it In Hade's house!"

Cerberus looked over, shocked, and bounced off the bed. The woman fell off, landing on the ground while the Demon muttered,

"Sorry, Boss, but she really couldn't wait, so I took her to the closes place I could, and well, I'm here." He muttered. The woman was shocked as she covered her naked body. Lee Couldn't help checking her out a bit though Lucifer snapped his fingers, causing them to vanish.

"I swear Cerberus is going to drive me insane. That horny Hellhound. Where does he even get these women?!"

"That's Cerberus. I mean, isn't he suppose to have three heads."

"He does; they are probably wandering around fucking other souls or those who find their way in hell."

"Oh… Okay." Lee wasn't sure if he could understand that. Lucifer waved his arm. The room is instantly cleaned, with no mess left by Cerberus giving out his pearl necklace. However, Lee didn't want to bring out a blue light to see what other mess might have been hiding in the room. This was Lucifer; after all, there might be some nasty surprise.

"Well, here's your room. Dinner should be ready in about an hour. Meet us in the Dining room. If you get lost, think of the dining room, and you'll walk into it sooner or later." It was there Lucifer had left him, and Lee stood there all alone.

CHAPTER 3

Lee examined the room after Lucifer had left him alone. The amount of silence was quite enriching as he looked around. The room was far from what he expected. It seemed almost modern compared to the rest of the Castle's more gothic nature; the bed was a double king size. As he explored, he couldn't help opening the dresser draws, not accounting for what might've resided there. But when he did. Lee found only an array of clothes.

He looked at the small shelves lined with drinks, mainly whiskey and Jack Daniels with a side of Ice. He reached over, grabbing one of the bottles, and pouring himself a stiff one. He looked out the window. He was looking off to the pits of Hell. He could imagine the torture going on out there—the horrors. Even now, Lee knew he was safe with Lucy around. It didn't bring him much comfort. His spine had a slight shiver. In most cases, the man knew he didn't belong there. At least not now.

"This feels like a dream. I mean, Lucy's dad is Lucifer. Why didn't she tell me?" Lee shook his head while sitting at the edge of the bed, trying to make sense of everything. Though he also wondered what they were going to do next. But the fact he was in Hell was overwhelming. Lucy had reassured him that it would be alright. But for a moment, he didn't know what to do.

He took another long swig of his drink. There was a television. Though when Lee went to grab the remote, he stopped for a second. He wasn't sure what might be on the Hell network as he shook his head.

"Maybe later." He soon proceeded to get a shower in since he had to get ready for dinner. He reached over and began undressing. His clothes landed on the ground as he walked to the side room and entered the shower. He started washing his body. There was no cold water. Thankfully, he learned the hard way it went from warm to scolding to lava. He didn't start all the way.

This place is insane, I mean, couldn't they have some cold water... Oh, right, Hell. Lee thought as he moved in, letting the warm water fall on him. His hand was grabbing the shampoo. It ran through his hand as he started washing his hair. He a scrubbing it through when he heard something. His head turned and called out.

"Is there someone here?" He yelled out, confused, but when Lee heard nothing, he sighed, returning to washing his body. However, Lee couldn't help but feel as though someone- or something was watching him. He looked off as he took a long deep breath, not noticing anything as he scrubbed his hair. His eyes closed as he felt the warmth running through him. It felt amazing.

Suddenly without warning, he felt something grope him, grabbing his cock, nearly freaking him out as he looked back, and suddenly, he wasn't alone. The figure that was behind him was tall, taller than Lucy. You could describe her as thick as she had a complete pair of hips. Her hair was long, and silver hair covered her eyes, and the steam from the hot water rose around her.

"Who the hell are you?" Lee muttered as he stepped back, his fingers reaching over to pull the shower curtains to make a run from this woman.

"Oh, come on, don't you recognize me? I mean, I will be your future mother-in-law." She smirked more, and Lee suddenly recognized her. She looked almost like Lucy when she had turned into her succubus queen form. Her crown of thorns had a gentle green flame atop her head.

"Oh, well, it's… nice to meet you. Lilith?" Lee winced some as he didn't know what she might say. How could you talk to Lucifer's wife? The way she stood there, naked, her whole body exposed, when he was about to shower. If he told her to get out would she be offended and say something to her husband? He was almost to afraid to say anything.

"It's good to meet you, and please relax, Lee, I just wanted to come and give you a personal thank you for what you've done with my daughter, and I have something special for you tonight.

After dinner." She smiled some, her breast swaying gently. Lee was doing all he could not stare, looking off towards the side only to meet a wall.

"Well, that's nice, but I don't need anything. I want to do what I can to make Lucy happy."

"Which I am thankful for. Though I'm sure you'll like what I have in plan. My husband has always been protective of his children. He is such an Angel. But unlike him, I don't mind my children exploring and enjoying themselves." Lilith smirked as she took his hand and pushed it against her ample bosom. Licking her lips, she leaned in, whispering in his ear.

"So long as they share their boy toys with their mommy." Her hot breath caught him off guard. He could feel his cock betray him as it became instantly erect. Almost poking against the mother of the succubi. Lee's eyes widened, his heart racing as his hands shook. He wasn't sure if this was a trap as he tried pulling away.

Her grip was tight as she leaned in,

"Don't worry about my husband. We have a special relationship. I can sleep with anyone, and he won't harm them, and he can do the same." She rolled her tongue more, causing Lee to groan, his cock twitching slightly. Arousal smashed into him; her essence was hitting him like a bulldozer.

Lilith looked down with a smirk seeing his member,

"Hmm, it's nice, though maybe it could be a bit bigger for my little girl. Oh, I know, maybe something special." She pushed Lee against the wall of the shower. His back pressed against the spout turning the water off as Lilith fell to her knees.

"Wait, don't!"

Lee grunted as he felt her licking his cock. A shudder escaped him as he felt her begin taking every inch of him as she hummed. Lee groaned more as he felt his cock tingling. Lucy was good, but her mother drove him wild almost instantly. Somehow she knew the right spots to hit as she lapped his member the long tongue wrapping around when she pulled back and gave him a wink. She

"I better stop right now. I don't want you to get too cocky. Besides, I can't ruin you for my baby girl." She licked her lips giving that wide smile as she got back up, leaving Lee behind as he had a confused look on his face. He looked down and suddenly realized His cock was far off. It was longer instead of being six inches hard. It was now nearly ten inches thick as Hell. Lee wondered how he could even think with all the blood running down his cock, but he gulped, knowing he had much to explain to Lucy. He just hoped she wouldn't be pissed off at him.

He listened as Lilith closed the door behind her. He stood there all alone, with a sigh as he turned over and began washing his body every inch he couldn't help but wish Lucy was here. She could drain him, all she wanted right now. But at the moment, his hands would have to do. His fingers were wrapping around his cock as he practically imagined how the scene would've gone. His newer, longer cock felt rather sensitive to the touch.

He would spend a good ten minutes relieving himself with his own hands. The memory of what Lilith did to him still echoes in the back of his head. To say this wasn't Lee's proudest fap was an understatement.

-000-

Lee walked out of the shower, the towel running through his hair as he dried it and noticed that his clothes were replaced, as what looked to be a bit more elegant as he rolled his shoulders.

"Well, It could be worst. I mean, I won't look out of place or look like too much of a goofball." He reached over and soon began putting them on. They were a tight fit, Making Lee wonder if he needed to hit the gym again.

Maybe? He thought as he motioned over and put on the button on the shirt. It was red as he buttoned it up and sighed, soon heading out. He was sure it was close to dinner time. He explored the hallways. He did not want to touch doors fearing he wanted to deal with another Hitler situation. Though admittedly, looking at some of the doors was tempting. At one point, Heck looked and saw a door with Trump written on it. His fingers close to grabbing it but pulled back.

"No- Nope, I'm not opening that can of worms." He sighed and motioned off as he followed the direction.

"Lee!" Suddenly a shout-out came off as Lee turned around and suddenly saw Lucy. She wore a low-cut blue dress that showed off a fair bit of skin as she moved in, giving him a tight hug.

"Lucy, heh, am I glad to see you." Lee was beyond truthful about that as he barely wanted to let the demoness go, but Lucy smiled some,

"Is that so?" Lucy smirked as she gave him a light kiss on the cheek as she pulled back, leading Lee towards the dining room. Lee thought about what happened and knew he couldn't hide it forever as he reached over, taking her hand. Lucy turned back towards him.

"Yeah, Lee?" She asked curiously.

"Um yeah, I wanted to tell you something quickly. Earlier, I took a shower and…" He gulped, thinking of the right words.

"Yes?" Lucy said, giving a slight nod and waiting for Lee to grow the balls to tell her.

"You're mother just appeared in my room, and she… Sucked my cock a bit. I never climaxed, I swear. I even told her to stop." At least, he thought he did. His head felt fuzzy even though Lucy blinked for a minute.

"And?" she was calm, a smile on her face. Lee thought it was a trap but was shocked.

"I mean, it's your mother, and isn't that kind of weird?"

Lee shook his head for a moment.

"Honey, Sweet pea. Remember, We're in Hell, and I'm a succubus. I'm not going to be jealous. About my mother doing that…." She reached over, caressing his arm and pulling him in closer, Yet there was a slight jolt in her eyes. Lee wasn't sure what it was, but he ignored it momentarily with how she whispered into his ear.

"It's kind of Hot. I wish I could've watched or joined, but the father can be such a spoilsport."

"So, you don't mind your mother tried seducing me?" Lee's eyebrow raised,

"Nope… not at all. I mean, I know Mom has eyes for only one man. To her, you're only food. In my eyes, you're the only one for me. If you want, we can perform a special ceremony after we get married."

"What would that be?" Lee asked curiously as Lucy turned back towards the door,

"I'll tell you later, sweetie. Though for now. We better get ready for dinner. I'm starving." Lucy would eventually head off, walking towards the dining room. Lee gulped and followed behind her for a moment.

The dinner was calm, Lee sitting on the other side. The room was quiet as The Angel Lucifer sat on the other side, his fingers twirling around as a fork floated with a smile,

"It's nearly time for dinner, and I'm sure we have plenty of time to discuss your wedding. Do you two have a plan?" Lucifer asked with a light smile. His hand was reaching over as he took Lilith's hand, who smiled warmly at her husband—such a passion in her eyes. Lee chuckled. It was almost enough to make him forget that she had taken his dick in her mouth not too long ago.

"Well, we don't have many plans now, Dad. We only recently got engaged, heh. You guys are the first ones we've ever told." Lucy smiled more as she sat back some. It was then that a set of chiefs began bringing the food in. In the center an array of apples is placed in the very center. It was pretty odd, as the apples looked almost golden.

"Lee."

Lee's eyes were on them, practically ignoring everyone as he watched them. They glowed a radiant light. It seemed they were calling him—wanting him to climb over the table to take them. Eat every one of them till none are left.

"Lee?"

His hands shook his face-covering in sweat as he reached over, taking some of the food. However, the Apples were what he wanted, so he came over and grabbed one.

"Lee!"

Lee's hand was suddenly slapped away. When he looked over, He was annoyed, wondering who had denied him this precious apple, as he wanted to get after who did it. The person who slapped his hand away is none other than Lucifer. The stern look on his face as he reached over, grabbing the bowel. A smirk spread on his face as he looked towards Lilith.

"I probably should've told The cooks not to bring these out." He pulled the bowel away from Lee's grip as he grabbed an apple and took a bite. He would practically throw them out the window to Lee's dismay. As soon as they were away from him, Lee shook his head.

"What just happened?" Lee muttered, rubbing his eyes.

"You almost took a bite from one of the fruits of the tree of knowledge. We don't need another incident like that happening again. The old man was pissed off at me for a long time for that fuck up."

"The fruit of- Wait, you mean those are the apples of

Eden?" Lee was stunned, somewhat shocked that something like that would be here. However, it made him question what would be wrong with him eating one of those delectable apples.

"Yeah, again, We'll have to make sure none of those get into your hands. It can really mess you guy's up." He took another bite and threw it out the window. Lee watched it in horror as he shook his head,

"I mean, what could be so bad? I mean, they're just apples." Lucy was rather shocked as she covered her mouth for a moment while Lucifer laughed,

"Well, besides, it might make you immortal. It could cause you to explode from all that knowledge rushing into you. Only divine beings such as myself can handle it. I once had the first humans try it. That got me in a lot of trouble for that and them."

Lee nodded, not able to find the right words to say. Lucy nodding,

"It's something I've never seen. I mean, Humans were eating an apple-like that is rare." She sighed some as she grabbed his arm.

"I'm sorry. It's my fault. I forget small things like this. Please Don't be angry with me." She chuckled while Lee nodded,

"No, it's fine. It wasn't like I nearly got blown up on my first day in Hell." He chuckled some, and Lucy giggled—the mood-lifting.

"Well, excellent since there's no more exploding. How about we get back to enjoying our meal? I'll grab some lamb Chops, and I swear, Lucy. This was an excellent offering." He grabbed some of the cut beef and began eating. Lee sweated some remembering the goat from just this morning and for a moment. He wasn't hungry. However, Lee pushed that feeling aside. Not wanting to be rude, he reached over, grabbing some himself.

Soon they would begin eating. There was an awkward

silence. Lee was taking large bites. He felt his foot tapping while trying to find the right words.

"Hmm, this is good." He muttered while breaking off something and tasting the corn.

"Thank you," Lucifer smirked.

Though it just went back to being quiet. Somehow Lee imagined that eating with the ruler of Hell would be more... Interesting. Yeah, those were the words. But it was just relaxing.

Though it wouldn't last long as, without warning, there was a crashing through the window. A massive beast that Lee could only describe as such. It looked as though it had a man's head, the body of a turtle, with tentacles wrapping around its arms and legs. His teeth were sharp like little needles, as it exclaimed.

"A human in the home of The Light bringer must destroy!" It screeched in a high-pitched voice as it started moving towards Lee, jumping on the table as it tossed the food off to the side.

Lee suddenly grabbed a knife. He wasn't sure he could take the creature, but Lee wouldn't sit by while it mauled him. He held it tight as he was ready to strike. His body was getting into a defensive stance. At the same time, he was prepared to stab the thing in its God damn eye. When it ran faster, he was letting out a harrowing howl. As it suddenly was stopped in place.

Not that it didn't try moving; it just couldn't get any farther. It scratched at the ground, growling spit and slime extracting from its body as Lee watched it.

"Well, are you going to attack it, kid? You've got the knife." He suddenly heard Lucifer calling, his head tilting, seeing Lucifer stand there drinking a glass of wine in one hand. (He hoped it was wine.) In the other one, a golden rope was wrapped around the neck of this beast.

Lee hesitated as he looked toward the beast. Looking into its almost human face as it growled out.

"I will skin you alive and feast on your fear and flesh!" Lee shuddered and suddenly stabbed it in the face. He stabbed it. Lee did not know how many times. By the end, he couldn't recognize it any longer as he took long deep breaths before falling.

Lee took a deep breath, his face covered with the blood of this creature. Eventually, it turned to dust, crumbling away.

"Well, with that out of the way, how about we eat." His fingers were snapping, and the ash flew out the broken window. Lee shook, shocked as he looked towards the Devil. Lucifer looked at him.

"What?" Lucifer asked as he took a bite out of his goat meat.

"I um- Is that normal?" Lee stuttered some as he had just killed the weird hybrid creature.

"Eh, once in a while, Don't worry, it won't come by for a good while. Besides, it wanted you. Now come on, let's eat." He chuckled as he tapped his glass, turning it into chocolate milk.

The rest of the night turned out quite simple. There wouldn't be another interruption for the rest of the night. Lee looked at his meal though it was clear after the attack. He wasn't as hungry as he was before. Though soon, the night would end.

"Well, that was delicious, though I must return to my duties. Please have a good night, everyone, and especially to you, my love. Please enjoy your night." Lucifer would raise Lilith, and they shared a kiss of inferno passion and burning desire. Lee could see flames shooting from out Lilith's ears. Soon the Ruler of Hell vanished without a trace.

-000-

"Well, that was interesting," Lee muttered, rubbing his head. Lucy was right by him, a smile on her face.

"Very much, though hopefully, we don't have to deal with

much. Maybe I'll have Mom put a barrier over the castle. Imagine what people would think if they knew what we're doing now."

"Yeah, I just never expected something like this. Heh, I mean, I imagine what my family might say, being married to the daughter of Lucifer."

Lee suddenly heard Lucy stop as he looked over, a sad look on her face as he felt a pain in his heart. He knew he was wrong.

"Lee, are you regretting your decision of wanting to marry me now that you've met my family?" Lee shuddered and walked back to her, his finger caressing under her chin.

"Listen, I don't regret anything. I want to marry you. I want to spend the rest of my life. Even if you drive me crazy and tie me to the bed for endless fucking, long as I'm with you, it's all that matters."

"You mean it?" Lucy said, a small tear in her eye.

"Yeah, you and me to the end. I wouldn't touch another woman without you."

"Good though, I don't mind if you fuck a girl as long as I'm with you, or you tell me." Lucy winked, and soon, they shared another kiss.

"Oh, I'd tell you. Besides, You'd know anyway." A small laugh as they soon separated, heading to their room.

"I'll see you tomorrow."

"See you then, honey buns," Lucy said as she went off, and they went off their ways. Lee was watching her walk off, swaying back and forth just as Lucy lifted. It had a slight bounce as he smiled with a light chuckle before. Lee made the journey to head to his room. He was cleaning up whatever blood that beast left on his face.

47

It took a bit. These goddamn doors were looking just the same. He grunted while doing so though eventually, He found it. As he sighed, the door creaked open though when. He stepped inside when he heard a voice.

"I've been expecting you, Mr. West."

As Lee looked in, the calming voice coming from his room was almost shocked, especially from who, or more about what he saw.

She was pink and very fluffy.

CHAPTER 4

Lee looked towards the figure lying down on his bed on her side. This woman looked like nothing. He had never seen a goddess in the flesh. Soft features, wearing a breastplate that Lee couldn't help but think made her breast look slightly more prominent. But the thing that caused him off guard as she had six wings. They reminded Lee of Lucy. The difference was this woman was hot pink while Lucy was black as the ravens.

"Um, who are you?" Lee asked quickly. His mind racing was imagining he was standing in front of another Succubus.

No, she's not a succubus… She's different, not like Lucy or even Lilith. There's a glow to her. It's kind of like, Lucifer's aura. The woman this being looked at him with a smirk on her face.

"I've gone by many names from long before your grandfather was born. Some called me Castella. Some called me Abbadon, but you may call me Cere. If you so desire. I am an angel of the lord. Well, I once was an angel for the lord."

Lee's jaw just dropped, and he shook his head as he realized that he was going mad,

"Sure, why not? I'm marrying a succubus; her father is Lucifer. Why was I even an Athiest?"

"It matters not what you believe in, good sir, but there is something I request of you." She crawled across the bed, her breasts exposing as she watched him hungrily like a man who hadn't had a drink of water in years.

Lee winced as he read a fair bit to know that she might ask him to betray his loved ones or kill the devil, and he hated to know what might happen if he said no. Lee winced

"What's the request?" He muttered as he figured he wouldn't even have a chance to run. Maybe he would have a head start with how she was lying.

"I want you to sleep with me fuck, me with all you have, and pour your seed into my body." She smirked, watching him. Though Lee was standing, his jaw dropped. You could almost see when the hamster stopped running in its wheel and spun in circles as he heard a long beep indicating brain death.

"Wait. What? You want to fuck me!" Lee was shocked. He wasn't sure what he was even going to do as he looked toward the Angel.

"Well, not Want per se. I need you to fuck me." Cere, the Angel, said, somewhat annoyed, though Lee sighed.

"Ok, Just why? I mean, it's weird." Lee took a seat on the bed while Cere let out a groan.

"It's complicated and rather hard to explain." Cere moved from her sexy position, her wings flapping as she sat beside Lee.

"How about you try telling me? I've been dealing with complicated things for a good while." Lee pattered her back. His fingers are brushing against her wings. Soft to the touch as he shuddered. It felt like a slight buzzing was running through his hand.

"Well, it started a long time ago when the world went through. I believe in the industrial revolution. I was up in Heaven, ready to bring love upon mortals. As per my duties back then. When I found myself seeing this man, he was handsome, wearing a fine suit, a bowler hat, and walking down the streets of America as though he owned the place."

Lee could practically picture this happening. Some Old-time mobster was walking down in a striped suit and a fancy bowler hat just walking down the place as he continued listening to her words. Lee couldn't help imagining her purring some as she went down memory lane.

"Well, I couldn't help myself and fell to Earth. Most of the time, angels are forbidden from coming down to Earth. But this one time. I was sure they wouldn't notice. We bumped into each other, and we got to know each other. Then we fell in love." Her eyes were looking almost like hearts as she got to it.

"There's a twist to this, isn't there,"

"Like you wouldn't believe it. It took us seven wonderful days to get to know each other. We were in love, and he asked me to marry him. I said yes, without skipping a beat. It's a beauty how it felt. I realized this was how I made you mortals feel. Falling in love and going crazy. But then he told me something."

"What was that?" Lee wondered as he watched the Angel, he had some idea, but he wanted to get the answer and not assume.

"He revealed he was a Demon, but not any ordinary one. He was Azazel, The Incubus General of Hell. Who was on Earth to tempt the souls of women? I was shocked; I didn't believe him at first. Till we met in his room, Such a scandalous idea at the time, he revealed his true form… You know what I thought at the time?" Cere looked at Lee for a minute, the soft look in her eyes with hearts in them, her body glowing a gentle pink. Lee tried to find the right words, but as he opened his mouth, he shut it close.

"I can't be certain. What was it?"

"I fell in love with him more, even in his Demon form. I thought he was an angel, his beauty, his handsomeness. I know we're meant to be enemies. He's an Incubus, a creature normally meant to force itself onto a woman or seduce them from God's light. But in many ways. I was more in love with him. I had cast away my mortal look and revealed my cherub form. He was shocked as well."

"I bet it was rough," Lee responded, interrupting. He couldn't help but begin imagining this as Romeo and Juliet their relationship.

"You could say so, but He told me I looked even more beautiful than I already had. Maybe it was a gift from The Father. But not long after that, we went to Vegas and well got hitched. We never looked back. Of course, I had to return to my duties in Heaven. He on Earth."

"So, what led you here?" Lee asked, his heart racing as he fell deeper into this Angel's story, though she looked down some While he looked into her eyes.

"I got impatient. I wanted to be with him, so I decided to do something few angels had done. Only a handful would even consider."

"That being?" Lee said,

"I decided to fall. I left Heaven for good and lept from Heaven. I renounced God and his ways. Taking only my Arrows and began to fall from Grace. I ended up here in Hell instead of on Earth. With only a parchment. A note from God himself was telling me this." She reached over and brought out a far older paper than Lee, stained with Yellow but well-kept.

'*When a man whose heart is pure of heart willingly steps into Hell*

If he shall lay with a fallen angel of the lord.

If that Angel is filled with his seed.

Shall have the power to escape the depths of Hell.

Shall walk upon the Earth. Never to be trapped again.'

Lee read the paper. Once, a second time, and a third before it finally made it through his thick skull.

"Oh well, I see what you mean." Getting the gist of things.

"Yeah, so please, fuck me, fill me with your seed so I may escape from this place. I desire to be on Earth with my lover. I want to always be with him and not wait for his return every fifty years." As Lee sighed, the tears in her eyes trickled down her face like those of sweet summer rain.

In his mind, he didn't want to. He wasn't sure he had the energy even to complete this task. But on the other hand, He couldn't leave her like this. He was hit with so much. He also began imagining what he would do if he never saw Lucy again. He a simple sigh as he nodded.

"Fine, but give me a minute. Lucy can take it out of me, and it takes a couple of days."

"Right ahead of you." Lee suddenly turned over to where the Angel was and found Cere was gone. Instead, she stood before him, whipping some of her tears away, a smile spreading over her face as she pulled out a bow and arrow.

Lee raised his hand, shocked.

"Woah, what are you doing there? No reason to get violent." Lee watched the Angel with a smirk.

"Relax there. I'm just doing a bit of Divine intervention to fix your problem." Cere smirked a smile that looked more devilish than angelic. Lee felt his heart racing as he was about to run right from the room. He wasn't planning to get shot, and the arrow pointing at him was killing any chance of getting an erection.

Cere smirked more as she muttered.

"Relax there. I'll fire my lust arrow at the count of three."

Lee nodded though he imagined he was going to dodge.

"1..2" But before she reached number three, she let go of her quiver, and the arrow fired. Lee screamed loud, almost like a girl. The arrow began flying through the air, glowing like a light beam as it struck Lee in the chest. Causing him to fall on the bed and groan.

Lee looked around and realized everything looked more pinkish. His sense of smell changed as he began smelling things he enjoyed, the morning rain and hints of ginger. But there was more to it as he heard Cere's voice. It was softer, well-versed, as he suddenly felt his heart racing and pounding more. It excited him like when he had first met Lucy.

He looked towards the Angel, and his eyes widened more. She looked more divine, more exotic as she looked towards him.

Lee groaned hard as he felt a shudder run down his spine. His pants felt tighter.

Take them off, and I don't need any pants. Lee shook his head, but it was clear his body was doing what it wanted as they reached down, undoing his belt, and began dropping them. His underwear was revealing an overly large bulge. That didn't hide a thing. His newly enlarged cock from this morning was spreading its wings.

"My Oh my, Is that for little ol' me," Cere said, giving a southern twang as Lee nodded, his head feeling fuzzy as he let his cock out from its binding? His shaft was bouncing as if it was waving to the Angel in front of him.

'Yes, all for you. Care for a taste?" Lee smirked, his voice calmer, clearly relaxed as he got on the bed though Cere smirked as she walked in closer.

"No, thanks. Let's skip to the main event." Cere pushed him back, Lee lying on the bed watching her. His lustful vision was watching over him as she turned around, lowering her thong. Lee hadn't realized she was wearing so little. Her ass was showing off, bouncing and jiggling with such a hypnotic beauty.

His hand reached over as he began rubbing it. Soft to the touch, His fingers rolled over the thick, soft mounds. He imagined Cere moaning. She started pushing her rear onto his lap, rubbing her ass against his cock. It wasn't long before his cock went inbetween her ass cheeks. She swayed her hips back and forth. She was trying to turn Lee on, which was already working. As Cere Lifted herself.

"Hmm, be a good mortal, and Fuck me with all the force a mortal can provide," Cere smirked as she reached around, positioning his cock over her anus. His cock suddenly felt wet to the touch, clubbed for what it was about to do. Cere began pushing down. Lee suddenly gasped. It had been a while since he did anything involving a woman's Butt, but it felt heavenly. Pun intended If you asked Lee. As he felt himself sinking deep into her ass. His cock slid down.

Lee reached over, grabbed her angelic hips, and pulled Cere down. His eyes crossed, thrusting into her warm ass as he grunted hard. Her body was pushing down. Breast bounced up as Cere looked back.

"Hmm, I see you like my ass Lee." She muttered in that sultry voice as she pushed herself up and slammed on his lap. The way their skin clapped was beyond words, like music playing, as Lee felt overwhelmed with lust and his body burning with such passion. His hips thrust harder as the bed began creaking.

Her body fell as Lee Gasped as he moaned, as Cere accidentally hit him with her wings as they unfurled out, flapping in excitement.

"Fuck yes, Harder Azazel… I mean Lee Faster! I want all that damn cum into me!" Her voice got louder as she exclaimed; it felt good to her. It wasn't anything like what her Azazel could do, but it would do for now.

She hadn't been touched in years. Lee didn't need to be told twice. Or even a third time as he reached around, grabbed those wide thighs and pulled her down faster. His balls tightened up as her ass was way too good. It drove him wild. He barely noticed how she called him another name. Pleasure overwhelmed his senses.

"Oh, God!" Lee moaned as Cere bit her lips, crying with desire. His cock spread her ass. Whatever Lilith had done to him was more than the Angel could handle. It had been too long since she had a dick in her. However, it wouldn't be the last. Cere knew who she would take next, making love to her love, Azazel. She shuddered to imagine the demon taking her rough like no being in the vast eternity could do. As she felt herself begin to orgasm.

"Oh, Lee, please Cum, Cum!" Cere begged. She couldn't fight back, taking him balls deep, her hot ass tightening around his meat. Lee slapped her ass as his eyes rolled in the back of his head. Cere's wings were flapping onward as though she was close to flying off him. But Cere looked back, her moaning profound as she looked towards him—a skip as she gripped the bed.

"Come on more, more! I want to go back to my lover's arms!" She exclaimed as she felt her pussy getting hotter. As she bit her bottom lip. Lee's felt his balls slamming against her as the Angel as he tried fighting his orgasm. In many ways, the arrow of lust had worked too well. He didn't want this feeling to go away. He wanted more, and He needed this.

The thing, though, it would never last as long as Cere screamed louder, a second orgasm running through her heavenly body as she pushed down. Feeling him balls deep into her. Lee was shuddering hard. He couldn't hold back. Not anymore; that was when Lee reached down, grabbing her shoulders. His fingers were brushing Cere's sensitive wings as he tugged her down. He began letting his orgasm go and filling her ass with his hot sperm. As ropes of cum shot up into her.

Cere's body began glowing bright gold. Her body rejuvenated like the shackles binding her down finally broke. Her eyes turned back to this mortal. Lee lay there, breathing heavily as he felt his cock sliding from her ass.

"Thank you, Lee, I wish I could do something for you, but as of now, I shall leave you. I have to return to my true love." Like that, Cere began to vanish in a spark of light as she raised through the room, gliding past it. Lee would lay there alone. Soon He let out a long groan, his cock softening. Wishing he had something to drink. Something to get him relaxed. The spirit is strong, but the flesh is easily bruised, especially when an angel gets ahold of your nether region.

-000-

Lee relaxed there for the longest time as he reached around, seeing the remote on the side desk. A small part of him felt curious as he grabbed it.

"I wonder if Hell has HBO?" Lee turned the television on and was met with a slight jingle.

"Hi there guys, welcome to the Lizzie Borden Cooking hour. Today boys and girls, we'll be making my favorite snack. Cupcakes! And our special guest, she's a former athlete who had decided to cheat her way to the top, betrayed her best friend, and committed the sins of murder and fraud. I present Mary! Now she will be in for a good time!" There was the sound of a chainsaw going off while Lee watched in absolute horror as the screaming commenced. He quickly shut the television off and shook his head.

"Nope, no T.V. while I'm here." He moved, putting the remote away, knowing he wouldn't deal with anything on the Helltube. He moved around and soon closed his eyes falling fast asleep.

-000-

There was a loud thump against the bedroom door.

Lee woke up from his slumber as he remembered what happened, a long sigh as he felt his body sore. It was clear fucking an angel had taken more out of him as he gave a long moan. His loins hurt the most.

"Well, it could have been worst, thank god."

"Oh, you should be thanking me, future Son-In-Law."

Lee suddenly shifted his head, seeing Lucifer standing before him in the dark side of the room, moving out of the darkness with a cocky smile.

-000-

Lee followed Lucifer out of his room. The devil hadn't really said much, just pointed towards the door and followed him as they headed off to who knows where. His heart pounded. Not sure what might happen next, the worry felt in his gut.

"I'm going to need your help with this, Lee," Lucifer said, a slight grunt in his voice as though he didn't want to do this but had no choice. The annoyance on his face while Lee. He was confused,

"Um, why is it you need my help?" A curious expression ran through Lee as he tried to think of what he could even do. But nothing came to mind. At the same time, he looked towards who would be at the end of all of this, his future father-in-law.

"Because I can't access all my powers while on Earth, and I need a human for this job. An important job."

"Wait… why can't you access your powers on Earth? I mean, your Satan? You're a damn Angel. You could walk in and drop everyone." Lee was confused but could hear the grunt and growl from the fallen Angel.

"I am not Satan! Why does everyone mistake me for my damn cousin? I swear it drives me up the heaven damn wall!" As for my powers, I can't access all my powers. I'm limited; for example, I can manipulate and make people do things they secretly want. But I can't say, drop a meteorite on someone or drop the wrath of Hell. Not like the old days. Nowadays, I need to be more clever."

Lee nodded though not fully understanding why he just sighed. Such a thought is trying to understand anything. Though coming along with getting used to dating a succubus was bizarre at the beginning, he eventually got used to it. He was doing this. He was sure in time and would become used to this if he lived long enough to do so.

They passed over as they moved into the throne room. The two were standing there. It was empty. No guards. He didn't even see the throne as he looked towards the devil.

"So, what're we be doing."

Lee winced as he began thinking, *Please don't ask me to fuck. So not gay, not gay!*

"We're going to retrieve a few of my daughters."

Lee wasn't sure what to say though he continued on watching Lucifer raise his hand, a claw-like finger appearing from his hand as he made it slit down, pushing down as a bright orange light followed behind. When he was done, he stepped back and appeared right between them; a portal appeared—standing in what looked to be a church.

"What is this place?" Lee asked, curious as they looked at the sizeable ram-shackled church that seemed to be on its final legs before collapsing in on itself.

"It's one of the hidden churches."

"The hidden churches? You mean the organization that insane priest worked for that nearly killed Lucy?" Lee remembered what Dawn had told them about the organization she once worked for.

"The same- this is one of their older ones, but I'm sure they've got some guards, secrets that they don't want people like me to find. They have lots to hide, even in the American section."

"Well, they have it well hidden. I mean, no one wouldn't look around in an abandoned church" Lee couldn't help but question it. He watched as Lucifer moved over, looking around the doors—such a moment as they prepared to find the entrance.

"Exactly, and they're paranoid bastards; whenever the organization loses a member, it might leave one or put more guards if they don't skip town just in case whatever they were hunting tries to come back. Ah, here it is." He approached one of the statues, one of an angelic woman whose breasts were gently exposed. The way it looked out at them, its heavenly glow—the kindness in this broken-down cathedral.

"Now watch this." He smirked as he grabbed the statue's bosoms and pushed down. It was there as if it was nothing. The breast collapsed down into each other, and Lee soon heard a loud click. The stairs began collapsing down long, drawn-out sliding of stone against stone. That seemed to go down. Lee watched this with utmost fascination as he would soon look down into darkness.

"Now come on- wait, no, not like this. Who knows what those nut jobs must've left down there to guard this shit." Lucifer chuckled as he snapped his fingers, and soon Lee suddenly found himself wearing a priest's gametes. It hung snugly around his body. At the same time, the devil wore one of his own, an inverted cross wrapped around his neck.

"An inverted cross. A little on the nose, isn't it?" Lee snaked though Lucifer only snorted that off.

"Please, kid, don't believe everything you see on t.v and the movies. This is the cross of Saint Peter. Blah blah- I don't have to explain Christian or catholic lore to you all day. I got my girls to pick up." He suddenly bounced down on the first step, third, and fifth. It was as though he was skipping along. Lee took long strides following behind him. While watching him, Lee couldn't help but think he saw a halo atop his head. Cracked but gently glowing.

Lee just followed the light. At such a time, he wondered if he could question his life. Not long before, Lee was having sex with an angel. Now he was following the king of Hell down into a church's hidden basement. To save another succubus locked in a ring.

Life was such an odd. Lee found himself thinking.

He would continue as he listened to his heels clicking against the marble steps. A chill ran down his spine from the wind passing him. His fingers felt numb from the sheer cold. Lee imagined he would soon see his breath if it got any colder.

They continued walking through the church, and It felt bigger inside. From the outside Lee thought they could've taken a minute or two to walk through this place. He wasn't afraid of this. But something about this place wasn't right. While he continued onwards, Lee soon watched as Lucifer stood before a wooden door.

"Now listen, act calm, and don't do anything rash. If there are priests in here, they might just shoot on sight. They gave up on that Thou shalt not kill, turned it into, Though Shalt blows thy heads off."

Lee almost wanted to laugh at that. It gave him a smith though he wasn't sure what the devil might do to respond to this. Lee kept himself going quiet with a nod. Lee took a hard breath as he somewhat imagined himself at work, doing papers and being yelled at by Grace. Though it was something he was sure to return anytime soon just when this was over.

Lee could feel his leg hurt. The moist musky place was getting to his ankle as he grabbed the doorknob and headed inside. Lee limped as he tried not to step on it the wrong way. Something he didn't want to deal with for some time, but here he was—the long pause as they moved inside.

The place was quiet. The stone walls just went off with wooden doors on either side. Lights are swaying back and forth with the cold draft and creaking. It was clear that the place was abandoned. Or felt like one. Such a place. It was creepy, like Lee had stepped into a horror film.

"Seems like they abandoned the place."

"Yeah, it seems like it. Though we should keep going, who knows what they left behind." Lucifer took the lead as he was ahead.

"I don't get it. Why don't you summon It or use magic to bring it to us?"

"Because if I could, I wouldn't need you. These churches probably have words that suppress my powers; they get benefits for working for the old man or, at least in their mind, think they work for the old bastard."

"Oh well, alright, then. I guess it'll take a while."

They began exploring the caverns moving through them as it was relatively silent between the two beings. Lee wasn't sure what he could say. It wasn't like he could ask him if he saw the game last night. How could someone talk to an archangel, let alone the devil? Lee just took a deep breath.

Moving deeper in, the few rooms they got into met with little to no resistance, though these rooms didn't have much in them, broken furniture. A bible is lying around on the ground. Nothing of importance though Lucifer still explored them leaving nothing unturned.

"So... this place is quiet..." Lee muttered while turning over a bed and noticing, Seeing a dildo and panties and not wanting to know who once owned this. He tossed it back in place. He pushed the bed back over it. He wasn't sure what they were even looking for. Was he hunting for another ring? Was it something more significant? Lee didn't know, and He continued as he approached the next door. His hand grabbed the handle and tried turning it.

"Locked... Weird." He tried turning it in the other direction, and still, it wouldn't budge. Now why would they lock this door? Every other door Lee had run into had opened. But this one wasn't.

"What could they be hiding in here." He turned his head towards the direction where Lucifer was before and called him out. Lee looked off into the distance.

"Is there something you need?" Lee practically bounced out of his skin as he looked back, and Lucifer stood there. He was leaning against the wall, casually posing with a relaxed smile. Lee couldn't think of how to respond. Not even asking how he just appeared behind him, as he realized he was talking to the devil himself. He decided to go with it.

"Yeah, This door. It's locked." He reached over, pulled the

door, and showed it was locked. Lucifer blinked.

"Here, let me help." The Angel grabbed the door pulling it. The Angel swung the door open with great ease, ripping it from the hinges—the sounds of nuts and bolts. Looking back, Lucifer pushed the entrance to the side. He was smacking his hands together.

"Well, that was fun. I wonder what's inside?" He turned, looking inside. Lee followed, doing the same as they looked on into the room.

The room was a cathedral in itself. Pews on either side, from one end towards the middle, were gaped for those who wished to walk across. Stain glass windows depicting saints, each staring off, almost as if they were judging. Such a sight made Lee's spine shudder—such a moment as he took the first step.

When he entered the room, nothing happened. Not what Lee was expecting, some trap or even an alarm, but there was nothing. Soon he and Lucifer proceeded inside. As they got in, Lee began noticing a pedestal. Off on the stage, it was black. Though something was on there, Lee moved in closer as he tried to see what it must've been. Only to realize that it was simply a black box, The same kind that must've held a ring in it.

Lee had run up towards it as he saw the thing. It was a ring box. His hand reached over but stopped before he could grab it. He realized it was far too easy. His fingers glided over it, tempted to grab an old thing and run away. But as he tried reaching over to grab it, he couldn't. Maybe he had just watched too many movies. He looked around, perhaps finding something that he could replace it with. But suddenly, Lucifer popped right next to him.

"What are you doing?"

"I'm trying to grab this box. It might have a ring in it."

"Well, grab it, grab it by the box!" Lucifer exclaimed as he looked at it, almost tempted to grab it himself. Though a Cheshire grin on his face as Lee reached closer and suddenly pushed the box over a few inches.

Lee's eyes widened as he practically bounced away in case a trap activated. Though nothing seemed to happen, Lee blinked a few times as he watched the box for a second. Sighing in relief, though, he eventually turned his head towards his future Father-in-law, giving him a dirty look.

"Hey, you were just going to stand there looking at it. Now come on, grab it, and let's go." He turned around walking out of the room. Lee only sighed as he reached over, picking the box up. He opened the box, examining it. The ring looked almost like the same one Lucy had when she was trapped in one. However, the difference between this and hers was that the ring was red and blue, with hints of silver. That was when the room began shaking. Luke looked around as he heard a crashing sound.

"Fuck! Lucifer, get back here! You coward!" He saw nothing when he looked over to where the archangel had been. The bastard had vanished without a trace. Lee couldn't help cursing under his breath. He heard glass shattering as he looked behind him.

The saints stood there, weapons made of glass in their hands as they began walking there. It was utterly queer, seeing the glass saints molding looking more three-dimensional as they began stepping over to him. There were five in total. They raise their glass weapon. Ready to strike. Lee did the first thing that came to mind.

He ran out of there like a crazy mother fucker. He ran out

the door and began running towards the exit. That was the problem, though, as Lee started to take a left turn when he found himself running into a dead end. Lee looked around back and forth as he tried grabbing one of the doors and hoping for a chance to hide. He turned the doorknob but couldn't make the door budge.

"Fuck!" Lee shouted as he imagined taking a good run. But as he did, he saw the glass Saints; they turned around looking towards him; the way they moved was unnatural. Each step pushed forward as they sounded like glass sliding against the ground.

Lee wasn't sure what to do. That was when he looked down, staring at the ring. He wasn't sure if it would work, and he wasn't sure what Lucy would say, but at the moment, he wasn't sure he had much of a choice. It wasn't like there were any rocks around. He grabbed the ring and slipped it on his right index finger.

"Come one, what was that spell? You know it." He muttered under his breath, watching the glass Saints move closer, dragging along, as Lee began speaking out.

"Oh, Demon of lust,

I free you from your prison,

Let this ring bind us.

Find our hopes and share this fire

As we are indeed the same.'

Nothing seemed to happen soon. Lee repeated the incantation though nothing seemed to happen. That was when one of the glass creatures through a knife at him. Lee dodged it though it managed to slice his cheek. That was when he realized what he was doing wrong as he grabbed the blood from his cheek, rubbing the blood around the silver ring. Lee began calling out the incantation one last time.

"*Please work fuck!*

Oh, Demon of Lust,

I free you *from your prison,*

Let this ring bind us!

Find our hopes and share this fire!

As we are indeed one and the same!"

His voice called out, screaming as he suddenly felt a fire running through him, his body heating up, as he felt as he had when Lucy was free from the ring. It was working, his body shouting more as he slumped back on the ground. Mumbling.

"Help me…" he whispered, holding consciousness as a shadowy figure raised up. Ram horns on her head, but there was something else, a hat. It looked like a cowboy hat, as the voice called out. It was female but a heavy southern draw.

"hoo, boy! Looks like I'm free, and we've got a Mexican standoff. But They brought a knife to a gunfight." Lee finally got a better look. This Succubus stood tall with long blond hair, Reddish skin, with dark freckles. Bright emerald green eyes, as she wore a dark uniform that looked ripped in different places. They looked almost like an outfit a soldier from the civil war would wear. Her breasts were mighty fine, not as large as Lucy, but they would be an eye-catcher. Her horns stuck right out of the hat. Sharp and pointy. She has the devil's grin.

As she suddenly reached over to her belt. She was pulling out a pair of Colt revolvers. The Succubus began firing away, shooting her weapon off as the bullets shot true and straight, hitting the glass saints and causing them to shatter into a million tiny pieces.

She kept shooting, the sound of gunfire going off, as the Succubus Laughed in much delight. Till finally, the last saint had fallen, and it was just between the two of them.

"Thanks…" Luke muttered as he pulled himself up. His legs were wobbling, though unlike when he freed Lucy, he hadn't passed out. In many ways, he was grateful for this.

"No prob, Sug, now I gotta ask you'll something?" The Succubus asked, raising her head. Lee couldn't help but notice her breast getting a bit bigger, as if a button would soon pop from her uniform. She turned over, picked him up, and put him over his shoulder.

"What year is it?"

"Um… Its twenty, twenty-three." Lee found himself answering while trying to focus on what she was saying while she nodded

"Alright now I've gotta ask. Who won? Was it the south or them damn Yanks?"

"Um… I don't know what you mean, ma'am?" Lee muttered, feeling emasculated from being picked up like this.

"Please call me Betsy, and who won the North or the South?"

"Oh well, the North won…" Lee examined the uniform more and cursed under his breath. It was than Lee realixed that She was wearing a confederate uniform…

CHAPTER 5

Lee wasn't sure how to react. The surprised expression on his face as he stared at this woman. Betsy was by far different from Lucy, who was her sister. Her voice was a heavy southern accent as she wore that grey uniform. She was soon holstering her colts while tapping her boots.

"So the Yanks won the war; well fuck me silly and call me Shirley."

"Alright, Shirley," Lee responded, trying to be funny though Betsy gave him a dirty look.

"Don't call me Shirley." She huffed hard, almost snorting, while she began looking around. Almost as if she was wondering where she might have been. Maybe, though Lee sighed.

She muttered under her breath as she looked around; she seemed to be examining the surroundings as The woman wondered where she was or when. So many questions were coming to her.

"Yeah, the south lost, though many things changed. Um, come on, Lucifers, waiting outside of this place." Though Betsy raised an eyebrow, he kicked himself in the foot as he imagined wanting to kick the Devil's ass.

"You mean, My Father is here? That no-good yellow-belly bastard finally decided to come and get me!? Ok, where the hell am I?" Betsy yelled out, annoyed and ready to kick someone's ass, her body sizzling as she grubbed her stomach, feeling hungry. Lee reached over, grabbed her shoulder, and wrapped his arm around her.

"Well, you're in the 21st century. It's 2021, and I Have no idea where we're, but I'm from Ohio."

"Yeah, yeah, yank, well, let's get going. I have a no good son of a bitch father to speak to." Betsy sneered in utter annoyance, not happy to see the man. Lee looked at her for a good second.

"Well, hopefully, he's out there waiting for us." Lee hoped though not sure. So far, today has felt like an eternity. Something about it was off, and now that he looked down at his hand, seeing two rings, he groaned in annoyance, knowing he was bound to another succubus again.

He wasn't even sure how he planned to explain this to Lucy. They began walking down the corridors. Not sure what would happen or who they might run into. All Lee knew was he didn't want to run into more traps. Even with Betsy here to protect him. Besides, how many bullets would those guns even hold now?

"So, How did you wind up trapped in the ring?" Asked almost curiously as he looked back at the confederate succubus.

"Ah, got ambushed. It took about fifty Yanks to catch me, though I took out as many as I could before they got one of them, preacher men to bound me. I'd have shot me right between the eyes if I caught that man of God." Lee barely understood a word she said, and that was saying something. But he shook his head and nodded.

"Well, that sucks. I mean, I found Lucy by accident, and well, we're getting married now. I swear, what am I even going to tell her?"

"Just tell her you got another Succubus; it should be simple," Betsy spoke while Lee shook his head.

"Again, this is the twenty-first century. There is nothing simple about this." Lee bit his lips as they finally found themselves at the door. Looking towards the thing as he carefully grabbed the door handle, his eyes closed as he prepared to open it, yet he imagined a rattlesnake right outside, ready to strike at any moment.

The door slung open; he let out a fierce yell. Running out there ready to punch, kick and bite if he needed to, there was nothing as he ran out there. Just a peaceful world. That chirped crickets and not much else. He took a deep breath as he sighed in relief. Lee let out a nervous chuckle. His guard dropped.

"Smooth move there, son." A familiar voice called out, causing Lee to jump in the air with much horror. He bounced around, looking to see none other than Lucifer and holding a pocket watch, looking impatient. Lee couldn't help screaming in pure shock. At the same time, Betsy stepped outside the door, looking at him with much annoyance.

"What's with all the yelling!" She muttered, crossing her arms. Lucifer snickered.

"Jesus boy, you don't need to scream! You've been in there for what seemed like forever. I was getting nervous like those glass saints had managed to get you killed."

"Well, I survived, no thanks to you." Lee groaned while just rubbing his face. The bags were over his eyes as he looked back at the devil himself.

"Why in the hell didn't you help me?" He complained while imagining kicking the devil in the ass. Lee West is kicking the devil right in the ass! He imagined his old Sunday school teacher would get a kick out of that.

"Woah, cool down there. One of the big guy's significant rules is not to allow messing with mortals. You're on your own and made it out in one piece."

"Yeah, with the help of your daughter." Pointing over to Betsy, who was polishing her Colt revolver. Lucifer gave his devilish grin happy to see his daughter.

"So you unleashed one of my daughters once more. So what are you planning on doing with her?" A wide chuckle while looking over at the mere mortal man.

"Well, I figured you'd free us from our bindings, and we could go. Lee pulled a hand up, showing the ring.

"Oh no, that's not how that works. Once you free one of my daughters from those rings, your stuck with her." Lucifer let out a broad, pleasant grin. Lee couldn't help but feel dread rising around him to realize what would happen. What was he going to tell Lucy? He shuddered, imagining the horrors that were going to happen.

"You have got to be kidding me."

"I'm the devil. I never kid."

-000-

"Well, I guess you'll have to find out; we're off to hell, and it's good to see you, Honey," Lucifer said with a broad smile. Betsy looked at him rolling her eyes in annoyance and not wanting to acknowledge the devil in front of them.

A portal began appearing before then, and Lucifer turned, smiling. The one, only the devil, could make itself as he turned around, stepping right through it. Luke and Betsy walked right behind him as they moved through the portal. Lee walked on through as they appeared in the dark castle of the Dark Lord Lucifer. Who smiled, sighing in relief. Lucifer looked back.

"Well, that was something else, but being in my sweet castle is good. The cold chill whistled in the air, passing by them. Lee felt an overwhelming calmness, and When he realized how relaxed he was, he couldn't help finding it ironic that being in hell somehow made him feel more comfortable than actually being at church.

- 000-

"Someone broke into the church, and our security system is destroyed, and something is clearly missing." Said one of the two men who walked inside, each of the old, with hair as white as snow and wearing black robes.

"So, It seems as though someone has broken into our chamber. Well, isn't that great?" One of the preachers muttered while looking at the broken glass of the security system. A thing they had spent months setting up and praying for forgiveness from the lord as they looked over and saw the vanished box. The one that held one of their greatest enemies, the Succubus.

"Who do you think it was, Father?" The preacher said while looking at the scorched walls. How they formed only added more questions.

"Truly, that is something we must ask. Ourselves and the Lord." said the older man who looked around the walls. As he imagined it was something, though turned back, "We'll have to consult the inevitable and track down the ring and those who broke into the church. Pray that they didn't release the beastly creature."

"Should we send someone? How about father Lucus? Has anyone been able to make contact with him?"

"No one has. We suspect Father Lucus failed his mission. There also has been no contact with the nun. I suspect they're both dead."

"Then what can we do? Father Lucus was one of our best Succubus hunters. If he failed, what can we do?" The younger man said while disturbed, imagining one of their best had managed to fall to such creatures.

"We'll send another one, and we can't rely on the past generation not to fall. If we must, send our next and pray to the good lord. Guild him to protect us." He turned, looking about as he knew that something was wrong, but soon, by the grace of heaven, they might be able to make a difference and save those who have lost.

-000-

Lee appeared in the dark palace, the room covered in darkness as he looked about for a second, sighing in relief, somehow glad to be located in Hell. Lee looked over, seeing the cowgirl succubus Betsy and Lucifer himself, who adjusted his suit.

"Truly, it's a time to celebrate; please take some wine, rest up, and enjoy yourself. I'm sure you both deserve a good rest after your difficult time." Lucifer said that wicked grin only the lord of Lies and evil could have as he popped his neck.

"Gah, I'll take some fine whiskey, old man," Betsy said while she looked around the room, clearly disgusted by all around her, while Lee felt his head fall. It was clear he was exhausted and needed to get some sleep; unlike these two, he was mortal, after

76

all.

"I think I'm just going to head to bed, I don't know what I'm going to say to Lucy, but she's not going to believe this."

"Believe what?" A familiar voice spoke up, causing Lee to look over and see none other than Lucy. She stood there wearing a red silken robe with just enough opening to show off her beautiful cleavage.

"Oh, Lucy, You look great there, honey." He smiled while looking at his beautiful fiancée.

"Well, thank you, now you were wanting to tell me? Also, why were you out so late?" She asked, more curious than anything, clearly not noticing the other succubus in the room for a minute,

"Well, I had to help your dad with something else, and one thing led to another."

"Howdy, there, little sis," Betsy spoke up as she stepped out of the shadows revealing herself.

"Betsy… You, How?" Lucy seemed lost as she realized she was looking towards her sister while The southern soldier tipped her hat up as she said,

"The varmint here got me out of that ring now; I'm stuck with him for now until we break it off or something. So how you been?" The Grey outfit hung off her as she adjusted it, Clearly giving her body a little more air while Lucy looked back.

"Lee, you helped her. Where did you even…." She looked over, seeing the ring on his middle finger; as she looked back at him, she became more surprised. "You released her… Bound her. I don't know what to say." She looked at him, and Lee felt a pang of fear on his face as he shook his head,

"We got into some trouble, crazy glass priests trying to kill us, so I did the only thing I could, and your dad there vanished on me." He couldn't help giving Lucifer a dirty look at that point, who quickly responded by raising his hand.

"Hey, Now, I was never there. I just helped you get there." That charming smile while he lies through his teeth. Lee couldn't have expected more from the father of lies.

"You're not mad at me, are you?" Lee said while he held her shoulder, wondering what she might say, as Lucy smiled gently.

"Why would I be mad? You're safe, and that's all that matters, though I wish you told me you were planning this. But also, I'm a bit annoyed that you're bound to my sister; but I'll let it slide, but you'll need to make it up to me for our wedding night." She poked his nose with that cute wide smirk as she rolled her red hair around.

"What would that be?" Lee asked while giving a gentle nudge against her. Imagining some of the strange things the Succubus Queen might try to do to him on their special night, she leaned in, huskily into his ears.

"You'll have to find out then, and it will be a surprise." She slapped him right on the ass as he bounced up. Her smack was nice and firm as she gave him that cheeky smirk. He'd grown to love more than anything.

"So, Old man, where am I going to be sleeping? I got stuck in that ring for how long, and I'll tell you what I want to get some into something nice and comfortable." Betsy looked over to the Fallen angel, who smirked,

"Well, you'll be lying down in Lee's room and your sisters

since you bounded to him at this point, and besides, we couldn't possibly have enough room to hold you in the castle." Lucifer chuckled while Betsy looked back over, clearly twitching her eye as if she were going to strangle the king of hell.

"You son of a!" But Lucifer had already vanished before she could finish that line, leaving the three of them there. Lee looked around slightly while giving a long sigh.

"I swear one of these days I'm gonna get dad and whoop him so hard Granddad gonna be jealous." Betsy grunted more annoyed while she looked back at her sister.

"This is just getting weird." Was all Lee could really say.

"Don't you know it?" Lucy snickered while she was ready to lead Lee off to their bedroom; the succubus's eyes glowed as she licked her lips. Til Betsy looked over at them,

"Uh huh, where the bloody hell is your bedroom, little sister, since the old Bastard is making me sleep with you guys?" She spoke with that southern accent that sounded madder than a bull getting stung on the balls by a hornet.

Lucy looked over at her sister, then back at Lee when she realized this was now a thing; she groaned, rubbing her head as she nodded.

"Sure thing, Betsy. Come on, and I'm sure we have enough room in the bed for one more." She looked around for a second and wondered how they would make it but soon moved on, dragging Lee; Betsy watched the two while rolling her eyes as she began following them.

-000-

Lee lay in bed between the two succubi, clearly shocked to

be in a situation. Sure The bed was large enough for the three of them. Lucy wrapped her arms around him as she lay there, her body close to his, as she shuddered. Her warm body against his felt nice, even with the sweltering heat of Hell. Betsy lay on his left and turned away. However, she didn't seem to have a blanket over her, which showed off her magnificent rear end. It wasn't something he could complain about.

Though Lee found he couldn't sleep, he just lay in the light darkness with the glow of candles. Lee was tempted to turn on the television, well, it was tempting, but because of last time. Lee wasn't going to take a chance of needing permanent therapy.

"To think, I was hoping to get a one-night stand and pay the bills a couple of years ago. I'm married to a beautiful woman, and my father-in-law is the devil." He said while looking at the ceiling. His head was resting back with a long smile. It was like God was gifting him. Well, probably not God; he wasn't sure what it was like to meet God.

"Oh crap, will he come to the wedding?" If anything, he imagined that it would be a shock, though, at the same time, it was a funny image, having the big guy in one of the pews sitting there bored while hearing the sermon read out loud.

Lee giggled under his breath as he felt something grabbing his sausage. He stopped right there, watching the ceiling as he spoke out.

"Lucy, it might not be the best time to do that." He whispered over to his future bride-to-be, but she never responded as he felt her hand going up and down. Slow at first while jacking his cock off.

Lee was tempted to smack her hand off. But it was beginning to feel good, her hands seeming rougher than average; it felt good as she continued to move her hand. Even playing with his head the way she twisted her hand over his thick shaft head. He let out a low moan.

"On second thoughts, just keep going. I'm sure we can clean this up later." He groaned, feeling her gripping him tightly as she jacked him off faster. Precum leaked from the tip Lucy had reached over, slathering it over his cock head, really getting his member lubed up as he moaned hard. His hand wrapped around Lucy as he squeezed and played with her firm breasts. She moaned,

"Keep going faster." He whispered in an audible, hoping not to wake Betsy. He groaned, closing his eyes as he felt his balls contracting. His breathing got heavy as he thrust his hip up into her hand, really getting into it. A part of him wished Lucy would go down on him. Lee wanted to fill her sexy throat as he let out a long moan.

"Yeah, like that; I'm getting so close." He said while feeling her tighten, her grip getting rougher on his cock, as Lee could feel his balls tightening up.

"Yeah, Like that, I'm almost there; yes, more, Lucy, I think I'm gonna." Lee found himself unleashing his load. His load was shooting into the air. He moaned loudly while feeling his load escape his throbbing cock. He didn't care. His load landed on his chest. The orgasm felt so strong he would ignore it. His heart felt like it skipped a beat as he collapsed there, his mind racing as he couldn't help but feel ready to fall asleep.

That was when he felt Lucy's hand reach around, circling where his load had landed on him as she pulled it towards his left. Lee closed his eyes for a minute when it struck him. *Please wait for a second; her hand pulled over to the left.*

He found himself looking over towards Betsy as he realized she had shuffled like she had wiggled in bed, causing Lee to pause for a minute and realize that the one who had given him a hand job wasn't Lucy but her sister. His heart skipped a beat as he laid his head back, soon falling asleep.

CHAPTER 6

"Are you sure you have to go? I'm sure your father can make arrangements for you. Send some imps in your place." Lilith said while hugging Lucy, a long hug while she looked over at her, Betsy, and Lee. The way she looked at Lee, it was clear she knew about last night, even if Lee wasn't sure what happened last night. A suspicion that he might have gotten a hand-job from the succubus sister.

"Yeah, we need to get home, work and all. But we'll send you a date for the wedding and where it will be." Lucy smiled as she grabbed Lee's hand. Betsy stood there, looking more refreshed than she was the other night. Lee wondered if last night had happened or if it had been his imagination. Lee decided to leave it be for the time being. They walked through the portal that Lucifer had created, transferring them back into Lee's Apartment. Lee gasped while looking around, finding himself shocked to be home already.

Betsy looked around as she touched one of the light switches.

"So this is the twenty-first century. Not that impressive." She mumbled while turning the light on. As she saw the illumination, Lee saw a flash of surprise.

"Hmm, light inside, and no need for fire, good to know."

Lee rolled his eyes while going around and putting some of his stuff up.

"I'm heading into the shower, no offense but the water down there is hot as well, you get the idea. So I'm going to cool down, babe. I hope I don't need to clean up the mess."

"No worry, save some of the hot water for me." Lucy smiled while she bounced onto the couch. Betsy tilted her head, looking out the window and seeing the modern world. Lee nodded as he began heading to the shower. Betsy looked over,

"So, did you marry some rich fella or something? Cause He isn't heading out at the crack of dawn."

"Oh, sis, the modern day is quite something; trust me," Lucy said while she patted her sister's shoulder. Their voices faded as he went to the bathroom, hoping he wouldn't need to clean anything up. Though when he walked in, he prepared a terrible smell. Imagine the dry goat blood left behind after Lucy sacrificed the goat. Yet Looking around, the bathroom looked clean. He tilted his head, more surprised.

"Well, thanks, Satan; at least everything cleaned up." Lee snorted at what he said and realized his mom heard him say that. She might have smacked him over the head just for that. Even then, he realized he needed to call his mom to tell her he would be marrying something. That was a whole different can of worms he'd have to open up later.

"Ok, shower first, then call mom." Lee jumped into the shower letting the hot water pour onto him. Somehow after being down in hell, it felt fantastic. Yet he didn't mind. It felt right; *It feels so good.* Lee thought while he began washing his body, closing his eyes, scrubbing his body down. He was starting to feel clean as he let the last few days fly away from him. The world is like a blur. The steam surrounded the room while taking his time.

He rashed his cock slowly, wrapping his fingers around the sensitive member. As he grunted. He slathered shampoo while he let the water hit his firm chest. It was one of those things that he enjoyed—a moment away from the world and everyone.

"So this is my life?" He said out loud to himself, wondering what would happen next.

-000-

Lee eventually got out of the shower and returned to the living room dressed while the two Succubus watched television. Luke noticed they were watching tv. Betsy watched it more surprised. Not able to look away, she pointed over.

"A black man is drinking from the same water fountain as a white woman; when did this happen?" Lee raised an eyebrow at that as he had to remind himself she was from the civil war.

"Listen, the world has changed. Black people have the same rights as white people. Heck, one even became president of the united states." Lee watched her while she had a surprised look.

"Well, good for them; that's quite shocking." Betsy's mouth dropped, "What's next? Are gay people able to marry? Cause that would be interesting." Lee had to fight the urge to snort while shaking his head.

"Yeah, you'll be surprised how much the world has changed. But I'm going to be keeping you away from Twitter. Also, the internet… Yeah, that's a good idea. But you're going to realize the world will not tolerate intolerance, got it."

Lee wouldn't be dealing with Racism, not in his house. The succubus might have come from a different period didn't mean he would tolerate bullshit. Betsy rolled her shoulder.

"Hey, now not all of us in the confederacy were into the whole slave-owning thing... That was why our stats leaders defected, but not every soldier agreed. We just followed orders... Some of us didn't have the nerve to kill our kin, which we might have done if we had gone with the north. I knew a few good ol boys who regrated their choices." There seemed to be sadness in her voice while she said that. Like she knew from experience. Lee nodded for a second when Betsy added in.

"Besides, a lot of them couldn't even afford to own a... Color fella? Is that the correct term?"

"No, that is not; they prefer to be called African American or simply person of color," Lee said as he resisted an urge to facepalm, as it was clear they had a lot to work on with her.

That was when Lee heard his phone ringing. Betsy suddenly reached over, pulling her six-shooter out while Lee raised his hand.

"Hey, listen there! It's just a phone. Put the gun down. No shooting!." He spoke out while he reached around, grabbing a hand ready to answer it and keeping his eyes on the woman while he answered it.

"This is Lee West; who's this?" Lee said, his eyes on the two girls, Betsy pulling the trigger back as she let the gun fall.

"Lee, it's Gracy; I need you to come to the office when you can. It's about the new manuscripts." Grace sounded far more concerned than she usually did. Lee wasn't used to this. As he nodded,

"You got it, Grace, and I'll be down there as soon as possible." Lee quickly hung up the phone as he looked back at the girls,

"Lucy! Grace called. I got to get back to the office." Lee cursed under his breath while he went over to grab his jacket.

"I'll keep an eye on Betsy, teach her a few things about the modern day, catch her up."

"Sounds like a plan. I'll get back here as soon as possible." Lee grabbed his truck keys and went towards the door. He couldn't help but pray she never found FOX new's last thing he needed to do was deal with that nightmare, especially if she started listening to someone like Tucker Carlson.

"I owe you one, Lucy!" Lee called out halfway through the door while Lucy giggled.

"You owe me more than one buster." She licked her lips as she imagined taking those favors from him sooner or later. At the same time, she looked back at her sister with a simple smirk.

-000-

When Lee left, it was just the two succubus, and Lucy was sitting there for a long moment as she looked back at her sister. This was the first time in nearly a century. She wasn't even sure what to say to her sister as she looked over.

"Hey, let's get you out of those clothes; I bet they're a little hot." She pulled herself up while Betsy looked over,

"Why should I? They fit and feel good. Besides, we're demons, and The heat doesn't bother me."

"Yeah, well, no one wears clothes like that anymore, and the world has changed, and I mean a lot. Stuff like that isn't appropriate."

"The fuck do you mean?" Lucy let out a long sigh as she realized this would be a long day.

"Alright, just, for the sake of argument, let us get something more comfortable, and trust me. You'll feel like you're in heaven when you try out a cotton t-shirt."

"Fine, but you better not be lying to me. Sis, you know I hate liars."

"Trust me, sis, you'll love these, and they'll show off your great body. Trust me; mortals will go nuts over you." Lucy tried to laugh but pulled her off to the bedroom as she imagined getting her in something more comfortable.

"So, Lucy, what's happened since I was locked away? Get any more wars?"

"Well, from what Lee's told me, there were two world wars, and Hitler led one."

"Who's Hitler?"

"A nonmagical Voldemort," Lucy said while she handed her sister a T-shirt that read, *Boobies make me smile!* It was black with Pink text. Betsy looked at it for a minute, judging while she put it on, not complaining.

"So, who the fuck's Voldemort?" Betsy muttered while taking her pants off. Lucy raised an eyebrow as she rolled her shoulder,

"You know he never told me, and I'll have to ask him about that one day." Betsy shrugged when she saw the pants thrown at her. They were a little big for her, but she placed them on.

"Well, I'll have to learn quickly don't need to get caught with my knickers down. So anything else?" Betsy said when they heard the doorbell ringing. Betsy looked around, ready to grab her gun, when Lucy grabbed her shoulder.

"It's just the doorbell, don't worry about it. Nothing is going to happen."

-000-

Lee parks his truck as he begins his way toward the office. He was crossing the road, avoiding the traffic as he looked around. Passing by the people walking around the large building, he headed straight toward the elevator. People were walking around as he slipped inside.

The large building was quite a sight, one of the more popular publishing companies for romance writers; they were the best for quality, especially picking out the top writers around the united states and Canada. There was no denying that working here was quite an honor.

Heading the elevator, Lee saw his boss, Grace, as most would refer to her, as Miss. Stone. Miss. Stone is a woman you dared not trifle with; she might have been a pretty face. But Lee, in his five years of working here, had seen the woman cause a grown man to cry and fall to his knees with little more than a few choice words, all because they were late on their deadlines.

She's proven to be one of the bests. Heck, Lee remembered when a writer had brought in fifty shades of Grey; she looked at the first five pages of the manuscript, walked it towards a window, and tossed it out the window, calling it absolute garbage.

Even when it hit the charts as the New York Times best-seller, she didn't blink an eye at it or regret it. She just laughed and went back to work. The intern who brought her the manuscript got demoted to delivering mail. Lee had honestly imagined he might have shared the same fate, being the nail to his boss's hammer.

"Mr.West, I requite you up in my office. Right now." Lee nodded. Soon his walk turned into a jog as he ran into the elevator. Her voice is tough and strong as she is around a group. It was only them as they stood there. Yet Grace kept that strong demeanor, her glasses perched while she adjusted them. The elevators closed behind them as they stood there while the music played awkwardly.

"So, what's going on with the Manuscript?" Lee asked while looking back at his boss.

"Well, there are a few problems, but also trying to communicate with the writers has been difficult, so I figured getting ahold of you to talk to him will be better 'cause you know."

"Cause they're being stubborn."

"No, I have no people skills, and you are probably one of the people I can trust to talk to people." Miss. Stone said while she stood there holding her hands while she looked back at him.

"How's your weekend been?" She said, seeming to break the more awkward moment.

"Oh, it's fine. I mean, I met my future in-laws." Lee said while rubbing the back of his head,

"Oh, how did that go? I remember the first time I met my in-laws, It felt like I went straight to hell, and for a while, I suspected his mother was secretly satan. Should have been a sign I should have run off instead of marrying the son of a bitch."

Lee was nearly stunned as he had to fight the urge not to

laugh if Grace knew who his in-laws were.

"They weren't that bad, but it could have been worse. Just a hell of a time." There, Lee wanted to kick himself, realizing he just said a pun.

"Well, that's good; any other plans for the wedding?" Miss. Stone asked while they stepped out of the elevator,

"Well, not much. Still planning some things out, but we're hoping it'll be within the next few months. Get it over with. Lucy isn't much for a grand show." In truth, he had no idea what they were going to do.

"Well, simple girl. I knew I liked her; she was good at her job and got it done. In more than one place." Hinting at some of the more private time the three of them had. Lee looked around, hoping no one heard as they headed down the halls.

"Might not want to say that too loud around here." Reminding her that she wanted to keep that side of her quiet."

"Not like they'll say anything besides; they know to keep their ears down when I pass by." She looked back at one of the employees who looked down. Lee just followed along.

"I mean fair, but still, you know how some people get." He kept a forced smile as they headed straight toward her office. Closing the door behind him, he sighed in relief before turning toward the older woman. She moved over, taking her business coat off, revealing the white button-up shirt as she sat behind the desk.

"So, where's the guy's number? I'll call him up." He headed towards the desk.

"I'll hand you his number in a minute, but I want to ask you something?" Lee looked at her for a minute, raising an eyebrow.

"What might that be?" Lee said while watching his boss lean over her desk.

"So when you get married, what are your guy's plans, move somewhere else? Finding a better job? …Leaving me?" there was a hesitation at that last part while she moved her finger in a circle against the table. Lee raised an eyebrow.

"What do you mean by that? We're going to be a married couple at the very most." Not adding that they were bound already, she didn't know about Lucy's status as a succubus.

"Yeah, well, it's not exactly like it means anything. You'll head off and find another life. You know, not since my ex-husband has I found someone quite as interesting as you two."

Lee nodded, admitting that she had seemed a bit nicer to him and Lucy. But that's the case.

"Well, it's not going to change much. You must change Lucy's last name to West when you sign the checks." He chuckled while Grace didn't smile at that.

"Yeah, well, I'm just getting older, and honestly. It gets lonely, Lonely on the top. You know, there were times I was tempted to call my ex-husband, sure he lazy, a dick bag, and cheated on me with our maid at one point." There was a moment of silence as she recalled that terrible night.

"He knew how to hold me, hold me on those rough nights when I just wanted to be held," Grace sniffed, looking like she was fighting the urge to cry. "When you came and well took my advances, it felt good. It's like I was wanted. Not just some old crow." There seemed to tear growing in Grace's eyes like she was finally letting out feelings she'd held back for the longest time.

"Then just having your Fiance, she made me laugh and was

a hell of a worker here and in the sheets. It's like she's not human. I don't think I can meet someone like you; I mean, It's hard for me; half the time, I barely get people. It's just hard for me.."

Grace rubbed her eyes as Lee found his heart hurting. He knew she had issues with her ex-husband and seemed sad on nights. Lee wanted to do more for her. He walked over to the desk. She was standing there while he reached down to rub her cheek.

"You know, if you talk to Lucy, I'm sure she can make a special arrangement, and She's a very good woman, and besides," Lee leaned in and kissed her lips. Their lips met as Grace let out a tiny moan, her hands reaching around and grabbing his cheek before eventually pulling away.

"I know Lucy would not want to give up her time with her. Just talk to her; there's always room for one more in our bed and yours." Grace looked at him, more surprised but nodded while caressing his cheek. She looked a the door with a long sigh.

"Lock that door there, Lee. Will you? We might have to discuss a few more things." She licked her lips, looking at him like a hungry beast.

"If you want boss, and besides, if the three of us don't work out, maybe I can ask Lucy to introduce you to a friend of hers. I'm sure she knows a few guys."

"Well, if they're as good as what I'm going to have you do, I might take the offer. But get down here." She sat down at her desk, clearly having something dirty in mind.

-000-

Lucy walked towards the door. Her heart is pounding while she looks at it. Wondering who it might have been and the last time someone came over when Lee left resulted in the murderous priest.

Who had tried to kill her and possibly Lee's friends? She worried about Such a thing until she looked back towards Betsy, imagining her by her side and her being a queen. She would be able to handle them if they tried.

Lucy reached over to open the door slowly as she prepared. Her hand turned into large claws as she pulled the door open. Lucy would strike at any second when the door fully opened. It was then she saw Dawn and Alice. Both of them smiled as Lucy sighed in relief.

"Hey girls, it's great to see you; um, where have you both been?" Lucy slouched while her hand turned back to normal.

"Where haven't we been? We've been everywhere, girl." Alice said, limping forward. Lucy watched her, raising an eyebrow.

"You ok there, Alice?" while watching the succubus Limping forward, Dawn walked to the right behind her.

"Let's say I'm getting out of my shell, and Alice is helping me. All she did was throw me off the Brooklyn bridge!" Dawn looked annoyed by this.

"Listen, will you let that go? I'm sorry you're now able to fly!" Alice said while she sat down slowly, letting out a sigh.

"Still didn't need to drop me off a bridge!" Dawn grunted while she walked inside.

"So, how's your engagement?" Alice said with a slight smirk. While taking a seat, Lucy chuckled.

"Well, you're not much of a nun anymore, now are you? Glad you're getting out of your shell, and yes, the engagement is going great." Lucy let out a sigh while she closed the door behind her.

"Well, that's good, though. Who do you think is going to be your maid of honor?" Dawn said, more curious as she looked back at the older succubus.

"Haven't decided yet, though that's probably going to come later if you don't mind."

"Hey, just send us an invite, I'm sure I can get me and Our Ex-nun a couple of plus ones, but I'm planning your bachelorette party, bring on the strippers!"

Lucy snorted as she imagined the Author would be bringing in hookers more than anything. She rolled her head around while Alice tilted her head with an expression that said; You what, mate! "Fine, but I'm not fucking any of the guys you bring; I'm sticking to Lee."

"Oh, relax there; I'll be screwing people, but that's with Lee's ok. We're a team, simple at that." She smiled while imagining Lee getting kinky.

"Well, that's fine, but I couldn't imagine being stuck to one person forever; I'm as free as an eagle-loving life and having my way with fertile young men."

"Best-selling author, folks," Dawn said while rolling her eyes. She got more comfortable while Lucy laughed at the two eyeing each other. Not sure if they wanted to knock the other out or get into bed.

"Who the bloody hell are these, sis?" The southern accent grew while Alice and Dawn turned around, seeing Betsy there, her gray hat on, while she looked at them with the boobie makes me smile shirt. It was almost comedic; the severe look on her face only added to it. While Lucy looked back at the others,

"Hey guy, this is my sister Betsy…." She held a hand up while The soldier girl gave them a nod.

"Betsy, your back? I mean, it's been what? Nearly 200 years ago? What the hell happened to you?"

"Got jump, my ass got shoved into a ring; nice to see you, sis, so you're going by Alice now?"

"Yeah, need to adjust to the time, see you still on the whole south thing, might want to drop that times have changed," Alice said while she leaned back on the couch.

"So I've been told." Betsy said while she looked at Dawn, "Who's the short stack?"

"Oh, that's Dawn; she's new, used to be a nun, worked for a real nut case, tried to kill Lucy."

"I see."

"No worry, she got better; she was a half succubus." Lucy quickly added while looking back at Dawn, knowing she regretted her past actions.

"Well, welcome to the family," Betsy said, raising a hand out while looking towards the former nun, who just reached out, taking it with a nod, clearly not sure how to feel about the other woman, but moved over, shaking it.

"Thanks, um, yeah, it's been a heck of a year finding out what I am," She gave Alice another dirty look while The succubus rolled her eyes. "Though I don't regret it. I feel so alive and not as hungry."

"That's the spirit; since you guys are here, maybe we can talk a bit about the wedding while Lee's out at work; speaking of work, how's the new book Alice been?"

"It's been fine, though, Miss. Stones riding my ass keeps going on about how I'm behind on my deadline; excuse me. I'm training a succubus and researching some material. Besides, art like this isn't finished in a day." Alice snickered. While she looked over at the suitcase, "Wonder what the old crone is doing?"

-000-

Lee thrust deeper within Grace as she moaned in ecstasy, her body covered in sweat as she screamed his name. Her half-naked body pressed against the bed as she panted. Lee continued moving his hips back and forth. Tightening his grip, he felt the older woman moan hard as he could barely hold it back anymore; feeling his nuts pulling,

"Fuck! Going to cum, Grace!" Moaning out her name, she screamed in pleasure, her pussy tightening around his member as she pushed back against him.

"Fill me up, baby!" She moaned, reaching down from under her shirt and playing with her breasts as she pushed back on him even harder. The sounds of their flesh slapping together, making loud clapping noises.

"You want my hot jizz in you? Well, you better take it all," Lee growled, clearly getting more into it as pushed his cock deep within his boss's pussy. Grace threw her head back, shuddering as she felt a powerful orgasm. She moved back one last time before collapsing on the table. Lee's thrust was as deep as possible. His cock pulsing, feeling himself being milked by Grace's pussy. Unable to fight back his want. He panted as he leaned down against her back. He freed his load into her and gave her a nice juicy cream pie.

"So, was it good for you?" Lee muttered while giving the back of her ear a nipple.

"Hmmhmm, we must do this more often; it feels so good." She rubbed up against him. Her shirt wrinkled up. Then without warning, they heard the doorknob starts to turn. Grace's eyes widened like dinner plates as she shot up in the air, causing Lee to fall back as she got on her chair. She quickly ran her hand down her shirt. Not wasting a second as she looked at Lee. "Get under the table now!"

Lee quickly went under the table and hid under it. As Lee got a face full of his boss's pussy, Grace pushed herself in. Watching his load leaking out as she sat there, he heard her speak professionally like she hadn't just gotten a load of cum shot into her.

"Yes, Beth? Is there something you need?"

"I've got those Manuscripts you wanted to read, also the letter for Satan reborn. You said you wanted to write the rejection letter yourself."

"Oh yes, thank you," Grace spoke with the refined form as she took the papers. Lee was too busy looking at her pussy, and an idea came to mind about fingering her. At the same time, they spoke but imagine if he did that, she would fire him just for acting that way while she was busy. He figured it wasn't worth it.

"Is there something wrong, Beth?" Grace said,

"Um, do you want me to open a window, boss? The rooms kind of musky?" Lee could feel his heart skipping a beat, hoping she didn't realize that musk had been the smell of the two of them screwing around.

"No, it's fine. Just get going; I'm sure you've got better

things to do." She lightly kicked Lee in the chest as he fought the urge to grunt while he looked back at her, his face expressing, " *Hey, what was that for?* Lee imagined he'd get back at her for that.

"If you want, ma'am, I'll get going." Beth's voice vanished as the door closed behind her while Lee sighed in relief, knowing they hadn't gotten caught.

Lee waited a good minute before Grace whispered to him, "She's gone. You can come out." Grace spoke under her breath while Lee let out a long sigh pulling himself out with a long groan, stretching out.

"Thank goodness." Lee popped out as he looked around for his pants. He quickly reached over and grabbed them.

"I better get going. That was close."

"Might be a good idea, Though give it a few minutes; I don't want others to notice." Grace reached over, grabbed her panties, and slipped them on while she looked over to Lee, those lush eyes. "If you don't mind." Grace seemed more exposed and vulnerable as she looked over at the man. Like she wanted to say more, do more with him. Lee just looked at her with that relaxed smile.

"I wouldn't mind for a few minutes, so how have you been lately."

"Good," Grace said as she sat back down, looking over some of the manuscripts.

"Here's the number; make those calls and set it up. I appreciate it, Lee." She gave him a wink before she went back to work. Like the excellent workaholic she is.

-000-

Off far across the united states in a place called Las Vegas. There was a poker game—a simple one in the back of a casino. Some of the men were playing with decent hands though there was one. Five players were in an intense competition, where the winner took all. There was more than cash, a few deeds to places. A pair of car keys. The whole nine yards. It was waiting for the correct winner. There at the end was a figure, a man who had a short black beard; he looked to be around his mid-thirties, but it was those eyes, dark brown, that seemed far ancient as he held his cards close. He looked at them intensely, not showing what he had, two aces and two eights with a jack of hearts on the side.

"I'll raise," The mysterious man dropped another chip.

"Woah, brother, you sure about that? You don't got much left, partner." One of the players said, a cowboy hat on his head as he tipped it having the time of his life.

"I'm sure I just want to win there, sir." The stranger said while looking over at the other players. He was getting a feel of them.

"Well, we like the guy's like you, always the intense type, best ones to lose." Another player said while chuckling at the other guys.

"Is that so?" He put his hand down, the cards were none other than the Dead man's hand, clearly ready to see how it went for the other players.

Each man smiled as it was clear they had better hands—one placed down a straight flush.

"Read em and weep, bub; that's game." There, the man with the straight flush pulled the chips and winnings in towards him when the mysterious stranger let out a sigh; for a second, the man thought his eyes turned green; instead of those dark brown, they looked like emeralds.

"You know, Joe, If I remember correctly, didn't you talk about you were jealous of Jack's Wife there?" He looked at one of the men who looked towards the others. It was almost like a trance was running over his face.

"Yeah, I mean, you seen his wife? She's a model, and those tits, fuck. Huge as fuck, like she could float in a lake with those life preservers."

"Dude, that's my wife!" the other man said looking more annoyed, he felt a growing anger in him while looking at Joe, the lust in that guy's eye.

"Yeah, and I want to fuck those big tits, Even if they are a boob job, I just wanna fuck em, then bend her over and give her a dicking you hadn't done in years." Joe growled while he looked back at the cash and everything Jack had won,

"I think I could pay for that one chick I'm seeing. Maybe I can convince her into getting a boob job; that would be great." It was like the two men were in a trance at that point.

"And Jack, weren't you talking about if you won, you'd be getting a bigger house?" The stranger added while looking back over,

"Yeah, I wanted a bigger house; I mean, Jims got a nice one; I hate living close; the only great thing is his daughter likes to sunbathe without a top. I'm so jealous; that hot piece of ass is there, and I'm stuck with an old crow." Jack wasn't even sure why he was saying it. He usually kept those thoughts locked away, but he wanted to say it.

"I want a hot wife with nice tits, and I want to bend her

over and fuck her in front of people and make them envy me."

"I want!" The group started looking over at the pile of winnings, getting jealous of Joe, who had won it. Their eyes grew green with envy and jealously. None of them thought about the stranger as they started moving towards it. Their hands grabbed the treasure when Joe called out.

"You sick son of a bitch, that's my money!" He growled while punching Jim. Soon the three men started to attack each other. Jack reached over, grabbed his metal chair, and he slammed it into Joe, trying to beat the other man to death.

They were trying to beat each other to death in their jealous rage. None of them noticed that the stranger had been scooping up the pile and putting them in a sack, Placing one of the car keys into his pocket while soon walking away.

Walking out of the casino, the stranger didn't even look back, not a care in the world if they followed them. Even if they did, the stranger could take care of them quickly. He looked around for the car he had just won as he pulled out the keys and unlocked the doors. The flashing of light appeared off in the distance. Following over, he found his car… actually his new car—a Dodge Hellcat.

"Very nice there, Joe, This will be very fun." The stranger was going to hop into the car was someone grabbed his shoulder and stopped him. He turned around, eyes turning a flash of green.

"Cain, we need to talk." The figure looking back at him for a short moment, as he sighed knowing he wasn't going to like what he was about to hear.

CHAPTER 7

Lee groaned while adjusting the tie. Standing on the altar felt like an eternity. Everything felt like it was driving him up the wall.

"I can't believe it's finally here." Lee groaned, looking at Beth. She was wearing a suit and looked like she was sweating off a storm, Lee had suggested she didn't need to wear it. Still, Beth had told him *I'm your best man, and by god, I'm going to wear the suit, buck-o* It was simple though he excepted it.

"I just can't believe I'm getting married." Looking over at the entrance of the church. Waiting for Lucy to come in, his eyes stumbled around, seeing Lucifer standing in the front pew with Lilith. He was whipping tears from his eyes. But Lee couldn't help but wonder how the church hadn't burnt down while the Devil had entered the sacred grounds.

In Lee's life, he wasn't sure what was right or wrong anymore. He turned, looking over at his parents, smiling at him proudly. The church is filled while he shuffled around, clearly nervous about what was happening.

"Still can't believe it took so long to get ready." He

whispered to Beth, who patted his shoulder.

"Relax, you're gonna be ok, so just relax." That was when the doors to the church opened.

There she was, wearing all white, a long flowing wedding dress with enough cleavage to show off to Lee. The groom couldn't help but smile at such a wonderful sight. How she walked down, Her bosom bounced, Made Lee's mouth drops open as he whispered; *Wow,* Lee had to admit his heart skipped a beat as the succubus bride got closer. Beth smiled as she looked over at her friend, his best man, or in this case, best woman. She gave a wicked smile.

"Save it for tonight, lover boy; I'm sure you don't wanna drop your pants here on the altar before your parents." It was clear that Beth was giving him that smile reassuring him. Though Lee only felt his feet getting cold.

"Yeah, I guess you're right, but it's weird. I don't think I could ever have imagined getting married." Lee smiled, watching the Succubus coming over toward them. His hand adjusted his tie. That was when she stood up there. Her head dipped down, that veil covering her face.

That was when the preacher looked over and let out a long sigh,

"Today, we gather to watch these two join in holy matrimony." There was something off about the priest as he spoke. As Lee turned over, looking at him, something about him seemed almost too familiar. The way he looked at him with his golden blond hair.

"For today, we unite these two, a whore, the daughter of the Devil, and her play toy."

"Hey, what's the big deal!" Lee said while he looked at the man, clearly ready to knock his light out for even daring to insult Lucy on their wedding day. Though once he got a good look at the man, it became clear just who he was, his heart stopped at that moment. The man in front of them was none other than Father Lucus. That insane preacher who had once tried to kill Lucy and his friend. Somehow he was back from the dead.

"How… you're dead!" Lee said, finding himself stepping back. His eyes turned around as he started seeing more of them, and he felt dread; nearly everyone in the church was dead, their necks cut open, his parents, his friends, hell, Lucifer was lying there, a cross shoved in his eyes.

"He who is without sin toss the first stone." Lee heard father Lucus say as he turned around. He wanted to scream. Lee wanted to do something, anything, but it was no use. The preacher laughed like a maniac as he pulled out a large bowie knife while brandishing it. His fingers gripped it tightly as he looked back at Lee.

"Are you prepared to join them?" As the preacher moved over, stabbing Lucy in the chest, the way a knife moved in, Lee tried running to stop him, save his bride, stop this madness. But as he tried running, he found himself sinking into the ground as it had turned into quicksand.

Lucus watched him with that dark smile while he moved in closer. The knife was shining wet with blood. Lee tried fighting off the mad priest but found he couldn't. The man wa strong for Lee.

"The lord has no mercy for those who lie with heathens!" Lucus brandished the knife clearly, ready to strike down at Lee, who was stepping back. The horror in his eyes as He watched Lucy Jump at Lucus, trying to save him. Lee screamed out,

"Lucy, run, just run!" But It was too late as Lucus reached around, grabbing the Succubus. His knife stabbed into the Woman as Lee watched in horror. Lucus's eyes turned back with that demonic smile, blood running down his face as he chuckled,

"You'll be joining her soon."

-000-

Lee woke up in a cold sweat, his hot breath turned to steam in the cold room. Lee looked around the room overwhelmed with fear. He could feel the dream fade away. He was sitting in a dark room. Everything seemed normal, all quiet on the western front. Yet something was itching at him, everything felt almost too quiet. Lee looked back over. Lucy was lying down next to him, looking as beautiful as ever.

"I need a drink." Soon he pulled himself out of bed, hoping not to wake the sleeping Succubus, and headed towards the kitchen. The apartment seemed quiet. Lee reached over, pulled out a beer, and quickly twisted it. He was taking a long drink. The bitter taste ran across his tastebuds. The dream slowly faded away when he let out a sigh.

"That was a weird dream; what does it mean?" He sat at the table, just trying to remember what had happened. Why was Lucus in there? Hadn't that man crossed his mind since dealing with him back at the warehouse? A part of him thought about it, wondering if he should go back to where they buried the man and see if his corpse was still there.

"No, that's insane; that guy's dead." Yet somehow, Lee felt a sense of dread, like something was coming for them. Something he didn't know about and would be his and Lucy's very doom. He tried pushing these thoughts from his head when he heard a loud crashing sound coming from the other room.

Lee picked up the beer still in his hand. He walked over, seeing what had caused the noise as he looked into the living room. Betsy stood before the window when she let out a light curse.

"Damn it!" She muttered in a harsh whisper while Lee reached over to turn the lights on.

"Is there something wrong, Betsy?" Lee asked, looking towards the cowgirl Succubus; she was wearing her confederate uniform, which was slightly modified, showing off her full cleavage. The way her hat was, it covered her eyes.

"Shit, you weren't supposed to catch me, partner." She muttered, looking annoyed as she looked back at the window.

"Maybe you should come over and take a seat; we can talk about this." Lee wanted to get to the bottom of it as he looked over, seeing the frown on her face as she nodded, taking a seat.

Betsy sat there, rubbing the side of her arm as she tried to get comfortable. Lee sat next to her for a minute as he shook his head.

"So, what were you planning on doing?"

"I'm planning on leaving, that's all," Betsy said while she eyed the window. Lee couldn't help but wonder if she would be jumping out of it.

"You know you could have just gone out the door. I don't think anyone would've noticed if you walked out the door." Lee said, giving a light smile.

"Yeah, I didn't think this all the way through." Betsy shook her head, feeling like kind of an idiot. Lee couldn't help but smile; somehow, it made the woman more human.

"Hey, we all make mistakes, so what's going on?"

"Nothing. I just wanted to get some fresh air, that's all." Betsy said, crossing her arms.

"While wearing your confederate uniform?" Lee quickly responded while she looked away.

"Hey, I like it, it's comfortable, and I'm used to it; not like your modern clothes. They feel soft."

"Soft; you think these are too soft."

"Yes, they're soft; they feel like they cling to my body. It's nothing like my uniform. It feels."

"It feels like home?" Lee interrupted, somewhat curious.

"Yeah, it feels like home, my time, where I belong." There was a moment of silence while Lee patted her back.

"Yeah, I mean, nowadays would be strange; I mean, I'm surprised you took we had a black president so well."

"I don't care." Betsy said, looking slightly annoyed, "Why would you even think I would care if some N... Black man became president." Betsy looked away, for a second as she was trying to break her habbits. Try and adapt to this world. Lee watched her for a good second as he reached over grabbing her shoulder. Trying to reassure her.

"Well, at the very least, you aren't dropping that word. I mean, it'll save us some trouble. But I mean, the Civil war was about slavery and all."

"Yeah, well, that was what happened, but not every last one of us fought for slavery; some of us had no choice, some of us had to fight for our home, or they didn't want to fight their family.

Other's were lied to, told the north was coming after them and the south was in their way. Its… It's not that simple."

Lee nodded, though wondering,

"So why did you join? I'm surprised you were even allowed, with you being a woman and all."

"Well, I wanted to; I couldn't sit back and watch people I knew go off to die. I might be a succubus, but I have the will to fight, and I just sat back while others did the fighting while I sucked on dicks to survive or fucked. I couldn't just sit back… Beside, why should the men go off and fight while the woman act barefoot, we should be allowed to kick Yankie ass." She turned the sad expression on her face to one of cockiness while she Looked back at Lee. Lee on the other hand didn't believe a word she was saying.

Yet Lee sat there simply nodding along almost imagining just that. Betsy sitting back and doing nothing. It seemed odd, but they found himself amused imagining her wearing a dress.

"Yeah, it doesn't seem like you, so where do you plan on going?"

"Out west, heard a few things about it before I sucked into the ring; maybe I could do something hunt for my fortune." She reached over, grabbing Lee's beer, as it rested on the coffee table. Lee didn't say anything, letting her drink it. He imagined she might have needed it more than him,

"Yeah, probably not going to be how you think it will be; times have changed. They might not like your confederate outfit, maybe Alabama, but yeah."

"Eh, I've been to Alabama; it ain't all that impressive back in the day." Betsy's stomach growled.

"Hungry there? Need me to make a sandwich or something?" Lee said, pointing back to the kitchen. Though Betsy shook her head,

"Not that kind of hunger; I haven't fed for a while. Well, not since before, and that was like… a snack?" She looked at him for a minute, and Lee saw the hunger in the Succubus's eyes. The kind of hunger only a succubus could hold.

"Oh, Ohhhh," Lee said, finding himself blushing. The cowgirl's breasts heaved up with each breath—such a sight, while Lee kept his calm.

"Do you need some help?" Lee offered, not sure why he said that. Lee felt his breathing getting heavy. Lucy was in the other room, and he was worried about waking her up. Though at the same time, this was her sister, someone she hadn't seen in a literal lifetime. But at the same time, Betsy looked like she needed his help. The hunger in her eyes the want like none other.

"We'll have to be quick about this."

His hand reached over, fumbling with his pajama pants as he watched the cowgirl eyeing him, that longing wants as she shook her head, focusing.

"I don't know you're marrying my sister,"

"I know, but I'm sure Lucy wouldn't mind; besides, all this is helping you out. It's not about me."

There was a momentary pause, silence filling the room as the tension between them could be cut like a butter knife.

"I wouldn't mind what?" Lee turned around, looking to see Lucy standing there, wearing a silk robe that barely covered her divine bust as she tapped her foot.

"Oh, Lucy, it's you; I didn't think you were waking up."

"Yeah, I just heard some noise and figured I'd check it out, is something wrong." Lucy looked over at her sister for a minute, noticing how she was dressed up and Lee, who was wearing just his boxers sitting on the couch, a beer in his hand.

"I was just leaving, that's all, Lucy; I mean, I don't belong here intruding on you and your lover's home; I should be heading out."

Betsy seemed down, like something was coming over her. She was about to head out, but Lucy raised her hand. The way she looked at her sister, Lee couldn't tell, as he looked over.

"Listen, Lucy, don't get mad at her; I was offering just to help her feed her hunger."

"I'm not mad, Lee; it's this situation; I never imagined you'd have another succubus bound to you. I know about the angel, but another succubus and my sister. My feelings are a little more wound up. I shouldn't feel this way 'cause of who I am, but." She rubbed her head and took a seat.

Lucy took a long moment of silence as she rubbed her head, leaving the two hanging.

"You're jealous?" Betsy was the first one to speak, cutting the silence, and Lucy shook her head.

"I don't know, maybe, but… You know what, I'm just used to just sharing Lee, that's all, sometimes I'm in the room, or sometimes he's on his own. It depends. But with us getting married, I'm thinking about what my future might be."

"I'm not going to leave you, Lucy, if that's what you're thinking." Lee looked at her, the beautiful woman who snored at random and sometimes kicked him while they slept in bed, the one who drank the milk from the carton. The Succubus he loved more than anyone else and would die to protect.

"I know that, but I'm just worried; what if you get bored of me? I don't wanna lose my hubby."

"Lucy, that would never happen." Lee found himself moving in, rubbing her cheek,

"I'd never be bored of you, and I love you."

"Yes, but I'm just worried about other Succubus, and I shouldn't be."

Lee moved in, giving her a long passionate kiss. Their lips locked as he reached around, pulling the Succubus queen in closer; their bodies pressed together as Lee held on for dear life.

Betsy watched the two with a long sigh as she found herself sitting down,

"You were supposed to help me?" The cowgirl said, watching both of them, her face turning bright red.

Somehow that rugged cowgirl had vanished as she adjusted her coat, letting it fall on her shoulders as she revealed her luscious breasts, the black bra barely holding on as Lee looked back with a light smile,

"I did promise to help you, Lucy? Would you like to sit back and enjoy the show?"

"I think I would enjoy that," Lucy said. Her mind was calm as she took the chair and leaned back, watching her future husband and sister, her legs crossing as she felt excited and nervous about what was about to happen.

Lee smirked while looking back at the cowgirl, who blushed wildly; though Lee took control, leaning in, he began kissing her neck. Betsy let out a light moan; the sensation was slow, something she hadn't felt in what seemed like an eternity, as Lee started to caress her side—pushing his hands under her arm as he caressed her moving his hands down to her thick waist.

Betsy moaned into his arms, her hands going up his shirt, caressing his chest. Lee felt her sharp nails scratching him, but he ignored the pain; he wanted to give her what she needed.

The two pushed into each other closer while Lucy sat back watching, biting her bottom lip as she imagined what the two might do. Her fingers rubbed against the armchair as she prepared for the little show.

Betsy was the next one to make their move. Pulling back, she grabbed Lee's nightshirt ripping it off; the sounds of fabric ripping apart as She tore Lee's shirt off. Lee reached down, pulling Betsy's shirt off, her breasts popping out; it was such a sight; Lee couldn't help smiling at them; they were nearly perfect. Lee leaned in as he started sucking on the right breast and massaging the left with his free hand.

Betsy moaned lightly, "Lee, what the hell are you, oh!" Her voice stuttered as she wrapped a hand around the back of his head, feeling Lee licking and teasing the soft pillows she called breasts. Lee nibbled on her nipple as he listened to her soft lustful moans while massaging her side. Betsy growled, wanting more as she found herself eyeing her sister, watching her with those beautiful eyes. Somehow this made her annoyed as she pushed Lee right down onto the bed,

"Get down there; I can't wait any longer!" Betsy reached down, pulling Lee down. She went down, bit his neck, and sank her fangs. Lee groaned hard, though he came around, grabbed her firm ass, and gave it a decent smack. If he could see it, he would have been able to watch how it jiggled.

"Give me a second!" Lee grunted, though he wasn't given any time, as Betsy grabbed his ass and pushed him against her. Lee could feel his sex made against her firm sex.

Lee grunted, his cock pushing against her slit; even now, the Confederate woman was wet, as he could feel her grinding against his firm, meaty member. He couldn't resist anymore, feeling The Succubus wrap her legs around his hips; without even thinking, he pushed in, entering her. His cock was consumed by Betsy's hot pussy. He grunted, feeling how tight she was.

"Fuck, You're almost too tight," Lee growled, trying to fight off the pleasure. His heart raced as he looked down, seeing the shocked look on Betsy's face. It was clear she hadn't been with a man for a while as she gritted her teeth, trying to get used to Lee's impressive size. Their bodies are close together as Lee prompts himself up his hands under her arms as he moves his hips. The thrust was slow at first, moving at a decent pace. He kept his eyes on the woman under him, making sure not to hurt her as he let out a grunt.

Betsy felt terrific as he grunted, wanting more as he could hear the couch beginning to let out faint squeaks. On the sofa, Lucy watched the intensity in her eyes as she placed her breasts, massaging them slowly with one hand. The other one moved down her pajama pant's as they moved down between her hips as Lucy played with herself. Moaning, watching her lover, she takes her sister without relenting.

"Keep going faster, harder!" Betsy moaned, her southern draw going longer as she found her legs wrapping around Lee; as she felt him pushing his fat thick cock deep into her, she panted, and her heart seemed to skip a beat. Her stomach felt the fire it had been missing for nearly a hundred years.

How he moved, and how Betsy held onto him as she moaned hard. Her body was grinding against him as Lee moved closer, sucking on her neck and giving it a light bite. Betsy let out a hard grunt.

"Fuck, come on faster! Faster!" Lee grunted, his head arching back as he pushed himself faster. She moaned, her hips pushing him more profoundly as she felt her orgasm build in more quickly. His eyes were on Lucy, who was fingering herself tighter, watching them give him a Sultry wink as she transformed into her Succubus Queen form. Her crown of fire illuminated the room.

Lust filled the living room as they continued their fuck fest. The couch seemed to hold out as it was jerking back and forth, going with the motions of the oceans as Lee grunted harder, pushing faster and harder. His balls slapped against Betsy.

Lee growled as he found himself unable to help it pulling her up. Betsy tried Protesting but somehow found herself pulled into the air as Lee pulled his cock out.

"Hey, what are you? Ohh. OH!" She moaned, finding herself pushed onto her knees, facing forward, forced to look at her sister as Lee got behind and started to penetrate her pussy, with no resistance. Taking her Doggy style as he pounded even harder than he had before.

"Do you like that?" Lee grunted, his voice husked as he kept pulling her back and found her shaking under him as he pulled her back, getting rougher. "Do you like how I fuck your tight little pussy from behind? You southern belle!" he growled, giving her pale white ass a firm slap.

"Yes! Oh lordy yes!" She screamed, not caring how Lucy watched her with that sinister grin, as she fingers herself faster moaning, as she called out,

"You take my sister Lee; show her how good your Yankie cock is!" Lucy teased her sister, feeling the dirty eye push on her as she moaned louder, enjoying the sight as she masturbated to such a sight.

"You got it, Lucy; I'll show her what she is missing, thinking she could join the Confederacy and get away with it!" he growled, getting more into this place as he slapped her ass hard, watching how it jiggles.

"Hmm, such a fine rear," Lee grunted, his hips sinking deeper as Betsy screamed in pure pleasure. Lee kept his hips moving, fingers gripping her plump ass, unable to hold back. Her pussy tightened around his dick as if trying to milk him dry.

"You want me to cum in you?"

Betsy could only let out long moans as she felt pounded into submission on the couch.

"You want me to cum in your pussy? Fill you with my American cock!" he grunted while looking down at his confederate Succubus. As she moaned louder, she wanted it as Lee gave her another fine-ass slap.

Betsy screamed, her voice echoing through the room as He pushed faster. They ignored his neighbor pounding on the wall, telling them to shut up as he thrusts more quickly.

"Tell me now!" he growled, his balls tightening, knowing he was close to achieving orgasm.

"Cum in me!" Betsy screamed, feeling herself squirting her

orgasm, overwhelming her. She felt herself shaking as she thought of Lee pounding into her; unable to hold back, he grunted.

"Fuck, You want it. It's all yours!" He called out, giving a strong thrust, pushing his cock in deep

His hot spunk shot out as he filled her tight pussy. It felt like she was milking him for every ounce he had as The demoness collapsed on the couch. Betsy's taking deep breaths as she lay there. Lee found himself asking the Succubus.

"Was it good for you," Lee said, giving her a smirk, as Betsy crossed her arms,

"It's filling." The cowgirl said as she took in another deep breath. It was clear she was satisfied while Lee chuckled,

"Well, I'm glad to help out at the very least. Lucy, Did you enjoy the show?" He looked over, seeing that Lucy was on the bed, looking relaxed as she had finished.

"Oh yeah, I think I enjoyed the show." She pulled her hand, revealing her wet hand as she gave him a wink while licking her fingers, taking a long time. She was being seductive while watching Lee.

"I think we should get some sleep," Lee said though some of him knew he might not get much sleep; if Lucy was still in the mood, Something told him He would need a lot of coffee today.

CHAPTER 8

Alice could feel something was wrong. Her fingers are on the keyboard, working on the next chapter of her book. But something was coming over her, feeling like something was happening with the world, as she looked at Dawn.

Dawn was on the bed of their hotel room, going through some pages.

"Is something wrong there, Dawn?" She asked, not sure what to say,

"It's fine, though. My legs hurt after landing in that cold water." She spoke, more annoyed at the fellow Succubus, but Alice wasn't sure about that.

"No, there's something else; you've been way too quiet."

"I have just been thinking about a few things that all," Dawn spoke while she looked at the magazine; it was an older one, where she looked at naked men; sure, she could have used the computer, but something about the magazine hit her right, the way they had posed and moved around. Plus, the articles were pretty nice.

She turned a page when Alice got on the bed beside her.

"You know we could just get any guy to come over; it's not that hard, especially if we use the internet; it's easier to feed that way than flicking the bean." She smirked, getting in closer, the snarky look on the Succubus as she looked at the ex-nun.

"I know, but I never got to experience things like this before; when I was with the church, we didn't get to do things like this; we had to be good; otherwise, they might bring him after us."

"Him, who the heck is him?" Alice asked as she looked over her shoulder, seeing the Adonis of a man showing off his fat pickle. She imagined by now the guy wasn't as good-looking as he showed in the magazine.

"Cain, we're always told if we misbehaved Cain would be sent after us, to punish us, for disrespecting god, and showing our sins."

"Cain, you mean as in Cain and Abel?"

"The very one," Dawn said while she turned the page; seeing an article, she moved in, reading it partially while Alice kept a slightly confused look.

"Why would the church threaten you with Cain? How would they even have contact with him."

"They have him do their dirty work; from the rumors of it, At least what I heard when I was a nun, when a priest wasn't able to do a job, or they found something they couldn't handle, they contacted him and made a deal so that he did something for them."

"You're just telling me this now? And why didn't they send him out after Lucus failed?"

"I'm not sure; honestly, I'm wondering, but maybe they didn't have something Cain wanted. I honestly don't know." Dawn muttered, trying to think of something as she read her short story.

"Maybe we should warn Lucy and Lee, though something they might want to keep an eye out for."

"Probably, for the best; shouldn't you be returning to your book or something." The fledgling Succubus spoke while Alice chuckled,

"Oh, I'll return to it, but I need a minute." The lustful smirk on Alice's face grew. She grabbed the magazine like she was about to pull it off.

"Hey, I'm still reading that," Dawn said, watching the horny Succubus over her.

"Oh, come on now, I'm sure you can read some old magazine about it later." She started transforming, her pale skin turning dark as she grew horns, clearly ready to turn into her far more demonic form.

Dawn rolled her eyes in utter annoyance when there was a knocking on the door without warning.

"Saved by the bell," Dawn spoke as she moved, pushing her sexy demonic teacher off the bed; a hard thump as Alice transformed into her human form.

"It won't save you forever, woman. I'll get you and that pretty ass of yours!" She cackled like a supervillain while Dawn shook her head.

"I swear, how are you a famous author? You literally wanna screw everything that moves."

"Hey, it's my curse as a succubus. Girls got to eat!" Dawn rolled her eyes as she opened the door. Standing there was a tall, well-muscular man with lightly dark skin. Those cold dark eyes seemed to grow by the second as he looked at them.

"Who are you?" Dawn said, ready to slam the door in his face. The man was too fast, grabbing the door and holding it in place.

"You may call me Cain." He spoke with a light smirk. Dawn found her blood go cold hearing that name, her heart freezing.

Alice looked towards the man, looking like she was ready to get into a fight as she popped her neck,

"Well, speak of the devil." She stepped off the bed and crossed her arm to the door. However, Dawn could see her claws growing sharp.

"I'm here to speak with you, and I have a few questions." His eyes turned green as he moved in. Passing the archway. It seemed as though he saw her claws as he spoke in a calming voice,

"I don't want to fight." His hands opened up. "You can check me. No weapons or anything." He smiles, showing off his white teeth.

"What is it you want?" Alice stated while she moved around, watching him with more contempt. Cain smirked,

"Just information, Margret; it's so nice to meet you." He spoke, taking her hand and kissing the back of it. Dawn watched in horror, realizing he had called her Margret, the name she had escaped from in her old life. A life she had before learning she was half Succubus.

"You know who I am?"

"Well, of course, I take time finding out who I need to speak to, and a nun who abandoned the church, well, that caught my interest." He spoke with the smoothness only a few had as his eyes transformed into a soft shade of red. He walked over to the chair in the hotel corner and sat down.

"So where's the missing Succubus? The one they stole? I know you girls can feel her returning."

"Why would we tell you that? You planning on killing her?" Alice asked, looking at the man, her eyes on the scar on his face, the way it formed on his face; it reminded her of a brand.

"Maybe, if it came down to it, but my job is simply to retrieve her; that's all I am asking to do; but I try not to kill unless I have to," Cain spoke in his calm voice while he looked at the girls looking into their very souls as Dawn shuddered, feeling emotions pulled out.

Dawn looked at Alice and felt slightly jealous of the other Succubus. Envy of her form body and how she was so calm doing the lewd acts as a succubus, something Dawn wondered if she would ever be used to. She hated it. Dawn imagined grabbing the television and dropping it on Alice's head. Though, the moment the thought came to her. Dawn instantly shot it out, knowing she couldn't do that.

"Try telling that to your brother." Alice spoke, giving a soft growl. She was slowly turning into a more demonic form, Her horns turning bright red as she looked at the first killer.

Cain let out a sigh thinking back to his crime, the first crime, while shaking his head.

"It was a mistake I made a long time ago. Listen, I'm not the bad guy. I have a job to do, and they want the Succubus back.

They offered me a deal, and I'm taking it." He tapped the desk looking back at Dawn for a minute.

"So, Margre—"

"Her name is Dawn. Respect it, Cain." Alice growled, protective of the young Succubus, as she let out a soft growl. Cain could watch the fire in her eyes growing as he flashed a light green at her, the emerald look shining bright.

"Fine, So, Dawn, will you be a good former nun and tell me where the Succubus is? Cause it can be the easy way. If not, I can do it the hard way. But I'll tell you this, I'll find them, and it might not be pretty." He clawed at the table. He was doing all he could to keep his voice steady, but even Dawn could feel the utmost malice in his voice like he was holding back a hidden rage.

That was when, without warning, Alice when to the mini fridge, pulled out a bottle, and smacked Cain in the face. The bottle broke over his head. Cain barely reacted as his face was covered with the content of the drinks, while Alice began stabbing Cain in the neck.

"We are not going to be dealing with your shit!" Her rage grew as she kept stabbing at him, imagining if she had done it long enough for his head to come off. Sure, they'd have to hide his body, but it would end his threat.

Eventually, Alice stopped as she took a hard grunt,

"There, Dawn, let's get a shovel; we'll bury him." She looked over, seeing Dawn look at her and the shocked expression on her face.

"Come on; we don't have time. Cain is going to cause more trouble." She then realized Dawn's face was twisting into horror as she turned back. Alice's face dropped as she realized what was happening. Cain's wounds started to heal. His neck moved back into place as he moved his hands around, adjusting his fine jacket.

"Well, I say, that was quite rude of you to do that. I came here to speak peacefully, and you decide to attack me like that." The scar on his face glowed bright red as he got up.

"If it makes you feel better, that hurts like hell, but I should be on my way. Before I get real mad." He started getting up. Alice brandished the bottle, ready to fight if he attacked,

"Place that silly thing down, I ain't going to hurt you, and I should especially Dawn there. I know she had something to do with Lucus's Death, and, sadly, he's gone; he was a good student, but he lost his way after her mother did the things she did to him." He watched her for a second,

"You judge me for killing my kin, but at least I didn't help kill my father; I don't know what's worst. But I'll let you go this time, but Let them know I will find them, and I will get the Succubus and the one Lucus. I think I'll take a bit of personal justice from their skin for Lucus." Cain shoved Alice away as he began walking out of the hotel room. He didn't say another word as he headed off.

Alice and Dawn stood there for a good few minutes. Not sure if Cain had left, but the tension he left behind made them worried he would be back. Alice imagined they would have to get out of there as they looked at each other.

"We've got to warn Lee and Lucy." They shudder at what Cain would do to them if he found them. He turned their blood to ice.

-000-

Lee groaned while walking back into the living room hours

124

later. It seemed that Lucy hadn't let him go that easy as he limped back into the room, but the two girls laid in bed this time as he got in his recliner, ready to try and get whatever sleep he could get before he needed to get back to work. Imagining what Grace might have him do. Lee hoped that the rest of the day would be pretty straightforward. Little did he know that wouldn't be the case.

Lucy walked out of the bedroom, letting out a long yawn and stretching out, giving him that knowing smile as she went to the kitchen to make them some coffee when the phone rang.

"Hello?" Lee said as he answered, his fingers tinkering with the side,

"Lee, sweetie, how's it going." He nearly dropped his phone, the thing fumbling as he spoke up.

"Mom, why are you calling so early?"

"Well, do I need a reason to call my son? You barely call now a day's, so I thought I'd call and check up on you." He could almost feel the Cheshire grin coming from her voice, even across the phone; he winced at it.

"Well, I'm doing well. Mom, how's dad doing?"

"He's doing great, but how's work for you? Meet a nice girl?" She snuck in while Lee could feel that smile growing even more expansive,

"Yeah, mom works going well, and as for meeting a nice girl, well."

"Lee, do you know where The coffee grounds are?!" Lucy called out while Lee winced as he turned around, finding himself answering,

"Second shelf to the right like always!" He winced while his mother spoke up,

"Oh Lee, who's that? Is she a new girlfriend?" His mom said as he knew what was going to happen.

"In a way, mom, um, Mind if I talk later or…."

"Can't I speak to her, at least know who she is?" She asked with a knowing smirk, and Lee groaned as he knew he couldn't say no to her cause she'd either call again or bring her up whenever they talked till he let her.

"Hey, Lucy, could you come over here." He resisted an urge to groan as he reached over, putting the phone on speaker. Lucy, who was wearing only a night robe over her body as she stepped in that wistful smile of hers, nodded,

"Is there something you need, Lee?"

"Um yeah, well… I'd like to introduce you to my mom." He held the phone up. There was a moment's pause when his mom started speaking up.

"Hi there, I'm Lee's mom, but you can call me Maddy, or oh, just call me Mom; it's nice to speak to you." Lucy looked at the phone a little confused, looking at Lee, who shook his head but quickly responded,

"Hi there, Maddy; I'm Lucy; it's nice to meet Lee's Mom." She spoke like she hadn't gotten put on the spot.

"It's nice talking to you, and I hope my son's been taking good care of you." The way she spoke it, Lee was tempted to hang up right then, feeling embarrassed as he imagined he knew what she was thinking

"Lee's been taking great care of me, don't worry," Lucy said, winking at him with a cheeky smile. A knowing smile while Lee knew he was trapped between the two women and felt he would hear about this later.

"Well, it's nice to meet you, Lucy, so when did you two meet?" Maddy asked as Lee tried not to say anything, the phone remaining in his hand as Lucy spoke up.

"Oh, About a year ago, we met at work." She spoke, knowing the story they devised back then since no one would believe that Lee had pulled her out of a cursed ring.

"A whole year, Lee; you never told me about her; how could you?" She spoke with a gasp as Lucy gave a long smirk.

"I know, Lee; how could you never introduce me to your parents? You met mine."

"That was completely different; they showed up by surprise." Lee lied while giving Lucy a dirty look,

"Oh, is that so, Lee? Why are you trying to hide this girl from your dear mom? Are you embarrassed?" It was clear his mom was teasing him,

"Things have just been busy. That's all mom, Lucy, and me, have been doing a few things, so it just slipped my mind."

"What might you be doing to distract you from talking to your mom?" She spoke while Lee groaned and thought, *I swear you're like a Jewish mother, yet somehow worst mom.*

"Just stuff going on, that's all."

"We're planning a wedding," Lucy said, giving that wild smile. Then the phone went quiet like Lee's mom had dropped the phone.

"Mom, are you ok?" Lee asked, but there was a shrill excitement. Lee had to pull the phone back to keep himself from going deaf.

"My baby boy's getting married. Oh god, I can't wait to tell your father and your sis; this is going to be Amazing; my little boy's growing up." She spoke so fast Lee looked towards Lucy, giving her a look that exclaimed, 'You did this!' There was a moment as they listened to the excitement from Lee's mother's voice,

"I've got to meet her; you've got to come down here this weekend. Heck, when is the wedding?"

His mom spoke like a freight train just going on while Lee spoke up.

"Mom, relax. We don't have a date yet. Besides, I don't know if we can drop everything just to come down; we've got a few projects at work we have to deal with."

"Well, when you get a chance, I want you two down here for dinner, alright." His mom said a bit more forcefully, and Lee knew she wouldn't stop till she met his fiancée,

"Well, I hope to talk to her more and get to know them." His mom said while Lee wanted to groan but nodded,

"Sure thing, Mom, we have to get going, that's all. It's almost time for work. Love you!" He quickly hung the phone up before she could respond, and he sighed, long exasperated.

"Mothers." He put the phone away while Lucy looked at him, nearly confused.

"Is there something wrong? I mean, you didn't seem happy about talking to her?"

"No, it's not that, just more so mom can be a little… Constrictive. I love her, but sometimes she can be like a Jewish mother, just overdoing it sometimes. Treats me like I'm a little kid."

"Oh, come on, it can't be that bad… Right?" Lucy smirked, moving in and caressing his shoulders,

"Oh, it can be, especially after my accident. I had to fight to get out of the nest. Thankfully my sister was there to take her time at other points. But she didn't happen when I moved out of town." He remembers hearing her cry and wanting him to call nearly every day. Now that was a pain, him trying to gain his independents fully.

"She still seems to care, and I wouldn't mind meeting her."

"Oh, I'm sure she would you, though I can imagine she might smother you a bit." Lee joked while Lucy smirked, moving in,

"Besides, if you don't want to hang with your mom, I'm sure I can be your Mommy." The cheeky grin on her face, as Lee watched her transform slightly, looking older, a real milf, for half a minute, he found himself responding.

"Oh, you cheeky Succubus." He moved in, wrapping his arms around his now older fiancée. He might have considered calling off work to have another round, but before the thought formed, he was interrupted by a call from his phone.

Lee looked annoyed as he reached over to answer the phone again and quickly responded,

"Hello?"

"Lee, I think you guys are in trouble." It was none other than Alice. Lee knew his day was about to go down the shit hole.

Alice told Lee and Lucy what had happened, their interjection with Cain, and that he was after them along with Betsy. Lee found himself shocked, looking towards his Succubus lover. He was not sure what would happen next as he didn't know what they could do. Sure, Lucy was strong, but if he could regenerate as Alice said, Would they even be able to stop him?

"This isn't good," Lee muttered, finding himself unsure about what was going to happen. His mind racing while Lucy looked back, grabbing his shoulder,

"I'm sure we can figure it out." Lucy had a puzzled look on her face while she was imagining dealing with Cain.

"I don't think we'll have to get out of here, at least for a while," Lee muttered while he looked back at the phone, his mother coming to mind while he took a deep breath.

"I hate to say it, but I have a feeling we will visit my parents soon."

"We better get to work. We'll deal with it when we get there." Lucy responded, and she was right, so Lee and Lucy grabbed their things to work.

CHAPTER 9

Lee and Lucy got up early as they headed to work, dragging themselves into the car. Neither of them looked forward to going. The phone call they had received from Alice and Dawn kept them on edge, unsure of what to do. The fact Lee didn't feel like going to work today, his body was sore from last night's activities didn't help much as he found himself driving down the road.

Lee looked back at Lucy and put on a smile even if it wasn't genuine cause if there were going to be a meeting, at least he knew Grace and Lucy would be suffering just as much as he would. He could imagine her sitting down, trying not to lose her mind. It was an almost comic imagination for his soon-to-be wife.

They made their way up to the office, the publishing company better known as Hornstone Publishing. The giant skyscraper of a building was impressive as they headed into the lobby, the room crowding as they fought their way into the elevator. The two of them stood there as they listened to the music coming from the elevator and how their day would go. Who knows, but Lee admitted many things were running through his mind.

"So, any idea what we're going to do? I mean, dealing with Cain and all?" Lucy asked; she had joined the company sometime after being released, taking on more menial work, something she did by convincing Grace. She claimed it was so she had something to do while Lee was working. It made him wonder if she had started doing that to sneak in some work quickies and even try and get him to get it on with Grace, his boss.

Lee found himself shaking his head,

"Not a clue, but we'll have to do something," Lee said while thinking back to the phone call. They were in big trouble if Cane was as dangerous as Alice and Dawn said he was. Lee tried to focus on something else as he realized it had been nearly a year since Lucy started working for the company. Suppose someone had told Lee that the two would be screwing at random points in his life. He found himself somewhat amused by the idea. Lee might have suggested you get your head checked out because you're bonkers. But now that he met Lucy, his life seemed to change more as Lee expected to do more than that.

"Do you think Betsy will be fine at home alone?" Lee asked as they headed into the elevator.

"I think she'll be fine. We left the tv and enough food. But she should be fine on her own." Lucy said, thinking she could trust her sister being alone in their home for a while.

-000-

Back at the apartment, Betsy was walking around the apartment feeling downright frustrated,

"What in the hell did they think leaving me here alone? I got nothing to do except this fricken tv, and nothing is even on." She groaned, taking a seat. Her hand is messing around with the thing they called a remote, turning it on. She had learned how to flip through the channels going over them slowly. The southern

Succubus is very much annoyed.

"Seriously, they could have just invited me over or something?" She wasn't sure why, but she found it fascinating as she leaned back and watched the race going back. She turned the TV, and there it turned on to Nascar; she stopped for a minute, delving into it, watching as the cars speed in a circle.

"Huh… this is neat." She muttered before going quiet, mesmerized by the show.

-000-

Lee would shrug,

"You have a point; what's the worst that could happen?" He shuddered, imagining that there would be so many things that could happen. They headed off working throughout the day while he leaned back, passing through the manuscripts and writing down the usual rejection letter.

There was a light sound trying to catch his attention; as he looked over seeing Beth, she eyed him with that smirk while Lee waved,

"Long time no see Beth." He said, trying to keep a cheerful smirk while ignoring the problems that the future held.

"Long time Lee, Have a good Weekend?"

"Yeah, nothing too much; how are you and Sharron doing?" Lee responded while just jotting down a few things,

"We've been doing well, and you know, lesbian stuff." She snorted while Lee couldn't help smirking,

"Yeah, Lucy and I have been doing the straight." He moved over, shuffling his papers.

"Ew, the straight; I hope it's not contagious."

"If it was contagious, I'm sure you would have caught it by now, but I'm guessing you've taken the gay shot." Lee snorted, sticking his tongue out at Beth, who returned the favor by throwing a raspberry. Beth groaned while she moved around her cubical.

"I heard a rumor that you asked Lucy to marry you. Did she say Yes?"

"What do you think? But if you have to know, she said yes." He said while looking over at his pal.

"Hey, that's good for you; besides, after all that…" you two deserve to be happy." She meant that the two had agreed not to talk about when that bastard Lucus kidnapped her and Sharron. It had been a hard time for the two, though eventually, they managed to get through all of it.

"I'm glad it's going well for you two. So, Lucy and I are getting married; wanna be my best man?" Lee asked with a light smirk; Beth looked at him for a second and gave a light squeal,

"Hell yeah, I'll be your best man… Or would that be the best woman? Eh, figure that out later." She moved, giving the top of his cubical a good smack, watching the thin walls bowing for a second,

"When are you guy's going to be married? When is the wedding?" She asked with much excitement,

"Damn, I've got to figure out what to get Lucy for your guy's wedding; then there's the Bachelorette party. I could get some hot chick to pop out of a cake. No, I should make sure it's fine with her heck; maybe Sharron knows a guy who can do it if we bribe him fifty bucks."

Beth seemed to think about this for a good second while she looked back at him.

"I am going to need a lot of Beer, Fuck, and this will be some interesting planning; I might have to ask Sharron to give me a hand when it comes to this. I mean, what am I even going to do to drive a succubus wild? I swear me and Sharron are going to need to get creative with this one."

Lee wanted to tell her about the incident, with Cain warning her about someone coming after him and Lucy. Yet simultaneously, he tried to keep his friend out of all the trouble. So he did what any good friend would do and kept his mouth shut about this as he would go back to work listening to his friend talk.

"Hey, No worry about it. I'm sure she'd be happy to have the two of you arrive there, but if you want, you can set up a bachelor party since you'll be my best man."

"What? Can't get any of your guy friends to come to help you out with it, bud." Beth snorted while she leaned over her cubical, poking him in the nose while Lee snorted,

"What guy friends? Most of the time, I have out with Lucy and you; half the time, I'm busy working."

Beth seemed to roll her eyes at this as she snorted even more while she stated,

"I swear, I have to go and get you some guy friends occasionally, so you must deal with a sausage party."

"Yeah, well, just get back to work. We'll deal with my lack of dude friends for a dnd night." He chuckled, blowing her a raspberry.

Work went pretty well, and Lee had to admit. Going

through the usual things while he tossed off a few manuscripts and sent some rejection letters. Of course, Beth had managed to get a hand on a couple they might have considered winners as they moved on. Lee saw Lucy passing by, giving him gentle winks and nods.

Yet simultaneously, he couldn't help thinking about Cain and what he might do. How far was he? Would he find them? He had managed to find Alice and Dawn, so what were his plans? These questions seemed to roam through his head as he typed away. His fingers hit the keystrokes. He was getting through the long day.

He couldn't help but pass through some of the various books as he saw the first one, checking over the letter and finding that it was a book about a man who found himself working for a vampire queen. Or as it described, Renfeild, but if he worked for a sexy businesswoman who sucked his blood.

"Well, this might be interesting." He muttered under his breath as he sent out a request to check out a few chapters from the guy via an email.

-000-

Cain is driving down the road. A slight grunt as he picked glass out of his beard. Cain hadn't expected the Succubus to try and cut his head off using a beer bottle. It was annoying as he cracked his neck—such a thought while he let his senses control.

"I should have taken care of them myself." He growled, but he shook it off. They weren't his target, and he wouldn't spill blood unless needed; he might have been the father of murder, as some people would call him. But he wasn't just some monster. He did terrible things, but Cain had a softer sight to him. Cain mumbled while he continued going off and imagining how his life could have been different. Suppose he hadn't taken that Rock and smashed his brother's head in.

Cain could almost see that life; maybe he would have died long ago and wouldn't have been known for the beginning of such evil. Perhaps the world wouldn't be as fucked up as it is.

Cain turned over to the side of the road as he saw a park. Resting there, he took a long deep breath as he watched the children playing. They were just having fun, not caring about the world or how close they were to its oldest murderer. It reminded him about many things as he took a minute to sit down.

"So, how are you doing, brother?" A voice spoke as Cain looked over; a young man who looked to be around his early twenties had light dark skin and wore a t-shirt and pants. The only reason Cain knew the man wasn't real was that no one was screaming as they saw that a side of his skull was caved in.

"What are you doing here, Abel?" Cain asked while he leaned back, watching the children play for the longest time,

"Just seeing how you're doing: you're my brother, after all," Abel said, sitting next to Cain; the two of them hanging out for the moment,

"Why, I caved your skull in; not like you have much of a reason to talk to me," Cain muttered while watching. Thinking back to when they worked the fields, their father walked past them when they were children. Back when work was hard, there was little time to play.

"Oh, what's a little murder to break apart a friendship, brother," Abel said, smiling but revealing the knocked-out teeth.

"It's not the same, Adam… Why do you haunt me? Haven't I suffered enough?" He reached over, feeling the scars healing, they might vanish, but he could still feel them in many ways.

"You, my brother, might not be my keeper, But I'm yours. We've got to stick together," Abel smirked; he sat there while he reached out, pulling out an old jug and taking a long drink before offering some to his brother, who held out a hand. Such a thing he didn't want to partake in. While they sat there for a minute,

"Cain, I have a simple question…." Abel asked, that calming feeling brushing over Cain as he heard those words,

"What is it?" Cain sighed, already knowing the question. It had been asked of him repeatedly, and he knew what he would say.

"Why are you going after those people? You don't need to do that; go off, go home, and relax… Maybe talk to God and pray to him." Abel spoke while he took another drink. Cain let out a sigh,

"I would, but he doesn't listen, he doesn't answer my prayers, He ignores me, He's always ignored me," Cain spoke while he thought back to the past, how he had begged for forgiveness, how he wanted to be free from this curse. To see his family, but all he ever met was silence and nothingness.

"There's always a chance; remember, he forgives." Abel smiled, but Cain looked at him, angry as he threw his arm at the other man, who vanished like dust in the wind. He sat alone with a long sigh as he got back up, popping his neck. He imagined he'd have a problem with it after the Succubus stabbed him with a beer bottle as he spat at the ground.

Cain gave a harsh grunt while he turned, walking towards his car.

"Besides, if I do this correctly, maybe I'll be free. Maybe

I'll be released from my curse." He got into his car and turned the engine, not even looking back to where he'd been, only walking forward as he drove off. The music is playing off in the background.

-000-

Lee and Lucy clocked out, sighing as the day had felt longer than it should have been. The two moved over as they thought to famish as they went to their apartment's closed diner. They grabbed a booth and sat back for a moment while the two sat across from each other.

"What a day, I'll tell you what," Lee said, smirking while looking at Lucy. The Succubus gave him a light smirk. Neither of them seemed to be busy cooking when without warning, someone sat with them. The moon rose off the horizon as they sat there deciding what they might have for the night.

"Hope I'm not interrupting you two." It was Ms. Stone. She whipped the sweat off her brow as she sat down next to Lee, her hand brushing against his knee as she rubbed her head,

"It's a hot day tonight now, isn't it." She smirked as she waved her hand to the waiter, who brought her a menu and waited for them. It seemed as if they were the only ones in the diner, which was strange considering the time it was. They didn't mind; the slow quietness of the day felt nice.

"That it was," Lucy said as she looked over at their boss, wearing her suit that clung to her body. She nodded,

"I have to agree, so how are you two doing." She eyed each of them for a second as she unbuttoned her top. Clearly, she was off duty and planned to remove her professional side on the matter while she let her hair down.

"Just getting something to eat and planning our wedding." Though this was a bit more of a lie, In all truth, they were going to discuss how they would deal with Cain. They weren't sure what he was going to do, but they imagined he wasn't planning on giving them a wedding present. Thought of taking on the Killer had loomed over them.

"Oh, that sounds nice. Are there any plans for bride maidens or where you will have it?" Ms. Stone asked, giving Lucy a light smile. However, Lee could feel her reaching down and rubbing his knee, clearly trying to be playful with him. Lee let her do it, not wanting to cause a scene as he spoke with a smile leaning forward.

"We're thinking of having it at my family's house; I just haven't told them about it yet and just thinking of what we will tell her." This was a partial truth, but with his mom calling. Lee couldn't help but think that maybe this would be a blessing in disguise, at least a way to hide from Cain, as he looked to Lucy, nodding some letting her know this was an idea.

"It would be nice to get to know my future in-laws. I haven't had a chance to meet them. As for brides made, I have a couple of choices."

Grace Stone smirked while nodding,

"Sounds like a good thing. Though I wonder if the two of you might be busy?" She moved her hand up Lee's leg; he was close to saying something when the waiter came over. Asking if they were ready to order. They did, moving around and making their order as the waiter headed off; Grace reached over and said,

"Dinners on me tonight, my treat." She said, placing her platinum card down; while the two looked, Lee might have said more, but she leaned forward,

"But enough about that, what have you two been doing? Lucy, you. I know I haven't been able to spend much time since you came to my beach house." She smirked, reminding them of the time they had there when they had spent most of their time in bed and a bit of time at the beach while they had that vacation. Lucy though smirked,

"Well, Me and Lee here mainly just been relaxing and working. Though My sister has recently been staying at my place, I haven't seen her in years."

"Oh, that's nice; I'm glad to hear that; where's she from?" Grace asked with a light smile, her fingers moving up lee leg as he could feel her rubbing around his crotch. He could feel himself getting hard while eyeing Lucy for a second, almost asking her for help.

"She's down south, been there for a while. I'm sure she would love to meet you," Lucy said while dropping her fork and picking it up; she saw what their boss was doing as she pulled herself up, giving him a knowing smile. Lee couldn't but eye her for a minute as she felt a foot move over, pushing between his legs; it was clear she would have fun while they had a chance.

"So, Grace, how has work been for you? I mean, is that too much to ask?" She smirked while she moved her foot around, messing with Lee, teasing him while he found himself fighting off a groan, while the waiter eventually came over,

"Here's your meal," The waiter dropped their meal, placing a bacon burger in front of Lee, Lucy having the chicken herself, and Grace, who seemed to take a steak. Grace took her hand off his junk as they dug into their meal. Not like she couldn't put it back there.

"Works, going well; our profit is going steady, thanks to

some of our sales; now don't tell anyone. I'm saving this for our quarterly meeting, but you will get a small raise." She moved to cut her stake, taking the knife through the meal.

"So what else is going on? You two weren't acting like yourselves. So what's going on?" She asked while she took a bite, the way she chewed slow and carefully while Lucy looked back to Lee, while they knew that they might need to say something,

"We've got a bit of a problem, Grace," Lucy said while she let out a small sigh,

"What kind of problem is that one guy again that Lucus?"

"Not exactly. It's more complicated than Lucus." Lee muttered, reminded about the time she listened in on their conversation,

It was around a month when they had managed to kill Lucus; they had talked about it for a minute while in bed, wondering if anyone would find the body. This was the time they had been staying at Grace's beachside home when she walked in at the worst time. One thing led to another before long. The two needed to tell her the truth. Lucy being a succubus, about the events that had happened since the two had met.

Grace, though, had managed to keep it a secret and barely spoke about it. Though, at one point, she had suggested turning it into a book, and if it was good enough, she might have made a deal making them some big bucks. Still, Lee had declined, not wanting to turn their lives into a fictional story. Grace was fair and willing to let it go.

"So it's the whole Succubus thing, huh?" She waved her hand around in a circle for the two of them while Lucy nodded,

"Yeap, someone after us… We might have to go

somewhere for a bit; this guy is dangerous." Lucy sighed as she moved back, taking a bite from one of the fries, finding them rather nice and extra crispy. Grace nodded while she moved over, cutting up her take more as she took a bit of a bite.

"So, planning on using your vacation days, or will this be around the wedding?" She muttered,

"The guy's planning to kill us, maybe Lucy's sister. We don't know where he is. That's the thing." Lee added as he leaned back, finding himself more annoyed,

"Does anyone else know?"

"Just Amy, she had to deal with him, and she also wanted me to let you know that her chapter might be late." This caused Grace to scowl at Lee briefly before shrugging it off.

"I swear she's lucky that she's one of our top-selling writers; otherwise, I'd drop her. Just let her know to get those damn chapters in." Grace seemed to be losing her mood as she took another bite but nodded,

"I'll see what we have in the budget for giving you guys time off. Though I think you'll both have to do something for me." She chuckled while eyeing Lucy momentarily before looking at Lee as he groaned.

"Are we going to be doing it at your place tonight?" it wasn't that he didn't mind sleeping with Grace at times, heck, he did it to her in her office at different times, but he just wanted to get some sleep tonight.

"No, not that, though. Thanks for the offer, sweet cake." She winked at Luke but looked over at Lucy.

"I'm curious about seeing your succubus Queen form, I

heard about it at least once, but you two have never shown it to me, and I want to find out." Lucy looked at her for a second and responded. She smirked while she continued eating.

"Is that it? I mean, sure, I don't mind. I thought you were going to have me do something crazy."

"Well, I can always have you give my ex-husband a gay scare. It'll make me laugh, but I'm sure you're not interested in that." Grace chuckled but nodded, "We'll do it at my house, though, if you don't mind; I don't want to disturb your little sister."

"She's older than me." Lucy quickly corrected her at this point.

"Oh, even better. Well, if you finish, we can return to my place."

-000-

When it was all said and finished, they headed to Grace's home; she lived outside the city, in a lovely house in the suburbs; while they sat in her car, she parked in the garage as they slipped out.

"You know it might have cost me a pretty penny, but I'm glad I got this out of my ex-husband, that's for sure." She chuckled as she led them to the living room as Grace turned on the lights. Everything illuminated as they looked around; nothing changed: the bookshelf on the side, some of the books she had published from the company, a television off to the side, and the oversized couch and recliner off to the side. The coffee table was covered in papers from work she had taken in the other night. She needed to bring it in.

Grace moved to take off her work jacket and toss it off on the coat rack, not even caring that it was getting wrinkled as she stretched out.

"Would either of you like some wine before we start." She smirked while she moved to the kitchen, pulling out a fine bottle and three glasses. Lucy smiled some as she nodded,

"Sure, I can use a drink." She imagined she might need one, significantly after she transformed, feeling low on energy, and she might need to feed soon after this was all over. With looking over to Lee, who nodded,

"Sure, not much of a wine drinker, but I'll take something."

"Oh good, this one has been in my fridge for a bit, nothing fancy, but it's more of a weekend thing." She smirked, pouring each a drink as she sat on the recliner. The glass of wine rested in his hand as she took light sips while she watched for a good moment. She crossed her leg while she looked back at them, clearly excited about what she was about to witness.

Lucy stood there, feeling herself being watched, It was one thing when Luke watched her transform, but it felt different when others did. Looking over to Luke, she took a deep breath, trying to relax, as she pretended that Grace wasn't even in the room. Letting the warm glow roll over her. Her skin crackled as she transformed, Feeling her skin slowly turning darker. The blue flames consumed her as her eyes changed to red. Her hair became a glowing silver white as her wings expanded, looking more angelic, like a fallen angel.

Then Lucy could feel her horns transform from those like a stag into the crown; as she felt them grow, she winced in pain. It felt rough the way they wrapped around her head. Like thorns as she stood there. Her body turned slicker and more sensual to the sight as the flames died away.

"How's this, Grace? Do you like my Queen form?" She asked while she felt her heart pounding. Lucy stood there, gripping her hands as she resisted the urge. She looked at Luke; that want and need to overwhelm her as she tried to jump him. Rip his pants off and have her way with him, Not caring that Gracy was in front of her. It wasn't like she hadn't seen her fuck Lee before. It probably wouldn't be the last time. Not now, Not while they had bigger fish to fry.

"Will that satisfy you, boss?" Lucy asked as she found her clothes burning away, standing there naked as the day she was born. Grace smiled,

"Very much, I swear, I wish I could get you guy's to write a book. I could imagine how sensual it would be." She smirked while she got right up, walking over to Lucy.

"Now I'm curious how hungry are you?" her fingers moved around her shoulder as Lucy moaned. The way Grace swayed her hips. The sensual move while she kept her eye on the two, turning her head. That alluring smile as she licked her lips. The way they moved slowly against her dark lips.

"Please tell me, what do you want." Grace moved as she reached down, caressing her breasts, clearly taking control while she looked at the Succubus queen. The way Lucy watched, gulping as she felt filled with sexual desire.

"Oh, like you wouldn't believe it, Grace." Lucy found herself moaning, taking in the cougar's scent. If Grace was a meal, Lucy could see her as a fine meal, the delicious stake that had taken hours to cook and get rightfully, with a side of wine. She wasn't a fast food burger, but something aged to perfection.

Lucy found her mouth-watering while she turned back, looking at Lee for a second, almost wishing he would join. She wanted him—she wanted Grace. Lucy wanted both of them simultaneously; she wanted to feel them against her, moaning as she felt Grace squeezing her breasts while she looked at him with a sensual want and desire. Her sex felt wet already.

"Lee… She moaned out, feeling Grace kiss her neck while Grace smirked,

"Do you hear that, Lee? Your queen wants you. She needs you?" She spoke with that sultry voice as she winked at him.

It seemed that Grace had something in mind as she slowly slipped her hands down. It's as though she could ignore the lustful heat. Grace moved down, caressing Lucy's thighs. Her fingers were slow, teasing, making Lucy moan; Lucy found herself releasing soft bits of pheromones. The way she sweats, feeling herself getting hot, the older woman knowing just how to work.

"Grace, what are you doing to her?" Lee found himself asking, seeing himself growing harder the bulge in his pants, watching how his boss/Lover was teasing his fiancée

"This, well, I figured I'd hand over my wedding gift, especially if you were off to your parent's house for the wedding. I don't know if I'll make it, so I figured I'd give it to you a little early." She winked as she moved Lucy's head around. The warmth came on as she leaned in, kissing Lucy. Lee watched his jaw drop at such a sight; he'd seen them kiss, hell there was once when Grace sat on his face, and Lucy was on his dick while they did it, but he was watching them now.

Lucy in her demonic form as she returned the kiss. Somehow it made Lee both jealous and turned on at the same time. He wanted to push his boss out of the way to kiss those delicate lips. He wanted to taste both of them while Grace smirked, giving him a seductive wink and inviting him over.

Lee found himself pushing against the table, consumed by lust. He didn't not caring what was in his way. It's the kind of Lust that Lucy had infected him with as he groaned, feeling consumed by want, a fine meal for Lucy as she found herself overwhelmed and growling to Grace.

"On your knees." She commanded, focusing on Grace as she smirked; the controlling woman who licked her lips excited told what to do muttered,

"Yes, my queen." She spoke sensually as she dropped down, watching the two of them. Grace felt a weight off her shoulders, watching the two stand before her as Lucy looked at Lee.

The hunger in her eyes that even Lee knew she would lose at any second. He reached down, undoing his pants as he dropped them in front of the Succubus queen, The way his member bounced, while Lucy watched her hand reaching down and caressing his thigh as she licked her lips.

"If the boss wants to satisfy her workers, we should let her." She eyed Grace. Her succulent powers overwhelmed everyone's mind as they felt a lustful hunger that could only match her's as she looked down at Grace,

"Now, Suck my future husband's cock." She moaned out as she leaned over, kissing Lee's neck. As she watched the older woman nod, looking excited.

Grace looked over at Lee's cock, that fat, throbbing member at eye length. She moaned as she moved in, giving a tip a long lick. Swirling her tongue, the way she was told what to do by the dominating woman standing over her. It excited her. She felt no control as she moved to lick the man's cock, as she moved in closer, while she groaned. Her pussy felt so wet, as she wanted to touch herself.

"Come on now, my Lee's can't wait forever. She smirked while watching her and adding more power to her suggestion. Though she wouldn't need to tell Grace again, she pushed her mouth down on his shaft, taking the entire thing down. Moaning with an untactful desire as she panted.

Grace sucked faster; she did this and soon found herself thinking about her ex-husband. The man hadn't done anything for her. The way he acted was submissive. He just lay around the house at times. Grace had to admit it, but the man was nothing more than the definition of a gold digger. He didn't do much for her. If it came to the bedroom, she had to take charge like always. It was one of the reasons she liked Lee; at first, he was submissive, but soon he took the reigns and gave her what she needed.

Heck, for a while during her marriage to the man, she thought she might have been gay. After all, she hadn't felt satisfied in bed with him for a long time. She never felt more alive. As she moaned, taking Lee's cock in her mouth and sucking on it eagerly, she couldn't help but be jealous of the Succubus next to him. Lucy could have Lee anytime she wanted to do what she wanted when they weren't on the clock.

Grace had to wait, find the right time, and sneak around. The woman had an image to keep up, and if people found out how much of a hungry slut she could be. Grace imagined it would cause her troubles in the business-dominated world. But for now, she found herself gagging on his member. She pulled back a hard moan as she jerked Lee's shaft. Grace could forget about all the pressure, enjoy herself, and let herself loose.

"So good, but I wanna taste something else." She growled as she moved in, sucking on his balls,

"Oh, fuck! That!" Lee found himself moaning as he almost stumbled backward. Lucy managed to help out using her wings to keep him from falling back. The way Grace sucked his balls felt exhilarating as he grunted more.

Lucy moved in as she gave Lee a long kiss, her lips moaning as she pushed in their hips meeting. He felt Grace's head going right down on his cock, When Lucy said something that caught his attention.

"Grace, don't forget to give me attention. I've got a neat trick for you." She smirked while Lee looked over as he saw it. Springing from between her legs was a giant dick sticking out. The more Lee looked at it, and he thought it seemed like a near-carbon copy of his own. He was tempted to jump back but reminded himself Grace had a mouth full of him in her. So there was a chance he didn't want to make any sudden moves.

"Well, that's a new t-trick you've got there." Lee found himself saying between a moan, soon feeling Grace pop his cock out of her mouth as she moaned,

"My, oh my, are you trying to hide something like this away from me now?" Grace smirked as she leaned in, soon gracing her member with her hot tongue. Though she didn't leave Lee alone, as she grabbed his member, jerking him, she used her saliva to get him primed and ready. Her tush wiggled in excitement with what might happen.

Grace moved to suck on Lucy's dick. She moved down by taking it down like it was nothing as she started bobbing her head. Lee watched, moaning hard as he felt her squeezing his cock. The motions of her soft hands went faster while Lee looked at Lucy. Her demonic form showed off as her crown set itself ablaze as she moaned, looking at the love of her life.

"You're not planning on using that on me?" Lee joked while Lucy smirked and moved him closer, whispering in his ear.

"Not if you don't want me to, but if you miss behaving, I'm sure I can punish you." She smirked as she grunted, "Though I will say I never realized how sensitive you guys had it. Woah, no wonder." She panted, feeling herself closer to climax already. However, it didn't stop Lucy from reaching around and groping Lee's ass. Lee felt something pressing against his butthole. Lee tried pulling back but couldn't escape Lucy's grip.

Though Lucy had an idea, she smirked, looking back at the table.

"Alright, Grace, you want to feel me, want my future hubby to give you a pounding; get on the table right on your back for us." She smirked as she raised a finger; whatever Grace was wearing was shot off her flying off as she stood there, only in a bra, as she found herself red with embarrassment. Though nodded,

"Yes, my queen." She muttered, her face turning more as she walked to the coffee table, Her ass shaking as Grace teased the two and licked her lips as she felt so excited. Lee couldn't blame her. He was also turned on, while Lucy smirked her seductive smile as she took control of the situation as she told Lee.

"Get on the other side; you've got her mouth. Me, I got that ass."

Lee nodded as he went around one end of the coffee table. Grace was lying there. Watching him as she let her head hang back as she relaxed. Gace looked with excitement as she opened her mouth. Lee knew what she wanted and was going to give it to her.

His cock pressed against Grace's lips as she opened her mouth, hungry. Her mouth opened as Lee groaned, finding himself pushing his cock down. Watching the light bulge appear in her throat as he groaned. How she hung her head and this position, he found himself going right into her throat.

"God damn, Grace, you've got a hell of a mouth." He couldn't help but give light pumps hearing her moan. Though he watched Lucy get right on the other side. Her hands ripped their boss's legs as she spread them apart. The rough feel as she held onto those legs, Her cock teasing Grace's pussy lips as they rubbed against her. Lee could feel Grace's mouth vibrating around his cock.

Lee could not resist; He began pumping his cock back and forth, matching Lucy's thrusts as she let out a moan holding onto Grace as if her life depended on it. The two rocked back and forth, split-roasting her.

Grace moaned hard as her tongue lapped at Lee's cock while he thrusts faster, his hips bucked. Even his balls slapped against Grace's nose as he pushed more quickly.

Lucy, on the other hand, was going wild. She loved every second of it. Lee watched how her breasts bounced as she fucked Grace with as much pressure as possible. As she moaned out,

"Hooh, yes! Yes yes! This feels so good, Soo, So good!" She moaned, her voice getting louder as she bucked into her, barely pulling her false member out. She jerked in more profoundly, feeling how Grace squeezed her member unrelenting.

Lucy pounded deep within the businesswoman, her hips bucking back in return as Grace could feel herself sliding on the smooth coffee table. The papers left on there fell to the floor with no care where they landed.

While Grace moaned, finding herself even more, she turned

on her toes, curling from such an experience. Never imagining this would happen as she felt her face pressing against Lee's member as he fucked her throat. The experience of being split-roasted drove her wild as her muffled screams went off.

Pleasure wrapping around her. Grace couldn't help but think that the two were like demons in bed; how they pleasured her spoiled her. In many ways, she imagined that the two had ruined her for other men and women. She found herself wrapping her legs around Lucy's hips as she bucked around, feeling herself wanting more, moaning more.

Lee couldn't fight it off. Her mouth felt so good as he found himself calling out,

"Crap, Grace, I'm going to cum. I hope you saved room for dessert!" He called out, his hand reaching down and grabbing one of her breasts as he found himself unleashing his load into her throat, as he groaned, pushing his member as deep into her throat as he could.

Hot cum spilled into Grace's throat. Moaning hard, she found herself bucking against Lucy. The way the succubus shecock filled her, The publisher found herself tightening hard around the thick member. As she began cumming. She squirted as she felt herself milking that cock for all it was worth.

Lucy's face twisted, clearly unable to hold back. The way Grace squeezed around her as she found herself bellowing out a scream. It was muffled by Lee's dick in her mouth. Grace imagined if she hadn't had something in her mouth, that scream would've gotten her a noise complaint from the more nosy neighbors. But she didn't care. She was lost in orgasmic bliss as she collapsed on the coffee table.

Lucy collapsed onto Grace, their breasts rubbing against

each over, while Lee let his cock slip out of her mouth. Lee landed back on the ground as he took a deep breath.

"Well, I never expected this to happen… I think I can cross split roasting on my sexual bucket list." He panted, feeling his whole body shaking from what happened. Lucy nodded,

"It was something." She moaned, feeling the face cock retracting as she pulled herself away from the businesswoman. Who groaned,

"Have to agree." She moaned while she reached down, her fingers sliding against her pussy. She looked over, seeing some of the stickiness from what Lucy had shot into her.

"What is this stuff?" Grace asked, her finger shifting around it.

"It's some of Lee's semen. I've had it stored in me." Lucy moaned as she walked over to the couch, sat back, grabbed one of the glasses of wine, and drank it.

"Wait, my semen? How?" Lee asked for a hot second finding himself not believing it. Grace was too tired to say much as she laid back, taking long, drawn-out breaths and enjoying the buzz she was experiencing from the fucking.

"It's how I keep myself from getting pregnant. When you cum in me, I use some of my magic to store it away. A slight trick Succubus did. Don't worry, and it's not potent anymore, So It's pretty much me shooting blanks." Lucy muttered while she patted the seat, clearly more inviting. Lee sat next to her as she handed him one of the glasses of wine.

Lee nodded, not knowing where to go from there, though a funny thought popped into his head,

"So Grace, is it possible with our good performance? We can get next week off for the wedding and all that."

Grace raised a hand with a light moan as she was drunk from the orgasm.

"I'll have to examine your work performance, but I'm sure I can do something about it." She collapsed down at that moment as she rested.

Eventually, she would pull herself off the coffee table, and Lee and Lucy would pull her off to bed, where she had the best sleep in a long time.

CHAPTER 10

They didn't get home till the following day. Grace dropped them off by the parking garage so that Lee could get his car; thankfully, Grace had been friendly to pay for the overnight draft from the parking garage.

"You guys rest up. If anything happens, give me a call." She spoke with that soft tone while she looked at the two of them.

"Don't worry, Boss, we'll make sure everything goes well…" Lee spoke though he hated to admit it was a complete lie. He had no idea if anything at all would go well.

They headed home, passing by Betsy, who seemed to be focusing on the tv. Her eyes glued onto it while she was watching a car show. Lee couldn't help watching her for a minute, finding it fascinating that she was watching it.

"You enjoying yourself there?" Lee asked while Betsy nodded, though she didn't say much. The show she was watching was American hot rod. The episode looked like they were working on a sixty-nine barracuda.

"Well, this is quite something, I mean…" her mouth watered while hearing the engine purring on the television. Such a thing while Lee snorted while shaking his head. That was when he heard the phone ring. He sighed, wondering who it might have been when he answered it.

"Hello."

"Lee, how's it going!" His mother's cheerful voice hit Lee as she spoke up more.

"Oh, Mom, it's good to hear from you." He admitted to it though he also knew that he needed to talk to her briefly, especially since they needed to get out of town.

"Sweetie, it's good to know, so what are you up to?" She said, almost like she was trying to pick up a few things.

"Oh, just the usual… Um, I've got some news for you. If that's ok." He turned, seeing Lucy, and she opened the fridge door while preparing breakfast.

"And that might be?" His mom said; Lee could almost see the smile growing on her face while he took a deep breath.

"Well, my girlfriend and I were thinking of coming over and visiting you guys. I hope that's not a problem?" He spoke while he heard the silence on the other end. The way it went before she spoke up.

"That shouldn't be a problem, and we can set up your room. When should we expect you?"

"Um, probably this Friday. That way, we can get a few things settled up… You might want also to get the spare room set up. Her sister might be coming with us." He muttered. He looked over, seeing Betsy off to the side, clearly glued to the television.

He knew he couldn't just leave her behind. If Cain came to the apartment, they would be in trouble.

"No problem; I imagine we can clear out some space. Just give us some time. I'm so excited to see you coming over and to meet your girlfriend." She added in as he could feel her excitement from the end of the line. While she called out,

"Your fathers calling; I'm going to let him know; oh boy! Love you, Lee, bye!" There before Lee could respond, he heard the phone click. He let out a long sigh.

"This is going to be a long week." He grumbled before he put his cell back in his pocket. He turned over, heading around to the kitchen where Lucy had started frying up a few eggs and Bacon on the side, as he smirked leaning over kissing her neck before muttering,

"Grr!

Lucy responded appropriately with a simple "Urrg!"

Grruuurgg grog!" Lee muttered as he moved to hand over the salt and pepper, while the two smirked while Lucy Howled and grunted like a chimp while they continued cooking breakfast.

Lee raised and moved his hands around the kitchen, going,

"Rrgger gerr hurry!" Responding more while scratching his armpits. This only made Lucy laugh hard at such a reaction.

Lucy snorted, flipping the eggs while she went,

"Greegs Greggs!" while she hooted, puffing her cheeks out. Neither of them noticed Betsy coming over. She watched them, unsure what they were doing, while He scratched her head.

"What in the... Why are you two acting like a pair of

howler monkeys?" She exclaimed, not sure if this was supposed to be expected,

"Is this some Mating charm mortals do now? Cause it looks weird?"

"Don't worry about it, but, Lucy, we'll stay at my parent's this weekend. Hopefully, it can give us a little time to think of what we might be able to do to deal with Cain." He moved around, grabbing some of the plates, while Lucy nodded,

"I mean, if it's something we've got to do, Sure. Are they alright with this?" Lucy asked while she found herself eyeing her sister for a minute,

"Perfectly, trust me; Mom will be excited either way when she meets you… Whatever you do, please don't use any of your magic on her guy. I don't want to imagine my mom…."

"Horny as a horned toad during mating season?" Betsy spoke as she found herself reaching for the bacon as the food was put in the kitchen,

"Exactly, and please do not put that imagery in my head.

"We can try, but I can't promise much, Lee. It's not how our magic works." Lee groaned, finding herself more annoyed but nodded,

"Fine, but as I said, we should be careful. The town is a bit old school, and Mom and Dad don't need to deal with some of the crap the town does." He muttered, almost thinking about his childhood, how even while he could have been considered a bit more popular, he felt more so an outsider.

"We'll behave, I promise, Lee, right Betsy?" She looked over at her sister, who was adjusting her grey hat as she ate up. At the same time, she gave them a firm nod while wolfing down her meal.

Lee shook his head but figured they would be safe for now. He just worried about what might happen. Though he knew simultaneously, they would be dealing with much more. Once they arrived, his mother discovered that he and Lucy would soon get married. There was no way to hide it. Lee looked down at the ring that bound him to Betsy as he looked at Lucy.

"Hey, do you think there's a way to remove this thing? I mean, we got yours off before."

He put his hand out in front of the others, letting them get a good look at it.

"I'll be honest, Lee, and I'm not even sure how the other broke; I imagined it might have been from my transformation. So unless we turn Betsy into a succubus Queen, I don't think there's a way."

"Nothing we can do, Betsy. Do you have any ideas?" He imagined asking her for a second since she was a bit older than Lucy; Betsy shook her head,

"Not really, this is some rather old magic. That was created. Most importantly, we could cut your finger off, but I don't think that will work out as you imagine." Betsy muttered, looking off at the ring, while Lee nodded, wondering what they could do. But for now, it wasn't hurting anyone, he sighed. Though it would be something they would deal with when they had a chance.

"We'll get everything set up and leave on Friday after work." Lee groaned as he imagined the rest of the week and wasn't happy about it. He moved around and ate his breakfast. His mind wandered elsewhere.

-000-

A week would pass by for the three of them. Lee had his mind on the fact he was going home for the first time in a long time. He shook his head while he thought more about going home. Lucy walked over, putting their bags in the trunk of their car.

"We have everything we need, right?" he looked over at Betsy and Lucy, the two noddings. Betsy was wearing some of Lucy's clothes. They still hadn't found the right time to get some of her own. However, she wore a Confederate hat. For some reason, she kept that one on. Thankfully no one mentioned it or asked about it. Lee sighed, needing to remind himself to get her a new one.

"Well, We better get going. It's going to take a couple of hours." He shook his head, hoping traffic wouldn't be as bad. While he turned and got into the car, Lucy sat on the passenger side as she smiled, looking towards him.

"Hey, it'll be ok; I'm sure Cain won't find us at your parent's place."

"I'll be honest, and I think I'd rather deal with Cain." He snorted while Betsy looked at him, more confused while she sat in the back. She was trying to find a way to get comfortable.

"I don't see why I have to go to this, and I'm sure I could handle being around your place. Heck, I could go off and check out America." She spoke up, somewhat annoyed, imagining she could have checked out some strange television. Lee only shook his head,

"Can't risk Cain coming around here and doing who knows what. Besides, we can't let you run unsupervised if you need to feed." With that, Lee could feel Lucy's eyes on him; while she looked worried and jealous when he mentioned feeding, he gave her a loving smile.

"Besides, it's nothing to worry about. You might like some of my family members." Lee moved down, taking Lucy's hand, reassuring her.

"Well, we better get going so we don't leave any crumbs for Cain," Betsy muttered, finding herself more annoyed than anything. At the same time, Lee nodded, chuckling as he started the car, and soon they would begin driving and heading off to their destination.

-000-

The hot afternoon sun blew through as Cain walked and exited the car. His eyes were on the apartment building, and he let out a long sigh as he entered. He could feel the wind blowing as he looked over, His eyes on the doors as he reached over pushing the door in. A storm was coming.

"Locked." He grumbled, finding that the doors didn't budge. It was the kind where you had to have the key or someone permitting you. He watched over it for a second as he pressed one of the buttons.

A pause came when he heard a voice,

"Who is it?" A rough voice spoke up while Cain keeping a calm demeanor, spoke up.

"I've got an appointment for room 3B. I'm the cable man." He spoke, making sure the man heard him.

"What again? I thought the guy had come already. Whatever, get in!" The man muttered at the sound of the door buzzing open. Cain didn't bother saying much as he walked in, hearing the door clicking behind him.

Cain smirked while he walked down the halls. He was taking in the scent. The thing about Succubus Cain had learned over the year that they left a particular smell. Humans couldn't sense it, but Cain had time to practice. Understand how it came and went. At the same time, he walked down the halls. The lights above him flashed on and off, over and over again. While he moved past, he imagined the people around him were curious about what was happening, but the killer didn't care. His hand reached over to the bowie knife in his pocket, ready to be pulled out as he took in the whiff of Succubus musk. He could almost taste the energy coming from the demonic beings.

"Now, where did you go? Come on, you two… Come to Cain." He smirked while walking up the stairs. He felt like a bloodhound. Though he didn't care, he was on the job, and the payment was something he desperately wanted, and the revenge might have been an additional bonus.

He remembers meeting Lucus as a young boy. It was a warm summer, and he was summoned up. The church of the Silver Cross, Its home base in Florida at the time, was called forth, where he met the organization of elders. They were youngins to Cain, but he called them the elders. To give them the feeling they were much higher than they were.

"What do you want?" Cain had asked; he remembered having a headache, a hangover he imagined after a night of Heathen practice, as some of them would call it, but the grand elders. They spoke to him,

"We want you to train someone." They spoke carefully with their words, knowing that if they displeased him, they might as well have dug their own grave.

"I don't train anyone; the answers are no," he spoke simply while he was about to leave when he heard them call out.

"This one is special if you will reconsider." They spoke carefully, looking down at him. A man older than them when their grandfathers weren't even a speck of jizz in their daddy's balls.

"You want me to train someone to kill? The answer is no; I don't care if you send me out to kill. I'm the saint of killers. But I won't train someone else to be a murderer." Cain remembered looking at one of the elders, who could feel his sin raising, wanting to admit how he had sinned as a young man and slept with a nun while weak.

"This one is different, and He might interest you." The elder on the right spoke, His gruff voice as he sounded like he was holding back something, but Cain raised an eyebrow.

"What might that be? Why would this boy interest me?" Cain asked, his blood boiling and his mark burning on his face while he stared off, feeling their sins raising their fear, overwhelming them, but he waited for their answer.

A young man walked through the doors behind Cain; he looked over, seeing him. He looked towards him and noticed something. Something that caused him almost to stumble back. The boy looked almost like Abel. The idea of him looking like a younger version of his brother scared him more than anything. The only difference between him and Abel was their skin color and hair; besides that, he was almost an exact clone.

"Who is this?" Cain asked—No, he demanded to know. At the same time, he looked over at him. His voice grew dry as he looked at that boy.

"His name is Lucus, and He wants you to train him." The

elder spoke, looking at Cain with a gleam in his eyes. While there had been a shock, Cain closed his eyes,

"Why does he look like My brother… How would you even know that?" Cain muttered while he looked back over. Watching them men as he found his eyes glowing.

"What in God's name have you done?" He spoke, anger rising over him while the boy spoke up.

"Father, Stone, who is this man?" The boy's voice was soft and careful while he walked over, soon looking at Cain; those eyes were innocent, strange, and familiar as he looked down at the young man.

"We've done a few things, but Lucus here might be the future for our endeavors for hunting down Succubus and demons."

Cain looked into the young man. Looking for sin, looking for what kind of horrors might explain everything… but he found nothing; he couldn't find the original sin. Cain couldn't find hatred or anger in him. Cain found nothing but a soul, a perfect one… A soul that somehow existed but didn't exist.

"What did you do!" Cain demanded, looking back over at the higher-ups. The elders watch,

"We've done, what few have ever truly done, created a soul. It's taken time, but we managed to make… A successful imitation."

"What were you thinking? Imitating gods! You've most likely damned your souls to the pit! Creating life, and what, how did you even do that!" Cain somehow found himself angry looking towards this child, born with sin but without any. Such a thing that should never exist, but here he was.

Then there was the fact it had the face of his brother. He wanted to destroy the child, remove him from existence into oblivion. Yet at the same time, while he watched him… He just couldn't, his heart twisting, as he couldn't repeat his sin, repeat the evil he brought onto the world while looking at this child.

"We want you to train him. If he succeeds, we might be able to make a group of them. Ones that might be able to take on the succubus. Will you train him?" The grand elder spoke up as Cain sighed. He didn't want to, but he imagined they would train the child.

"Fine, but this will be the only one. If I find out that any of you make another one of these… Abominations, I'll come back and end every one of you."

He reached over, grabbing Lucus's shoulder, watching him with resentment in his eyes. The reluctant looked at him, feeling his sinlessness of him, while he shook his head for a hot moment. The fact that he looked so much like Abel infuriated him yet somehow brought a hidden calmness to him while he walked to the child.

"Come on, Kid, If you're going to learn. We start now."

"Yes, sir!" The young boy spoke, barely questioning this man and his trust in Cain. Cain didn't understand it, feeling a weak bond with the child. He didn't know why, but he knew if he didn't train them, the organization would have someone else teach him. So that was that he would make sure to prepare the boy. Though he looked back at the silver cross, somehow more disgusted than anything else. In contrast, he could imagine their very souls being damaged for eternity.

-000-

Cain snapped out of his train of thought, Looking towards the door, and grunted. This was the room. The succubus stench was powerful. As he moved around, grabbing the handle and finding it locked. Of course, he knew that but reached down, picking up the lock. Nothing complicated while he looked around.

The Apartment hallway was empty as he walked inside.

The apartment was empty. Though he wasn't too surprised by that, Cain imagined that The two succubus he talked to had managed to call and warn them about his arrival. It didn't matter. Cain would eventually catch their scent. He took in the smell. Basking in it while he looked around, imagining what he might be able to find. He chuckled while looking around, seeing that the stove had gotten left on. He imagined leaving it there and letting the place burn to the ground.

Don't do that, Cain; others will get hurt. Come on; you're better than this. He imagined hearing Abel's voice telling him not to do it. He groaned, rubbing his brow, while he looked at the place.

"Why should I? They left it on by accident. They should suffer." He grunted, but he was met with silence; Cain blinked for a minute but shook his head.

"Fine, whatever you cricket." He would quickly turn the stove off as he explored. He wasn't sure why he did it. He wasn't some bleeding heart. He grunted while he looked across the room.

-000-

Lee continued driving off; they were on the road for an hour. Driving with the traffic. The radio played music while he sat there. He listened to the girls. Lucy managed to fall asleep. Lee couldn't help but find it cute; when they went on a long drive, she just zonked out. It amused Lee that Lucy could ride his dick for hours on end. But the moment she drove for twenty minutes, she got drowsy and fell asleep.

He leaned back as he drove on when Betsy spoke up a whisper, at first where he barely heard her.

"So I've got to ask… What do you see in my sister?" Lee had to resist looking back at her, keeping his eyes on the road,

"What do you mean?"

"I mean, why do you love my sister? Did she use magic on you, or did she do something? Or is the sex just that good? Most men don't normally marry succubi." Lee could feel the cowgirl watching him while he drove a bit faster.

Sex isn't always everything. "I just did; at first, the sex was great, it was fun, but then she fascinated me; Lucy, she's just something. I'm not just some sex-obsessed Incel, It's hard to explain, but Our relationship is more than it seems. She's more to me than just a succubus." Lee found himself pouring those feelings as he moved around a car going a bit slow for his liking.

Betsy didn't seem so satisfied by his answer egged on.

"What do you mean by its hard to explain? This should be simple, why do you want to marry her?" Betsy said, almost pushing the seat against Lee as he got annoyed.

"I just want to marry her, and She makes me happy; I make her happy. It's straightforward, But there's just this spark. The way she talks how she makes me laugh. I'm just happy around her. I could care less about the sex. Heck, if I lost my dick, I'd be happy just being with her," He spoke up, trying not to wake Lucy up while Betsy watched him some and nodded,

"I suppose so, though if you lost your dick, you'd have to find another way for her to feed." She smiled at him; Lee found himself somewhat wanting to pull her over, but he took a deep breath holding back his temper.

Why was she asking him these questions? It got on his nerves when he glanced over at Lucy. The way she slept only made his heart flutter at the very sight of her while he gave the nod.

"It's just love, that's all. I don't think I can explain it as easily. Sometimes two people on the opposite side fall for each other, and they make it work. I might be human, she might be a demon, but we work." He smiled as he continued driving.

Betsy didn't say much after that, but Lee could feel her watching him, staring at him. But he found himself ignoring it while he continued down the highway.

-000-

They would drive for another hour, with only the radio making noise; they listened to the music while Lee hummed away, barely thinking about their past conversation. Such a thing when he saw the radio tower, The red blinking light on top, like a lighthouse, and he knew that soon he would be back home.

Did he want some to come back here? In some ways, Lee was conflicted. The town he grew up in and returned to. He shuddered as he took another turn and saw the sign,

Now entering Hillsboro, The sign was rusting away, vines creeping up the metal bar that held it up. Lee drove past it. The town was sobering while people walked around. Over the last few years, the city had been hit with bad luck, the local factory closing down. Though it slowly recovered.

Sadly, it would never be the same vibrant small town it had been though Lee shook his head. He imagined that there might have been more to it. At the same time, he looked at a few of the run-down houses with boards over the window.

Kids played off to the side as they passed by the baseball field, throwing and hitting the ball. Lee felt tempted to pull over and watch them play. He loved baseball; besides Boxing, it must have been one of his favorite games. Yet he drove past. Knowing he shouldn't waste time. There was always next time. At least, that's how Lee imagined it.

He drove around town as he made his way home, Seeing the bank. He saw it. It was still vibrant as usual, somehow untouched by the test of time or depression. It was a sign he was nearly home while he drove past it with another right turn.

The two-story white building lay between two others. Sure, it was a bit dirty and needed a power hosing, and the windows cracked; Lee saw the stained glass window off near the attic. Lee slowed down as he pulled into the drive-through and down the hill. The driveway was relatively comprehensive since it was shared between him and the neighbor. However, Lee pushed over to the side. He was looking at the willow tree. The long thin branches looked like a mess. He remembered when he was a kid and the times he sat under it enjoying the shades. Pretending he was going on an adventure through the vines of the jungle.

Those were just simple times when life was just a bit more normal. Lee giggled while he parted at the end right in front of the double-ride garage and stepped out. Lee reached over, nudging Lucy as she snored rather loud.

"Hey, we're here. Time to get up." He chuckled, nudging her with that long smirk. Lucy grumbled while she pulled her head up. Her pitch-perfect hair seemed all over the place as she ran her fingers through them.

"Already… yesh, didn't realize." She muttered while getting out of the car. Betsy joined as they all got out, stretching their legs. Lee felt his knee popping at that. A hard groan while the girls walked around for a second.

"Lee!" A woman called out when the girls looked over, seeing her descending the back porch stairs. She seemed excited.

Her hair was a bright blue on the older woman's face, and she was wearing a rock and roll shirt as she bounced down as she came over, hugging Lee tightly while she smirked,

"It's so good to see you, honey." She muttered while patting his back. Lee found himself giving a light grin while nodding,

"It's good to see you also, Mom." He reached around, patting her back briefly while Lucy realized this was Maddy. She chuckled, seeing how the woman reacted seeing her son.

"It's great, now. Have you been eating? You look like skin and bones." She muttered while she looked over, seeing both Lucy and Betsy. The smile on her face was nearly infectious as she ran around, giving them a broad hug.

"It's so nice to see you also; one of you must be Lucy."

Betsy pointed towards Lucy, simply stating,

"That would be her." She found herself jumping out of the way, getting right out of Lee's mother's grip as she hugged Lucy passionately. Lucy looked like her eyeballs would squeeze out of her sockets with the force Maddy was doing with that single hug. The woman was strong, as an ox.

"It's nice to meet you also." Lucy barely said as she tried to breathe, caught off by such a hug from the woman.

"Oh Shucks, meeting my Lester's girlfriend is nice." She said while waving her hand. Lee found himself embarrassment already coming. What she

"Well, it's good to meet you; I bet you've got many stories to tell about Lee." It seemed like Lucy was watching him smiling almost evilly- clearly showing her more demonic side at this point. Lee watched her with an almost don't you dare."

"Oh, plenty; I remember when Lee tried tipping over this cow before us. He was so mad 'cause he couldn't push it over."

"Mom, I was like Four." He groaned, somehow still imagining that. But his more scoffed it off.

"Please, it's not like I am telling her about when you nearly broke your father's penis." It seemed like Lee's eyes were twitching at that one, clearly not wanting to hear about that time again, while Lucy snorted more, giggling,

"Now, that has to be a story to tell, Lee. Why didn't you tell me about when you nearly broke your dad's Weiner." Even Betsy looked like she was about to laugh at the idea.

"Oh, trust me, plenty of time for that, come on. Let's get comfy. You've had a bit of a trip."

They began making their way off to the house. Lee watched them in pure contempt, wondering if he would have instead taken on the killer, Cain. He looked back to the car and let out a sigh.

"No, I prefer to live." He muttered while he moved over, grabbed some of their bags, and headed right onto the house.

CHAPTER 11

"Come on in; you two can sleep in Lee's old bedroom, while Lee, well, you can sleep on the couch in the living room," Maddy said as they walked through the back door and right into the kitchen.

"Mom, we're adults; we can stay in the same room," Lee complained, annoyed that his mother was treating him like a kid. He walked in carrying two suitcases, one under each arm. His mother smirked at him.

"That might be, but neither of you is married, so It simply won't do." She gave Lee a knowing smile as they walked past the kitchen and into the living room. A large room that was reasonably simple. An oversized leather couch against one wall, with a TV on the other side. An ice chest, and Victrola, Ye the walls were lined with pictures, some of Lee, others of him with his parents and just his parents.

"Who's that?" Betsy said as she looked over at one, where Lee was standing in a black suit next to a girl in white; the first thing that someone could notice were her eyes, bright blue with long brown hair and a cute button nose. She was the definition of cute as a button.

"Her? Oh, that's Samantha, her and Lee used to date. She's such a nice girl." Maddy said; while she appeared next to Betsy, Lee found himself nodding, some not thinking about it,

"Yeah, she was a nice girl," Lee said, remembering the night they took that picture. It was on their prom night.

"Oh really, what happened to you breaking up with this nice girl?" Lucy said, teasing the love of her life, giving him a good shove with her elbow

"Well, we broke up after I left town, you know; Long distance relationships never really worked out," Lee said, but he knew that wasn't the whole truth. Yet Maddy smiled while she said,

"She's doing great. I'll see her by the library on Saturday. She works there. Though on the weekend, she's reading to the kids. You have to see her son Lenny. He is just the cutest little guy you've ever seen." She spoke up in awe while Lee found himself hearing something pop, but he wasn't sure if that was somewhere else or if it was just in his head.

"Oh, that's nice, is she married?" Lee found himself asking, not sure why he even was. But somehow, hearing about a kid caught him off guard. His mom shook her head,

"Nope, a single mother, sadly. The poor thing, she needs a good man, if you asked me. Oh Lee, go and show them your old room. I'll grab some blankets for down here." She headed off to the hall closet, while she turned back, remembering something,

"Oh, and if you are hungry, dinner should be ready in an

hour. Your father should be back from work by then also." Lee only found himself nodding in agreement while feeling like something was buried into his head. He wasn't sure what it might have been.

They walked up the stairs and went straight to the right. Lee pointed to the doors explaining that was where the bathroom was. The other door on the right was his room.

Lee reached over, opening the door. When he did, Lee couldn't help but feel he traveled back in time. The room looked just like how he left it all those years ago.

"Dear god." He exclaimed, finding himself cringing over his past self's choices, besides the punching back that hung over to the side. The room was covered in posters. A few tasteful, a few not so, as he felt embarrassed while the girls looked at it. Betsy didn't give much attention to it. Lucy found herself resisting the urge to giggle.

"Well, this is interesting." She looked at one poster, which showed two women naked and pressed against each other, their breasts obscured by their hands. The way they looked off, it was like they were looking at them.

Lucy found herself snickering seeing that,

"Hmm, ever imagined doing it with those girls." She muttered, her red hair turning blond as she mimicked one of the girls in the poster, while Lee couldn't help but smile at her suggestions.

"I mean, I won't say no." He chuckled, rubbing her side briefly when he saw the Nickleback poster.

"Oh god, I forgot I was into that." He groaned in annoyance as he found himself wishing that he could have pulled the thing off. While Lucy laughed,

"Lee, no reason to be embarrassed. I mean, I don't even know who they are." She patted his shoulder.

Betsy looked around the room for a second, finding herself examining the room a bit more.

"Well, I'd say you guys should settle up a bit. I'm just going to pray that nothing else can get worst." He joked but winced, imagining he would reject saying something like that. Those things always managed to come back to bite him in the ass.

"I swear, I was such a dork back then." He muttered while feeling a bit nostalgic; it was a simple time. Maybe one he wouldn't have minded returning to though he shook it off while looking back to Lucy and Betsy.

"Well, you've seen my room; I'll let you get settled out, have dinner, and do whatever you guys want." Lee found himself saying while he turned around though Lucy found herself stopping,

"Hey Lee, what happened in the living room? You kind of went blank there?" she asked, worried about her fiancée. Lee shook his head. It wasn't something he wanted to answer,

"Oh, I'm fine, just something that surprised me. That's all, beside haven't heard about her in quite a while." He muttered flashbacks to his ex, A long smile on his face while he remembered the times they spent, how she was. It made him wonder what she was going right now. All he knew was she had a kid.

"I should talk to her when I get a chance." He mumbled, thinking about it, but he was curious when she had the kid. But shook his head,

"Let it go, Lee; it's nothing besides that had been years ago; it couldn't possibly be." He heard the door opening when he looked over and saw who walked in.

A large muscular man wearing a flannel shirt, making him look like a lumberjack, heck. If someone looked at him the right way, they might have thought he was a black bear. As he moved on, calling out,

"Maddy, you wouldn't believe how my day was." He groaned while he headed into the living room, a hard sigh as he took off his flannel shirt, tossing it right onto one of the couches when he looked over seeing Lee. The stern look on his face lasted for a second as he gave out a big ol smile.

"Lee, how's it going!" he reached over, giving his son a big ol' hug and a hard chuckle as he patted his son back,

"Oh, nothing much, Dad; seeing you is great." He muttered, reaching around and giving his father the same hug while they patted his side. There was a good minute as he pulled away from Lee while he popped his neck.

"So, how was your trip, any problems."

"Nah, not really; traffic is just about as normal as it normally is," Lee smirked while he moved around slightly,

"Well, at the very least, you managed to make it, all that matters." His dad said a hard chuckle while he looked over at his son.

"So from what your ma keeps reminding me, you've got a girlfriend. Did you bring her here, or did you leave her back at home to protect her?" He chuckled while Lee had to fight off the urge to laugh.

"No, she's here." It was like magic as they spoke about her; some might have imagined it was like speaking of the devil when Lucy walked down, Betsy joining her while she smiled at Lee,

"Woah boy, Lee, you sure knew how to pick 'em." He said while looking over to the two, "How are you two doing? I'm Lee's father." He spoke with a slight accent, The thing that Lee's father was he was handsome. He looked like Bruce Campbell if he had a Southern accent.

Lucy smiled more when she reached the bottom step.

"Hi there, and I suppose you're Lee's dad, right."

"Yes, I am, and you must be Lucy?" he said while he reached over.

"Yeap, and this is my sister, Betsy, and It's nice to meet you." She spoke up while Lee's dad nodded with a smirk,

"Well, you can call me Dad, or Rufus, whichever makes you comfortable." He said, giving a hard chuckle while patting Lee's back,

"No problem… Dad." Lucy said while Betsy let out a small sigh as she wasn't sure how to react to that but nodded,

"Nice to meet you, Pardner."

"Ohh, Pardner haven't heard that since Lee was a little kid; speaking of which, Lee is still working on your moves." He chuckled, glancing at him. Lee nodded,

"Every so often but not as much as I used to work getting in the way."

It seemed Rufus nodded,

"It's a shame you were good at Boxing, but those things happened. Wish I could get my hands around that Kenny Shoemaker." He muttered while you could see the silent rage in his eyes. While wishing he could have gotten the guy who hurt his son.

"Yeah, though can't change the past," Lee muttered while he thought back to that day, how the guy had screwed over his chance for a better future. Yet, in many ways, if it had never happened, he may not be the man he is today, with Lucy by his side.

"True, though; what's your ma cooking 'cause I'm starving." He chuckled while he went to the kitchen. The smile on his face as Lee heard his mother giving a light, playful scream,

"Unhand me, you brute. Our son is in the other room." A light laugh came from the old man, who bellowed loud,

"Can't help it, my sweet southern queen!" Lee found himself resisting a chuckle as he heard Lucy snickering,

"So I guess I know where you get your charm from, babe," Lucy smirked, bumping her hip into his side, while Lee groaned,

"Be thankful; hopefully, he will wear clothes while he sleeps." He snorted at the thought though Lucy raised an eyebrow,

"What are you talking about?"

"Trust me. I grew up with him; he slept naked and had some interesting habits." Remembering his childhood, for the most part, he wonders if he should warn Lucy about the fact his dad, yes, slept naked and walked around… He doubted it when he remembered his dad would wear something when they had guests over.

-000-

Dinner would eventually be ready, as The five of them sat at the dining room table. It seemed Maddie had decided to cook up steaks tonight as a celebration as they passed out the well-cooked meat. There was corn, and mashed potatoes, as they passed it around. Maddy smiled more, looking over at the three of them. Rufus smirked more while he grabbed him a few spoonfuls of beans.

"So, How has been your job, Lee? Get any promotions?" His mother asked while Lee found himself rubbing the back of his head,

"I got a few things, and the boss does notice me."

"Well, that's great; got to rise in the company, even if you start at the bottom; I remember when I started working in the plant, just a sweeper." He turned, looking to Lucy, "How about you? What is it you do for a living?" There was a moment of silence while Lee expected Lucy to answer by working in the exact location, but what she said next caught him off guard.

"I'm a sex therapist." She spoke with a light smile as if she glanced at Lee, clearly teasing him. Lee found himself coughing a bit, unsure why she even said that. Maddy found herself almost dropping her plate in utter shock.

"Well, that's something," Maddy said before realizing she had dropped her plate; luckily, she managed not to break the thing as she quickly grabbed it.

"Is there a problem with what I do?" Lucy asked, concerned by her reaction.

"No, not at all; I'm just surprised. Lee has always been a bit of a shy kid. I've never pictured him being with a girl of that profession." Maddy said, pulling a smile on her face; Rufus cackled at the reaction.

"Lee's always been a bit weird. I'm trying to say that We aren't judging you; Maddy's best friend used to be a porn star." He found himself snorting so hard that he started to let out a cough. Lee had to move over, giving him a firm pat on the back.

Lucy found herself giggling at that while she looked over to Lee.

"Now, Lee, you've never told me about that; I didn't know you knew Porn stars." She smirked, glancing at him with a wink.

"You never asked, and she's my godmother; not something I talk about. Besides, she's a Sunday school teacher nowadays." Lee blushed more as his face turned bright red while they talked about his aunt, Millie. Something that he wished remained in the past. However, everything seemed quiet as they continued eating dinner and having a good laugh. At the same time, Lucy learned a bit more about Lee's history.

Rufus brought up the time he and Lee started to try out Boxing and how Lee took that shit like a champ, in his father's words.

Then Maddy brought out the desert. A nice Lemon cream pie. Lee saw it.

"Oh, Mom, you didn't have to," Lee said while slicing the pie for everyone.

"Oh, it's no problem, Lee; lemon cream pie is your favorite." She said, and Lee could see the succubus' smile as they heard the word cream pie.

"Lee, how come you never told me you loved cream pie?"

Lucy said with that coy voice as she seemed to nudge him with his foot, almost teasing.

"It just hadn't come up beside. I can be picky." Lee found himself mentally smacking himself at that response. In contrast, he could almost hear Lucy giggling at that. Betsy had taken a slice while she let out a moan.

"Wow, Lee, your mom's cream pie tastes great!" The Confederate Succubus said as she took another bite, amused by Lee's suffering as they talked about his mom's cream pie. Lee imagined he'd get her back for this when all this was over. He just had to wait for his chance.

Lucy seemed to be adding fuel to the fire as she asked Maddy.

"This Taste's so amazing. I'll have to find out how you make it so I can give Lee some of his favorite homemade cream pie." She gave Lee a wink, even causing Rufus a hard cough as he almost choked on his drink, trying to suppress a laugh at his son's embarrassment and blatant teasing.

Lee felt himself fighting off a groan at such a thing, as he wished a meteor would somehow fall from the sky, crushing him right then; his mother, though, somehow not realizing the dirty jokes she had unleashed upon them or knew what she was doing and hiding it pretty well.

"Oh, it's not that hard, just a half hour of your time, some lemons, cream, and lots of love. Would you care for some strawberries?" she asked while she looked over at the tabletop. "Try some. It goes well with whip cream." Lee found him wishing to put a gag on his mother as the succubus barely held onto their laughter.

Rufus seemed to go in to be his son's hero and save him from the madness his wife was bringing onto Lee.

"So, Lucy Lee? Is there anything that you two might be planning for the future? Like anything special." Maddy seemed to agree as she went quiet, almost leaning into this, wanting to get the juicy gossip of what her son and his new girlfriend might be doing.

"Actually, yes, we do; well, Lucy and I are engaged." There was a moment of silence while Lee gave an awkward smile. Lucy smiled more as if on pure instinct showing off the engagement ring that had never left her side. If anything could be said, Lee's mother took it pretty well.

"Oh my god! My baby boy's getting married!" She jumped into the air and hugged Lucy, who was more shocked than anything as she found herself squeezed like a doll. Looking over to Lee, almost begging for help from the women, strong bear hugs. Lee, couldn't help but find himself amused by Lucy's expressions. It was what she deserved for the cream pie jokes.

Lee's father moved, giving him a hard slap on the back.

"Congrats, so when is the wedding? I'll make sure to bring in the strippers." Lee found himself snorting at this, but it did bring up a few things. As he decided to bring up an idea,

"Well, we're hoping to have it soon, maybe around here, in a week or two… Nothing too wild. We're thinking about making it simple." He pulled out his best smile, though a part of him felt guilty; it wasn't the whole truth, but the expression on his parent's faces was quite something. While his old man nodded,

"Hmm, seem's like a stretch, but I think we might be able to set something up. Call some of the family in. I know there are a few of your cousins from out of town. Oh hell, we'll make it a big

Redneck wedding in the backyard." Rufus chuckled while Lee nodded,

"I'm sure that could work. It's at least something." In truth, they hadn't thought much of the wedding, but they might be able to use it to help their stay, for the time being, while they could think of something to do with Cain. Betsy watched them for a second, raising an eyebrow as she seemed confused.

"Redneck wedding?" She asked while Rufus nodded,

"Yeah, it's like a traditional wedding with more rednecks, Moonshine, and guns. Trust me, and we must ensure cousin Leroy doesn't bring his squirrel Riffle; last time, he got me in the butt, and I still can't go through metal detectors."

"Moonshine?" Betsy asked again, finding herself more confused by that as Rufus nodded,

"Oh, trust me, the kind of Moonshine my cousin Leroy makes is the stuff that can cause you to knock your socks off. You've got to try it. I remember this one time when Lee snuck into the stash he left; he was drunk as a skunk and walked around the house naked when we got home."

Lee groaned in horror as it started over again while Lucy giggled.

-000-

Dinner was finished, and Lee and Lucy took care of the dishes while the rest went to the living room. Lee hummed off a tuneless noise as they listened to the water splashing against the plates while Lucy dried.

"You're parents are something."

"I know, embarrassing I mean, I love them, but sometimes I wish they'd calm it down." He muttered, looking behind his back, hoping neither had walked in at the wrong time.

"That's not a bad thing. I mean, think about who my father is. Do you think they're embarrassing? My dad caused human disasters because he thought it would be funny." She smirked, giving him a giggle. Lee didn't need to be reminded that her dad was the devil himself.

"True, though, some of those stories; I was such a cringy kid." He groaned more while Lucy giggled,

"I mean, at least you had a normal childhood. Remember, I'm a succubus and spent nearly a hundred years trapped in a ring."

"You have a point. However, it's just a bit strange sometimes. They're supportive but have a habit of overdoing things. As you can see." Lucy found a slight chuckle.

"Guess so, though. Like I said, Dad… Lucifer wasn't much around ruling hell. We normally had to raise ourselves, except our mothers or trainers teaching us how to become full fledge succubus and survive out here in this world." She remembered meeting the priest before she'd gotten shoved into the ring. She traveled the world. She passed by those countries and slept with various men, seducing women away from their husbands. She regretted sucking some of them too dry. It sickened her when she left her past lovers as husks. She wondered what her life would have been like if she had never been captured or met Lee in the first place.

Then there were nights when she dreamed that she did the same to Lee, where one day she'll wake up and find him as nothing but a husk of nothingness. A fear of those questions made her stay awake at night when Lee had slept soundly. Lucy buried her face in his chest as they cuddled.

They heard Betsy's laughter. It caught her attention as she looked back at Lee, the way he smiled at her. He didn't need to say a word. Her heart skipped a beat. The long motions as she dried up the last plate, putting it away.

The two of them would soon head into the living room, finding out what was so funny that Betsy sounded like a hyena.

-000-

Lee groaned, waking up the next day; his back hurt from lying on the couch, so he sighed. His leg hurt as he limped to the kitchen, grabbing a drink. It hadn't settled that he was back in his childhood home. That was until he saw his dad in the kitchen butt-ass naked.

"Gah, Dad, put some damn clothe, son." Lee found himself covering his eyes. It wasn't like it hadn't been the first time he saw his father walking around the house naked. The old man had a weird thing about being naked at home. Heck, his whole life was something like this.

"Oh, relax, son, this is my house. I can walk around naked we're all adults. It's not like when you were kids and brought people here."

"Clothes now!" Lee found himself almost raising his voice at that while his dad nodded,

"Fine, but this is my house. I can walk around naked if I want!" He spoke up while walking through the kitchen, his dick swaying while Lee tried his best not to look at or even perceive. Such a thing he imagined would drive him crazy even if he were now numb to the sight of it at his age.

"Just put on some pants, alright." Lee groaned in annoyance before turning around to get in the fridge. Shuffling over, he grabbed a drink and popped his neck while he saw his old man heading out of the kitchen and hopefully back upstairs where he could get some pants.

The silence came over him as he decided to go on a run. If Lucy needed to contact him, she could call him, but for the moment, he needed some time to think. He reached over, grabbing his phone and headphones as he left.

He left the front porch and began running.

The feeling of the cool air against his face as he took a stroll, he remembered the time Lee did this when he was younger, passing through the back ally as he let the music flow in his ears. Listening as he matched his steps with the beats of the song. Letting out a long, hard grunt while he turned to the left, where he passed the local Arrow Tax and headed down the sidewalk. Barely anyone was out. The stores were closed at this point.

He was tempted to come back here more often. The crisp country air felt good. It was one thing he had to admit, thinking about how much the air was different between the city and the countryside.

He moved around, passing old-man johns out. Though he had to admit looking at it as he passed, the place had seen better days. He noticed the town was a bit off from how it used to be. The place had more life to it. But still, he kept running. He would go on for nearly a half hour before stopping with a hard groan as his leg finally felt ready to give out.

"Well, that was something." He groaned, his leg aching, imagining he might have to get some aspirin when he returned to the house. Yet, for now, he decided he needed to take a seat. He looked over, saw the library, and decided to head inside.

One thing for sure, the library hadn't changed much. The place was just the same as when he was a kid. The computers are off to one side of the building while on the other side. Books lined the walls. The cool air hit him as he stepped inside.

The place was empty, As Lee walked through the library. Examining over some of the books on the shelves. He was hit with a wave of nostalgia as he remembered times being in here. Looking over some of the books. Lee moved down the shelves. At the same time, he embraced the cool air beating down on him while he got comfortable.

He barely paid attention to where he was walking into someone.

"Oh, sorry." He said, finding himself looking over to who he ran into.

She was a simple redhead woman, wearing a button-up shirt that hid most of her features and a pair of black-rimmed glasses. Suppose Lee had to describe her. She was the definition of a librarian, trying not to be noticed by the masses. But Lee could see right through it. Instantly knowing who she was as he found himself saying in a calm voice,

"Samantha, is that you?" Lee was somewhat surprised; it had been long since he'd seen her. Samantha blinked for a second, finding herself looking up at him. The shocked look on her face as she took a step back.

"Lee, is that you?" She had to resist raising her voice while Lee nodded,

"Um yeah, it's me. I mean, how long has it been five… six years." He muttered while looking at her. Somehow Lee found her looking perfect.

"It was six years, so what are you doing in this little town? If I remember, you were determined to get out of here." She said, crossing her arms, more annoyed as her moods changed.

"Well, I came by to visit my parents. It's been a while since I saw them." It was a lie, sure, but it was also the truth at the same time while Samantha watched him.

"Well, I'm glad to know. Are you looking for a book or something? You might need to renew your Library card." She said as she went back to placing books on the shelves.

"I'm just looking, you know, going through memory lane. So you're the new librarian; whatever happened to Miss Blob." He chuckled remembering the old librarian, while Samantha looked over,

"It's Miss. Blaub retired last year. We had a party." She said though she gave herself a light smile, as she hadn't heard the old librarian's mean nickname.

"Well, it's good for her, heh Glad she could retire." He chuckled while he could almost hear the clanking sounds of the old librarian's tea cup as she stirred sugar into it, reminding him of the chains of a spirit screaming for freedom from its eternal prison.

"Well, she was also, though I'll be honest, hate to see her go. She grew on me a little bit." Samantha chuckled while moving around and putting the books up. It was those silent moments that Samantha enjoyed letting her have time to think.

"So Lee, how's your life going? Finally, make it big even after your leg injury?" She asked, finding herself noticing the limp he had while Lee nodded,

"It's been pretty well. I'm not some famous person." He chuckled as the two made small talk. Lee, actually moving in, giving her a hand and putting some of the books away for a short bit. Just talking about how their life was.

They had a good time, talking about the good old days, when a small voice called out,

"Mommy!" a small boy ran over, almost knocking Lee into the bookshelf as he moved in, hugging Samantha.

"Al, don't be rude. You nearly knocked someone over." She spoke, giving him a firm look as the little boy looked over at Lee; there was a guilty look on his face as he spoke up.

"I'm sorry, Mr," Al said while Lee watched him for a second, the shocked expression on his face as the little boy looked almost like a direct clone of himself from when he was his age.

"Um… It's no problem. Just be careful where you're going." He said while looking at the little clone of him.

"Ok, Hi, I'm Al, it's short for Alexander… My mommy said I'm named after the guy who invented the tellyphone." The way he said telephone made it sound exotic, like he was pronouncing it tell-e-phone. Lee somehow found it cute while shocked by the little boy.

"Well, Al, I'm Lee; it's nice to meet you." He chuckled, letting his hand shake the young boy's hand. Al reached over and shook it, his smile showing he was missing his front right tooth. The way he shook his hand, Lee found himself smiling,

"Oh wow, little dude, you've got a strong grip. You're crushing my hand." Lee spoke up exaggeratedly, making the young boy giggle like a goofball.

"You're funny." He turned over, looking back at Samantha.

"Mom, are we going to be going swimming soon? I wanna go to the beach." Though Lee had to fight back the urge as the way the kid said beach almost sounded like he said bitch.

Lee grabbed his side, fighting the urge to laugh at how the kid spoke. It was adorable and funny as all hell.

"Al, I keep telling you it's beach... Not bitch... that's what you call a female dog." Samantha said while she rubbed her forehead like she had to explain this to him once before and had to do it yet again.

"Oh, Sorry, Mommy, can we go to the beach today?" He spoke more slowly, trying not to say the other word. While Samantha chuckled,

"If you behave. But I've got to work. How about you go over and play with some of the puzzles, alright." She said with a light smile to the little boy, who nodded and ran off.

"Kids, I swear," Samantha said with a light smile as she looked back. Lee nodded, watching the kid heading off.

"Yeah, heh, so he's yours... When did that happen?" He asked while looking back at the young woman, who smiled.

"Oh, it was about six years ago; it was a one-night stand, and well, Al wasn't planned, but I don't regret having him. I wish his father had stuck around." There sounds to be a twinge of annoyance. Lee wasn't sure if that was pointed at him or if it was contempt for someone else. He felt a cold chill running down his back.

"Um... the kid looks familiar, is the father someone we know?" Somewhat pushing the subject, Samantha shook her head.

"No, not really. I'm Al's mother, and if the guy wanted to

be in his life, he'd be here. Besides, the guy was more of a sperm donor. I can handle myself." She spoke while she put up the last book.

"I mean, fair unless he doesn't know, but… well, he's a cute kid, and it looks like you are raising him right." He spoke carefully.

"I try my best, but trust me, and he can be a handful." She smiled at him though she looked at the clock.

"Listen, I have other things to do, I wouldn't mind staying all day and talking, but I've got to work." She moved passed him and started to head off.

Lee stood there, and one thing he knew, he would have to talk to Lucy. If what he was thinking was correct. He might be a father. Now that thought terrified him, especially with everything that was going on.

CHAPTER 12

Lee would eventually leave the library walking back home, his leg hurting the way there as he limped around as climbed up the stairs.

"I swear, if I see Lucy's father, I'm gonna ask him if he can fix this damn leg." He groaned while he walked through the door. It was a moment of silence though it didn't last long without warning. Maddy came in calling out,

"Hey, get out of here; we're getting Lucy's wedding dress worked on!" Lee found himself pausing there as he shook his head.

"Wait, Wedding dress; there's no way you found one already. It's?" Lee moved over, checking his watch. Seeing it was around noon,

"It's noon; where did you." He said while, without warning, his mother was pushing him back.

"Don't question this; I'm prepared; we're just sizing it up. She's going to look stunning." His mother said while she led him out the door.

"Well, what in the world am I supposed to do?" He asked, finding himself more annoyed while his mother rolled her shoulder.

"No idea; go to the lake, go fishing for a few hours; we wanna get this ready for your guy's wedding." She moved, pushing him right out the door. Lee found himself both annoyed and amused by that as he saw the door slammed shut—such a thing as he let out a hard groan turning his head.

"I'll go fishing if I want, just don't tell me what to do." He mumbled under his breath as he headed back down the patio. He found himself letting out a long sigh. Lee headed right out, guessing he would need to do something for a while.

-000-

Cain was sitting in the diner, a long sigh as he waited for a cup of coffee, a good drink as he would make his way off to hunt after the succubus. He had a light moment of tapping his finger while listening to the people walking around the small area, talking about their little problems.

The waitress moved in, pouring his coffee; the steaming black liquid smelled good. At the same time, he heard the waitress speak.

"Is there anything else you need, sir?" She asked. She seemed to be rubbing her side, Feeling anxious, like she was hoping for the man to leave while Cain drank his coffee.

"Mostly, I am; this is fine coffee." He exclaimed while he sipped his drink. He was taking in the taste. He paused for a minute.

"Is there anything you might recommend me?" Cain asked, keeping himself calm, though a part of his was frustrated, hunting down his prey—the fact they hid from him while he tried keeping his cool. Then Abel popped into his head; now, that wouldn't do.

No, it wouldn't do at all. But he kept himself focused while the waitress stood there, her foot twitching,

"Well, you can always try our Apple pie; it's got to be one of the best versions around." Though she leaned in.

"But to tell you the truth, I like sticking my finger and tasting them. Though don't tell anyone." She smiled, licking her lips as if thinking about trying one of those bosses.

"Hmm, that sounds tempting, though not fond of you sticking your finger in there," Cain spoke while he felt his power running over the whole group.

"Well, if not, you can try our burger; trust me, I don't stick my finger in there; I'm a vegan and can't stand the stuff… Would you like to know something?" She said with that broad smile like she had been hoping to tell someone about it while Cain watched.

"What might that be?" This seemed to excite the woman as Cain scratched the mark on his face. The way it itched as he felt her sin and secret desires run over her.

"I want to eat meat, So badly. But I feel bad for those poor animals when someone wants meat. I just want to stab them! Why can't I have some of those tasty foods? It drives me up the wall; I want to beat them. We need to protect the animals." She spoke up with a smile as innocent and careful as anyone while Cain nodded.

"I might have the burger, though I wouldn't recommend stabbing me," Cain said, giving her a smirk, As he looked over at the others around, feeling the rage the jealousy in each of them while he drank his coffee. "Besides, if you'll stab someone, do it alone. I don't have time to deal with the drama."

"Ahh, alright there, Mr. I'll let that son of a bitch in the kitchen start cooking it up. Or my Ex, who cheated on me with a man, and I wanna kick in the balls till they stop working." She said with a light laugh as she moved to the back, walking around as Cain sighed.

"I swear, mortals sometimes give me way too much information." He moved over, grabbed his computer, and typed away. It was time to do research. He was going to figure out where they went. While going over the apartment where the succubus scent was, he discovered the owner was Lee West.

"Hmm, now where are you, Mr. West?" he asked, skimming through the net as he started going over Facebook. A short time later, he found Lee's mother face book as she raised an eyebrow.

My son's getting married. I'm so proud of him; we're having the wedding at my house! Cain read this with a slight smirk as he moved over, checking out the rest of her Facebook. She had plenty of things on there, including a house picture. He had a slight smirk on his face while he popped his neck.

"Well, I'm sure it won't be a problem." He chuckled while he took another drink of coffee, his eyes glowing when the waitress moved in and brought him a burger. It wasn't bad, in his opinion, as he took a bite and turned to leave. He was leaving a fine tip to go with the bill. The door slammed behind him as everyone returned to their usual selves, no longer affected by their sin.

-000-

Lee found himself coming back home a few hours later. His Fishing pole is hanging over his side while he lets out a light sigh. "Not a single bite; I guess today was not my day." He groaned while he moved around, walking through the door; he was sure he had given them enough time to work on the wedding dress.

The man was somewhat curious as to how it would look. He stepped through the door. Everything seemed quiet. Almost too soft as he walked through the house as turned on one of the lights. The kitchen was cleaned up, except for a note as he grabbed it and began reading it.

Lee, your mom wanted to show us a local bar called Judoon's Legends in town so we can drink; I left a note to let you know where we went if you wanted to join us.

- Lucy

Lee found himself chuckling while he shook his head. Of course, his mom would do that, as he looked over. Lee could make it over if he wanted to; as he put the note away, he remembered Judoon's legend wasn't exactly that far away, as he could jog over there. He remembers passing by the place when he was walking to school.

He pondered if he should go off and meet up with them. Indeed he wasn't going to leave Lucy to get drunk; who knows what chaos that would ensure with her being in a small town, with her abilities. She could almost picture there being a scandal or something like that. *An orgy happened the other night at Judoons Legend; everyone was arrested for indecency.* At least, that story came to mind as he put his fishing pole against the wall and headed right off to the Bar.

Judoons Bar, Lee, was suitable. It wasn't far, as he strolled over, walking down the road; it had taken him nearly fifteen minutes as he moved in, pushing the door open. The music hit him when Lee walked in and heard a cover band of ACDC playing off. They sounded fine as he looked over, seeing a girl sitting behind a small desk; she looked bored out of her mind like she'd come to do this so often. Nothing phased her at this point. There was a moment's pause as she looked up to see Lee.

"Hey there, you here for the cover band?" she asked, looking at him somewhat blankly.

"Why yes, I am," he said for a good minute as the woman behind the desk nodded,

"That'll be ten bucks, don't I know you?" She asked, looking at him like she was remembering something while Lee shook his head.

"Don't think so; I just got one of those faces." He muttered while he reached around, handing over a ten-dollar bill as he stepped in. The woman just nodded while she seemed to try and remember just who he was.

Lee walked in through the Bar, hearing the sounds of bowling pins being knocked over. As he turned, seeing a bowling alley. He shook his head and chuckled.

"I almost forgot this place had it." Reminding himself of the time, he was a teenager and got a hold of a fake id. Ordering a few drinks, and when he got caught. Oh, that was a night he wouldn't forget, especially when the bouncer gave him an ass-kicking he wouldn't forget.

He passed over the place, heading straight to the Bar. The Bartender was pouring a few glasses, a blond hair bombshell wearing the bars uniform, a tight white t-shirt with the name Judoons Legends plastered over her tits, as she put them on full display for everyone to see. He couldn't help but peek at them.

"Hey now, buddy, my eyes are up here." The Bartender said, clearly in a joking fashion, while Lee smirked.

"No problem at all, boss." He said while the Bartender motioned over, watching him as she was ready to take his order. "So what are you having there, cutie?"

The Bartender asked, Lee only noticing her name tag that read *Sandy*.

"Well, Sandy, I'd like something to start the nice, simple, so how about a beer." He reached over, bringing a few bucks and a bit for a tip.

"No problem at all." She reached under the counter, quickly pulling out a long-neck bottle, taking the money from him, and putting it into the register. Lee moved, opening the beer and taking a quick swig, when he saw Lucy approaching him. She had a smirk on her face as she hugged him, Bouncing in his arms as she said,

"Glad to see you finally showed up." She muttered as Lee tried not to spill his beer all over them.

"I didn't think you would be here so soon." He said while the succulent succubus was holding him.

"Well, I figured I'd have a beer check out my sexy fiancée and make sure she wasn't doing anything too crazy," Lee smirked as he moved, giving her rump a good smack; as he gripped it. Lucy just blushed and smiled,

"Cheeky bastard, I can get you later for that." She smirked while looking over at the bartender.

"Hmm, check out her tits?" She asked with a light smirk while Lee shook his head. He wasn't going to fall for that trick.

"Nope, just getting a beer. Your tits are good enough for me." He flirted as Lucy nodded, not believing him.

"Oh, I'm sure you just love playing with my tits, but I will say the bartenders got an amazing rack I wouldn't mind burying my face into." She teased while winking at him. Lee snorted at such a response.

"I swear you confuse me sometimes, Lucy." He smirked while they took a seat, Lee drinking his beer as Lucy managed to get one herself.

"Is that so, Mr. West? How do I confuse you?" she smirked while she took a drink, her lips pressed against the long-neck bottle, as Lucy winked at him, teasing him as she wrapped her lips around the tip.

"You're fine with me sleeping with our boss, but when I had to... feed your sister, you were beyond jealous." He chuckled, leaning back and taking another drink.

"Simple enough, I was jealous, other succubi can do different things, and I don't want another one taking you; as for most mortals, I have no reason to be jealous." Her eyes flashed, giving a lustful smirk. "I can make it where you don't want anyone else and mine if I desire."

Lee smirked while he leaned in closer, "How do you know you haven't done that, alright? Let me tell you a secret." He chuckled momentarily while looking at the beautiful woman, his Succubus queen. Lucy looked over with a small smile, imagining what he might say.

"Well, I don't want any succubus other than you. Your sister, I feed, though not without you." He chuckled, looking at her, the passion in his eyes while Lucy smirked.

"Heh, Lee, you cheesy lover boy." She winked while she took another drink as she gave him a wink. It seemed as though life was going well. However, Lee nodded but remembered this morning.

"I do have to tell you something, Something I saw this morning." He imagined he couldn't hide it. He knew if he tried, it would somehow come back to bite him in the butt.

"What's that, Lee?" Lucy asked, overseeing him, her head tilting at this point. He let out a sigh and started telling her about his morning run. He went by the library and saw his ex and her child. Lee described how the kid looked almost like him when he was younger.

Lucy would sit there for a second, blinking at him. It was a bit to take in as she muttered… "Oh, is that it?" She asked though Lee wasn't sure how to respond as he spoke up.

"I just told you there's a chance that I might have a kid, and your only response is, "Oh, that's it?" Lee somehow felt astonished by such a response. Lucy raised her hand for a second while she shook her head.

"It's just kind of surprising; I'm not mad, this was before you freed me from the ring, but did you know about this kid?"

"No, Bit it does—"

"Then it's fine, she didn't tell you, and you had no idea he existed, but I want to ask… Do you want this kid in your life?" Lucy leaned forward, looking at him for a good minute like she was looking deep within his soul for a good moment. Lee found himself pausing. He wasn't sure himself. Could he have been a good dad? What if he fucked the kid up. There were questions that he wasn't even sure about.

"I mean, I don't."

"Lee, it's a simple answer. Would you want to be in this kid's life? Cause whatever you choose, I'll fully support you." She moved in, rubbing his hand while he nodded.

"We should talk to her first, but if she wants me in his life, I think I can handle it also." He smiled at her, a part of him, that tiny sliver. I liked the idea of him being a dad. Maybe this wouldn't be so bad, so long as he had Lucy by his side. In some ways, he felt like he could do almost anything.

"Well, I'm glad that you understand," Lee said, giving a light while Lucy nodded,

"Though the thought of you being a dad is funny." Lucy giggled while she covered her mouth.

"Are you sure I could come up with some bad dad jokes? Maybe get some food? I'll give myself a dad body." This caused Lucy to laugh as she grabbed her side and giggled like a storm.

"Oh, you." She smirked while leaning in closer, "Though maybe if you're a good boy, and after the wedding, maybe we can make a baby... At least we can try to; I'm sure it'll take a few tries." She winked at him while Lee could feel his cock hardened. While the succubus chuckled. "So how about it, Daddy?"

There was a moment's pause as he was close to thinking about it when someone grabbed his shoulder, jerking him back.

"Hey there, are you Lee West?" Lee turned around seeing a man wearing a black leather jacket and a white T-shirt. His hair slicked back with a golden blonde look as he smirked.

"Yeah, and who's asking," Lee said, finding himself more annoyed as he talked with Lucy.

"Come on, Lester; you don't recognize your old sparing

partner." The man chuckled while he beat his chest. Lee looked over at the man for a second. Lee's face turned pale.

"Jack Winslow…"

"The one and only motherfucker." There was a light chuckle on his face while he grabbed his shoulder.

"So, how're the years been treating you? How's that leg." There was a cockiness in his voice, and he found his eyes turning to Lucy. He looked at her like a piece of meat ready to be chowed down.

"Yeah, my legs are fine, no thanks to you." He muttered while he pulled back.

"Come on, your still not mad about the whole leg thing that was years ago? It was an accident." Jack said while he kept his eyes on Lucy, "Now, who is that Lovely lady? Do you know Lester over here?" Jack said with a cocky smirk. Lucy watched him, not giving him much attention,

"Lee, Who's Jack?" She seemed to be interested in giving Jack much attention. Though Jack just chuckled while looking back at Lee.

"Come on, tell the lady, we used to be on the Boxing team back in school. Lee and I used to be rivals." The smirk got On Lee's nerves while he nodded,

"Yeah, we were; then you decided to break my leg with a tire iron so you could stay on the team." There was a bitterness on his face.

"Hey now, The courts said I was innocent, and we both suffered from it; I also lost my scholarship. So we're even." Jack said before he turned, looking over.

"So, got a name, pretty lady?" Jack showed off his white smile.

"It's Lucy, and my Fiancée and I were talking. Would you mind leaving?" She said, her eyes flashing red as she watched the man, clearly showing her disdain for the other man.

"Whoa, Lee, you managed to get your hand on this pretty thing; congrats." The smug smile grew on Jack's face. Lee shook his head,

"What are you doing here fucker?" Lee found himself more annoyed that he was even talking to this guy. The fact that Lee was sure he might end up in jail for the night, why he hadn't punched the guy out already?

"Listen, I simply saw an old pal of mine and wanted to see how he was doing. Is that so wrong?" Jack smirked while patting Lee on the shoulder.

"Well, thanks, now if you excuse me, my fiancée and I are about to have a few drinks and listen to the band," Lee said, unclenching his fist. However, Jack saw that with a smirk.

"Still wanting to fight, I see."

Lee said, walking past Jack. "Dude, we're out of high school, and adults, I don't feel like fighting, so how about this, go off and live your life, and I'll move on with my life." Ending the conversation while smiling at Lucy. Lucy had a smile that lasted for a few seconds When it turned to shock. Lee barely had time to react, as without warning, he felt a fist slam right into the back of his head.

Lee shook his head. The hit was hard against his head, and he felt himself slamming against the table. The beer bottles bounced over as they hit on the ground. Lee managed to look over, seeing Jack—the anger on his face as he propped himself up, ready for a fight.

"Jack, you trying to fuck up." He felt his body swaying from the surprise punch. Lee pulled himself up from the ground. The customers are watching him. While Lee wondered where the bouncer was, *What happened to them?* He groaned while watching Jack approach him and throw a quick right hook. Lee dodged, putting his fist up as he returned with a quick jab, pushing fast, as he knew Jack had a week left.

Lucy watched as she stood up, watching her husband throw punches quickly. At the same time, Lee managed to make a quick turn dodging a few points.

"Wow, you've gotten rusty there, Lee; what haven't you thrown a few punches," Jack said when he moved, throwing a left hook right into Lee's ribs, causing him to double down. A hard grunt, when without warning, Jack through a stiff right jab, hitting Lee in the jaw.

Lee groaned, but he pulled himself right up. Such a thing. While Lucy pushed herself up. Such an action as Jack smirked more.

"Come on now, stay down." Jack was ready to throw another punch when without warning, a beer bottle came right down on Jack's head, knocking him down. Lee wasn't sure how to react when he looked over seeing Betsy. She stood there with the broken bottle while looking at Lee.

"Need some help?" She asked, giving a simple look; it was clear the fighting didn't amuse her.

"Thanks, that will do." He groaned, feeling himself sitting down right then. He was standing up for a short moment. Jack groaned as he stood up, barely thinking, looking at the three of them.

"You bitch!" Jack growled, looking like he was ready to throw down. He took a few steps when he felt a hand on his shoulder. He looked over and saw none other than Lee's Dad looking at Jack, the anger in his eyes like he was about to send Jack straight to hell himself as he growled personally.

"Hello, Jack… are you causing trouble?" he asked while he popped his neck. Jack saw Rufus, and there he hunched down, looking small.

"Oh, Mr. West, is there something you need?" There was a moment of pure silence, watching him. Rufus didn't show much emotion. It looked freaky as He looked down at Jack.

"Well, you attacked my son and called the pretty lady a b-word. I think I have a problem." There was a minute where he barely even reacted, picking Jack up and carrying him to the front door. Everyone watched the sight. Some of them found it hilarious how Rufus held him by the scruff of his neck. Jack tried to squirm away. But there was no use. The young man was caught in the trap as Rufus opened the front door and tossed him out.

Rufus clapped his hands while he turned back to his smile, the relaxed look on his face as he called out.

"Come on, let's have some beers and listen to the band!" Rufus laughed while the Bar nodded, raising their glasses. Lee sat down for a minute while he took a deep breath, clearly cooling down from the fight.

Rufus came over checking over on them.

"Lee, you ok? Need us to leave?" He asked, patting his shoulder. Lee shook his head.

"I'm fine; besides, I don't need to ruin your guy's fun; just buy me a beer." He muttered while rubbing his rib. A light smirk on his face while Lucy nodded,

"Thanks, sir, thanks, sis." She looked over at Betsy, who shrugged and joined them, sitting down.

"No problem, total yuppie," Betsy said as she held a glass of whiskey; Lee wasn't entirely sure where she got it, but she drank it with a smirk.

"I swear, Lee, I like this girl. She knows how to drink a fine whiskey and is not afraid to fight dirty. Lucy-girl, you've got a great sister." Rufus said, smirking as he looked over and saw Maddy dancing on the floor. "Look, I'm heading off. I gotta dance with a mighty fine lady you have fun, guys." Rufus pulled himself up and headed back over to Lee's mom. Lee couldn't help but chuckle, finding the whole thing funny. The rest of the night seemed to go well without a cause.

They drank, laughed, told dirty jokes, and enjoyed each other's company time before heading off and walking back home and not worrying about what might happen in the world— forgetting about Cain himself. Besides, if you couldn't drink with your family. What was the point of having fun?

CHAPTER 13

To say everything was simple when planning a wedding within a week could be like saying that pulling out teeth without any anesthetic would be pleasant. It wasn't, and Lee West learned it the hard way.

If anything, Lee made a deal that he would never get married after this. However, it wasn't like he would be leaving Lucy, not in her life. Though they were only a few days till the wedding would be here.

Lee had been out here since the crack of dawn. He was in the backyard, working on the yard and cutting the grass. Fixing up the tree, doing whatever he could to ensure the place looked proper, his dad was overworking the fence while they felt the sun beating off their brow. With just a few days to the wedding, he knew he had to get dirty. When Lucy came over, she had a cold beer in her hand as she brought it to Lee.

"Hey, thanks," He said, smiling as he took the beer getting a good drink. He let out a long sigh as he put the beer down.

"Well, Darling, ah figured that since you've been working hard, I'd get you a nice cold one." Lucy tried speaking in a more southern twang. Yet it failed, as she sounded more like a British person trying to say American. Lee found himself cringing at how bad it sounded but snorted.

"Nah, that ain't how you do a southern accent, Dear, yee got to add more lick to it. See you all." He returned, sounding far better, causing Lucy to giggle at such a response while she shook her head.

"I love it when you talk southern to me." She snorted while bending down more to his eye level.

"You know you don't have to do this; we could have just married at some building for all I cared. We don't even need a party." She smiled while she helped, grabbing some of the weeds, Her fingers scorching some of the ground just enough not to be noticed as she pulled some of the weeds out.

"I know, though I can imagine my mother might kill us if we don't." He chuckled while he could smell some of the food cooking. To say he wasn't happy to be home was an understatement; the dinners at home were great. Sure, he could some, but as the old saying goes, There's nothing like family dinner. At the same time, he looked over to his future wife.

"So, um… have you told your parents yet?" He asked while imagining how this would go. The fact that Lucy's father was the devil himself, Lucifer. He was hoping the rest of his family wouldn't find out. Though if they did and acted up… He wouldn't care; it wouldn't be so bad if they accepted them. But for now, they would keep it to themselves.

"Well, They'll be there but weren't expecting it to be so soon, though I'll have to find a few goats around town. Hopefully, No one notices; it's either that a cow goes missing. But they should arrive." Lucy said with a smile. Lee found himself thinking more about when they had to visit hell and the fact the bathroom was covered in blood when they left. It made him shudder to imagine what would happen if his mother saw that. She might lose her shit at that one.

"Um, just in case, might want to set that up in a hotel. So that you know…" He pointed towards the house. It took Lucy a second to realize what he was talking about, and they nodded,

"Oh yeah, I know that. I've also called Dawn and Alice; they'll be with Beth and her girlfriend. They'll be on their way also."

At that point, Lee wanted to kick himself, completely forgetting about them but nodded.

"Shouldn't be too much of a problem, besides. Well, I forgot about letting them know." However, Lucy gave him a knowing smile.

"So, any plans for tonight, since If I remember correctly, you'll be having your bachelor party." She smirked, moving her fingers; Lee looked at her confused before remembering that it was tonight; he and Rufus and a couple of others were heading off to a strip club to get a good few drinks, watch some naked woman, dance overall a good night for a last night of freedom.

"Thanks for reminding me." He said while he pulled out another weed as he looked over his work. It was clear that it was done.

"Now, while you're doing that, the girls and I will have fun. You're mother coming also. So I'm sure she'll embarrass you." She chuckled while Lee groaned, knowing she would tell stories and he wouldn't like it. Not one bit.

"Just try to keep her from embarrassing me too much, ok,

babe."

"No promises." She chuckled while she moved around and headed back inside, Lucy was dealing with other parts of the wedding, and he wondered when she would be going out and getting a goat. However, some part of him wondered what would happen next.

When he heard yelling behind him, he finished pulling some of the various weeds. When he turned around, seeing what else he might have to do. When he felt a moment of silence, he closed his eyes taking in the crisp country air; when Lee was startled back into reality when he looked over seeing Betsy, who looked at him almost hungry. The way her pupils looked small as she stared at him.

"Betsy, are you alright?"

"Hungry… So Hungry." She moaned; Lee thought he was seeing her body transform, turning from looking human as horns started to grow from her head; how long had it been since she fed? He remembered it was the night the two had done it. Lucy watched him as his face went wide.

"Don't worry; I'll get Lucy, we'll." But before he could finish that sentence, Betsy grabbed him by his arm, dragged him into the two-car garage, and locked the door behind him. The window brings light into the room. Betsy reached down, undoing his pants as he let them drop.

"Betsy, we've got to be careful if my family walks in. This will be hard to ex—" He gasped as he felt her grabbing his dick, Running down his pants as she moved, stroking his member as he walked back deeper into the Garage, as they moved around behind the blue Dodge truck. His back against the hood, as she Betsy fell on her knees, his cock bouncing in front of her as she licked her lips. Smacking her lips like she hadn't eaten in weeks as she moved in, pushing his member against her lips as The succubus took his cock deep in his mouth. Sucking slow as she took in his scent. Her wings expanded out as he looked at those black raven wings. With a hard groan,

"Fuck!" He groaned as she was going to town on him. Barely tasting her food, she sucked on him, bobbing her head back and forth rapidly. The way she sucked him. The way her wings flapped, sending wind against him as papers behind flew into the air, as he groaned hard. His balls slapped against her chin, and she went down on him nonstop as he let out a hard grunt.

"Shit! Betsy, If you keep going like this, I'm going to… I'm going to." He groaned, feeling her grab his balls, squeezing them. His cock forced down her groan as he gasped hard. The way she slurped on his member as she went down deeper.

Keep going, keep going, Betsy!" He let out a hard groan, his hand reaching around and grabbing the Demoness by the horns as he pushed her down on his cock as started throat fucking her. Her arms turned more muscular as he gagged on his cock with a hard bounce. His member was as stiff as a board as she pulled out his cock, popping out of his mouth. The garage was filled with the sounds of Betsy's moans and slurping as her body transformed, as she turned into a succubus.

"I need more feed me! Fill me up." She turned around, bending over the work table as her plump rump wiggled for him. Lee watched, almost hypnotic, as he felt himself at the point of wanting it and being able to think.

"We've got to be careful if someone walks in."

"I don't care! I need feed. I'm starving if you're so worried here!" she suddenly started to burn into a blaze of fire; Lee almost had to cover his eyes as he saw her transform, looking almost like a perfect replica of Lucy. Her tits sway like a pendulum as she bends over for him.

"Don't make me beg. Let me keep my dignity." She groaned as her ass bounced, jiggling with each movement while Lee nodded.

"Alright, but remember you asked for it." He moved behind her. His hand gave her rear a firm smack. Betsy let out a light moan, feeling his hand giving against her ass. As she panted, her hands holding onto the work table as she felt her legs wobbling; she felt Lee still pumping his fat shaft into her pussy. When he let out a hard grunt, he called out.

"Here's the meal you wanted, Betsy!" He shuddered, letting out a powerful orgasm. His load shot deep into Betsy as he filled her pussy with every ounce. To the point that when he pulled his cock out with a soft plop, he watched bits of his load escaping from her cunt.

"Just fuck me, please I don't have time!" Betsy moaned while feeling her pushing back against him. The head of Lee's dick pushed against her clit, the way it resisted him, as he pushed against the Lucy-Betsy, who moaned hard the way her hair hung down her back as Lee growled,

"Such a tight little pussy." He moaned, feeling his cock penetrating her. The way his cock spread her pussy as he sunk in was more profound, and she let out a harrowing moan. The screams of pleasure as he didn't waste any time. Lee took her like tomorrow, the way his hips moved, thrusting against her as Betsy held onto the table. Betsy held onto the table as she moaned, looked at the wall, and panted more,

"Keep going faster, harder!" She moaned more as she could

feel him pounding against her like there was no tomorrow; the southern dame groaned as she rolled her hips. The sounds of their skin slapping against each other. He a hard groan as he thrusts faster. Lee groaned harder as he moved his hips moaning. Lee felt his cock squeeze between her tight pussy, as he reached around, his hand wrapping around. While Lee began rubbing her clip. His finger rolled around it as he leaned in, kissing Betsy's neck. Her moans were like music to his ears.

"Keep going, oh god!" She moaned. Her pussy felt so sensitive, and the way Lee kept thrusting his hips jerking up as he teased her clit, she could feel herself absorbing his energy as she moaned more, her horns sprouting from her head as she moaned even more; they glowed bright as Betsy felt filled with sexual energy, as she screamed in pleasure. She came in pure bliss as her pussy tightened up around him.

"Fuck Betsy, this feels so good." Lee could feel his brain growing wider as he fucked the succubus harder, his ass hitting the front of the car as he continued taking her like no tomorrow, her insatiable pussy. The way it held onto his cock. Lee could barely move as he groaned. His eyes closed as he heard her moaning. Lee loved every second of it. He just hoped no one walked in on them. He wasn't sure what would happen, but he knew it would lead to trouble even with Betsy disguised as Lucy.

"Getting close there; where do you want it, Lucy." He groaned while he gave Betsy another ass slap. Betsy screamed, feeling a second orgasm running through her body. Her body felt sensitive from the lack of eating, but now she felt like she was given a five-course meal as she moaned.

"Put it in me, come on, fill my hot wet pussy!" She groaned as Lee nodded, his balls tightening as he could feel his orgasm slowly growing; he let out another hard thrust pumping into her before he unleashed his load into the southern woman as she screamed in bliss.

The two stopped as They took deep breaths; Betsy looked back, her body transforming to human form, her hair falling over her face as she panted out.

"Thanks, I needed that." She moaned while she reached around, summoning her clothes back, her mouth feeling dry while she looked over to Lee, who nodded.

"It's no problem; glad to help, but I wish we didn't do it in my dad's garage." He groaned, taking in the smell of sex that went across the room while Betsy rolled her eyes.

"It'll be fine. Besides, I needed to eat; you saw what happened if I didn't… it could have been worst." She muttered, biting her lips.

"How so?" Lee asked, raising his eyebrow as he became more curious about what the Confederate succubus might have meant.

"You mean Lucy hasn't told you?" She tilted her head. Lee shook his head as Betsy sighed, "When we don't get enough to eat, we not only use our more human form for a while, but we can also go feral. Well, in a way, we go after the closes dick around. So it's why we try not to go hungry." Betsy sighed while remembering the times back in the old war when she didn't get her hunger in check and nearly killed some of her brothers in the war while they slept in the middle of the night.

A hard groan while Lee nodded, but a thought came over them. Betsy imagined it was because of what she did. They lost a few battles, barely surviving. At least the ones she was in.

"But Alice told us about how some of the succubi had

managed to be cursed where they couldn't fill themselves; how come they hadn't gone feral by now?" It was an interesting question as he thought about it.

"The Spell, most likely, just set it so they can't consume as much as they want. While they can't eat enough to fill themselves, they can still feast. It's like being given limited portions; you can eat, but you're never satisfied." Betsy said while she thought more about it, but felt pity for her sisters and brothers as those who weren't luckily roaming this world, never fully fed, just barely holding on." Betsy wondered what would have happened if she had been one of the unlucky ones.

"Hey, at least you guys are safe," Lee said as he pulled his pants back up. His cock dangling there, covered in Betsy's juices for a minute while he buckled up.

"Yeah, for now, but what about Cain? What if he finds us? What if he..." she trails off as she imagines what the first killer would do. In many ways, she knew what he was going to do for the time being while she let out a sigh.

"Hey, he doesn't know where we are; we've got time to figure it out. But let's relax. The wedding is coming soon, and we have time to relax." He imagined it didn't help much, but Lee was trying his best.

"Yeah, we can only hope," Betsy muttered, rolling her arms.

"Trust me, as long as I'm alive, I won't let anything happen to you; besides, we're family. I won't give up on anyone, not you, Lucy, or Alice. We'll stick together till the bitter end."

There was a momentary pause while Lee looked around his surroundings. "We should get going before someone notices." Lee headed out first while Betsy nodded, though she felt uneasy. As something would happen to them, it was only a matter of time before she turned, looking back at the garage and towards the American flag. A part of her looked at it while remembering the four years she had gone against it. Fighting for her home and not her country.

Betsy stood there watching it feeling foul and guilty. Realizing as she looked back, she was very much a young fool. "I'm a rebel soldier, and I might have betrayed my country, But I'll fight for my family." She felt warmth as she imagined she would redeem herself. At the very least, she would do what was right. For once, the succubus would do the right thing. She rolled her neck as she would fight.

Betsy turned around and was put into that cursed ring for the first time in a long time. That the former Confederate soldier felt like she was full. Not just sexually but emotionally.

-000-

Lee and his old man turned into the building as they approached the Strip club. The building was simple, though they got out and headed inside since this was a celebratory night. The neon sign reads The Succulent succubus. Lee found himself amused by the irony of the name.

They paid for their entrance and were met with the music playing and the girls dancing. The skimpy outfits, as they moved around smiling while the patrons handed over their money. As they continued, two girls led them to the back room for a more private dance. Lee smirked while he and the old man got a drink.

"So, when's your one pal coming?" Rufus asked while he raised a finger to one of the waitresses, a blond with big ol titties, a black bikini, and a smile on her face as she took their order, a couple of beers, and a shot of whisker.

"They'll be here, I'm sure of it." Though without warning, Beth appeared right next to them.

"Hey there, guys." She said with a smirk as Rufus jumped into the air, more startled than anything.

"Oh, Hello there, Miss." He tipped his hat in respect while Beth chuckled,

"No worry about it, Big man, Name Beth. I suspect you're Lee's dad?" she asked with a smirk; Rufus nodded while he chuckled.

"So, this is going to be your best man? I mean more like the best lady, if anything… you are a lady. Nowadays, you never know." He spoke in apparent politeness.

"Yes, I'm a woman, no worry about it." She snorted more while she checked out some of the waitresses, a part of her admiring their assets. The three would begin talking, having a good time, and sharing stories while watching the woman dance and pulling their tops off. Beth had gotten a lap dance from a cute brunette as the night went on.

Lee leaned back, enjoying himself while he popped his neck, having a few beers, as he sighed. Watching the woman dance around naked, Rufus leaned in.

"If your mother asks, let her know we went and saw a movie got it? You know how she gets some time."

"You got it, captain." He chuckled as Rufus nodded,

"To be fair, she'll be mad that we didn't invite her, but hey, that's just supposed to be a guy's night." He chuckled while noticing Beth, "Um, no offense."

"None was taken, though; it's interesting; got any fun stories about Lee, here I can blackmail him in the future." She chuckled while Lee looked at her, almost like he was trying to communicate about not doing that. Rufus, though, gave a challenging smirk.

"Well, there was this time, when he was around a year old, I took him to a strip club. I think it was Diamonds then, and all the ladies around wanted to see him and hold him."

"Dad, wait, please don't." He called out, trying to stop his old man from telling him what happened. Though Rufus kept talking, "Oh, it was a fun sight, The girls were all over talking about how much of a lady killer he was, and when he got over to this one girl, she just tickled his cheek, and Lee accidentally puked on her. Like it was something out of the exorcist. Just green, and it got all over her!" Rufus found himself snorting, but Beth, hearing that started laughing like it was some of the funniest things in her life. Lee almost imagined that she would fall right out of her seat at that point.

Lee just watched, finding himself more annoyed, but a smirk passed his face as he chuckled. With all things considered, it was a funny story. Especially with it about him being a baby.

"Alright, you two, I'm gonna grab another beer; try not to embarrass me any further, Dad." He chuckled while pulling up from his seat and headed to the bar counter. The pretty thing stood behind the counter while cleaning some of the glasses; she looked at him. She was wearing a cowboy hat that covered her hair, and she wore a cow-patterned bikini as she nodded at him.

"Is there anything I can get you, pardner, names Daisy, Daisy Ducane?" She gave him a wide smile while Lee nodded.

"Just gonna need another beer." The Cowgirl nodded and quickly poured him a fresh brew as she dropped it. He reached over, handing her a tip.

"Here you go, a fresh cup of Guinness with a hint of Minotaur milk." She gave him a wink as he found himself stopping there.

"Wait, what was that?" He asked, unsure he heard that as Daisy spoke up the southern twang, reaching a high point.

"Ah, said it was a Fresh bit of Guinness, with a hint of our special brew. It's the pub's specialty." She smirked, winking at him. Lee nodded, though he became more curious as he took a sip. Not bad, if you had to ask him, as he headed off, when a hand grabbed his shoulder.

"Listen, bub, I've got to talk to you about something." Lee turned, seeing the man sitting there, a clean look to him, well-shaved with dark hair and light brown skin, like he had been in the sun too long. Something about him seemed somewhat familiar. Lee couldn't put his fingers on it as he looked over at the man though He pulled back.

"Thanks, but no thanks, I've got a few things to do." He pulled himself away. He could feel the stranger's eyes while they watched him. Such a thing made him shudder when Beth came right up, a slight bounce as she smirked.

"Lee, got you a special gift? Now come on." She dragged him to the back, where she'd been walking for private dances. She raised her hand as one girl stood leaning against the wall. She was a tall figure, with raven black hair with aqua blue highlights slender body as she gave him a bit of a smirk. She wore a red bikini and a g-string that barely covered anything with how her ass looked.

"So, is this the groom to be?" she asked, her eyes on him as if taking in his sweet, succulent scent.

"Yeah, he's the future groom, Lee; this is Mirage; she's great." Beth winked at the stripper, who nodded,

"It's nice to meet you also, Lee." She smirked as she moved over, taking his hand for a second. Her hand was warm as she led him off to the back.

The back rooms had booths; he could see how the girls danced as they walked past. The men were mesmerized as they kept their eyes on the girls dancing. For a second, Lee thought he noticed something off about the girls. But shook his head, ignoring it, while Mirage pulled him to the back corner. She pushed him into the booth as he landed on his but, feeling her lick her lips. The music slowly started as she swayed and moved her hips around. Her breasts bounced with every move as he thought himself lost to her grace.

A feeling came over him while he watched her, the way she came in closer as she licked her lip. As he found himself sitting back. She straddled his lip as she moved, caressing his cheeks. The way she watched him, her eyes flashing as the tiny lights passed over.

"What do you desire." She moaned as she moved in close, grinding against him. Lee found himself taking in her scent. Somehow this felt familiar, as he let out a hard groan. Somehow this woman felt familiar, but he knew well that he'd never met the woman as she leaned in and whispered in his ear, that hot succulent voice,

"What is it you desire? What would you like to do to me before you get married, groom?" she showed off her teeth in a white smile, showing a pair of fangs, as Lee felt he was under his spell as he heard a small voice telling him.

'Some succubus can use tricks to get food; some are desperate.' As he found himself reaching down to pinch his hand. The pain was still there as he let out a hard groan.

"Are you a succubus?" he said as he felt himself finally able to focus. This caused Mirage to stop, and she blinked at him for a minute while looking at him.

"No, of course not; why would you suggest I'm a succubus…. I'm just your average everyday stripper." Her voice cracked there, clearly nervous as He looked at her.

"Listen, my fiancée is a succubus; This isn't my first rodeo. Also, you're a terrible liar." Lee said while she looked at him, her eyes flashing more as she groaned.

"You've got to be kidding; today been a dry spell, and a succubus takes the first customer I get and him." She groaned rather annoyed,

"Dry spell? I mean, can't you… Oh yeah, the restrictions." He pointed out while she looked at him, more annoyed.

"Yeah, those things had to get caught. Now I can't access my full power; always hungry. Fuck, wait, your fiancée isn't stuck under the same condition… How?" She asked, forgetting she was supposed to perform a strip tease for him.

Lee rubbed the back of his head.

"Well, apparently, she was shoved into one of the rings before she could have that cursed put on her… same for Her sister Betsy." It seemed Mirage's eyes twitched hearing that while she crossed her arms.

"Well, good for her. She's one of the lucky ones. Sometimes I wouldn't have minded being shoved into one of those rings." She muttered while she looked down.

"Hey now, don't say that; it was rough on her, being trapped." He remembered the few times they talked about it and how she described it as feeling like absolute nothingness.

"Well, there are times when I'd rather not be in this state. I feel trapped as well." She muttered while shaking her head, "Sorry, I'm being unprofessional. How's this? I'll compensate on another song." She was about to go back to dancing as she tried to hide the sadness on her face.

"Hey, It's fine; I'm the one who fucked it up."

"Yes, but your friend paid good money." Mirage pointed out at that as Lee nodded, knowing she had a point. The woman moved, dancing, her top coming off, revealing her perky breasts, the way they pointed at him. Her nipples were sadly covered up with pasties as she smiled.

"So tell me about your succubus fiancée; Bet she's a fine lady?" she winked while she blew air into his ear. A play she did on her customers to get a raise out of them. Lee shuddering.

"She's great; I'm lucky to be with her, even if it was an accident." He smiled, feeling his cock hardened, the succubus working her magic.

"How did you meet? I mean, you claimed she was trapped in the ring?" she asked as she began to grab the edge of Lee's seat and started to flip herself. His face is getting a full view of her pussy. The soft look as she sneaked around, pulling her underwear around and showing her fat pussy.

Lee found himself looking at it while telling her he bought

the ring off an auction site and released her. However, leaving out some of the more private things.

"Aww, that's so nice." She smirked while turning around and rubbing her ass against him. The way it pressed against his groin while they talked. "Like a knight in shining armor… In a way." Lee found himself chuckling, finding it funny the way her pussy was near him while she said that.

"Yeah, and well, as I said, we'll be getting married soon. So hopefully, it'll be a good life."

"Well, congratulation." The succubus said as she plopped onto his lap, Lee letting out a hard grunt as she giggled lightly.

"I hope you have a fabulous honeymoon… Oh!." She reached around. Lee wasn't sure where, as she brought out a small card and handed it over. Lee found himself looking at it, as it read, *Bordello of desire.* The card was lined with gold engraving. He looked at it curiously.

"A brothel? Um, a little weird for a wedding gift to a married man."

"Trust me, and it's a great place; work there on the side. Just let em know, and I'm sure they'll give you a night." Mirage winked as her eyes turned dark red, looking into his soul. Lee found himself nodding. In contrast, slipping the card into her pocket.

The music seemed to stop at this point while the succubus chuckled.

"Well, our little dance is finished. Would you care to have another one or anything else?" She moved in, kissing his cheek at that point while Lee shook his head.

"Why, Mirage, why would you insinuate that I'm almost a married man." He found himself joking, making the other succubus giggle at his response while nodding.

"Fair point. Well, have a great night." She turned and put her top on. Lee would sit there for a good minute before getting up and walking away. He let out a sigh while she rolled her shoulders for a good minute when a hand grabbed him. Lee turned and found himself looking over at a man, a man with a scar over his face.

Somehow Lee knew that he was looking into the face of Cain. The first killer and he knew right then, and there he was in deep trouble.

CHAPTER 14

It was late when Lee dragged himself back to his parent's house. Rufus helps him up with one arm and Beth with the other. They opened the door letting out a cheerful tone. Lee, however, remained silent. At the same time, he let out a hard groan. The door closed behind them while They stumbled in.

Lucy was sitting in the living room, wearing a white robe over her. In contrast, she looked at the two of them, smiling.

"Finally, I was kind of worried for you guys." She muttered while she went over, seeing Lee slumped over.

"Lee, are you ok?" she asked, noticing how quiet he was.

"Oh, he's fine. Just had a little too much to drink. It was a great night." Rufus let out a severe hiccup while he swayed. He was helping Lee get onto the couch. Lucy sat next to him for a minute while he took a long deep breath, feeling himself relax. But if anyone looked at his hands, they might have seen him shaking.

His Dad would head upstairs, a spring in his step, while Beth looked back,

"Hey, I'll head over to my Hotel. I'll check on you guy's

later." She spoke up while looking at him. Her face was concerned as if she hadn't seen Lee so quietly. But she wasn't entirely sure what was going on. She hadn't drunk as much as the two guys had. Yet she was sure she could trust Lucy to get it from him. She had ways Beth wasn't quite sure about as she headed back out the door.

So there it was, Lee and Lucy sitting there for a good minute while Lucy wrapped an arm around him.

"Is everything alright?" she asked while rubbing his shoulder; Lee sat there for a good minute while he responded.

"I'm fine for the most part, but I ran into someone…." His mind drifted off, thinking about what happened a few hours ago.

"Do you wanna talk about it… I'm here." The Succubus said while looking over at Lee, her heart fluttering while she felt worried for him. What happened that left him so quiet as she leaned into him?

"Do you wanna see my tits that usually cheer you up?" She asked, a small smile on her face as she was about to open the robe for him, but Lee shook his head.

"Not tonight, no offense, it was a great night… I need a moment to think about some things." He muttered, his voice sounding monotoned while Lucy looked at him. I was feeling worried about her husband-to-be.

"Alright, but I'm here to talk, Don't forget about it. I'll be heading up to bed… If you want to come. Betsy decided to sleep outside after the party we had… I think she and Alice left with one of the strippers. I don't know what happened to Dawn; she passed out somewhere." She muttered while feeling more concerned.

"I'll be up. I need some time to think about a few things." Lee muttered while he looked off into the distance. Lucy looked at him for a hot second before nodding. She leaned in, kissing his cheek. She imagined his skin felt cold for a second, but she kept it to herself. Soon the Succubus headed upstairs and off to bed. She didn't bother if his mother said anything when waiting for him. Lucy knew she needed to be there for him and have him in her arms.

Lee would sit looking off into nothingness, remembering what happened a few hours ago.

-000-

He had come out of the back room, as he was adjusting himself and going back for a beer, when without warning, Cain. The man who was coming after they arrived grabbed his shoulders.

The man looked at him, that broad smile on his face. If anything Lee could describe, he looked like John Wick, though browner, as he gripped Lee's shoulder. While he spoke up, simply saying.

"Hello Lee, mind if I call you that? Let's sit down, and I'll buy you a beer." He squeezed his hands to empathize as he walked to one of the tables. Rufus and Beth not even noticing this happening as they were busy talking about something. What It might have been, he wasn't entirely sure. But right then, it was clear he had bigger fish to deal with.

The Waitress came, and Lee started to notice she had one eye and handing over a couple of beers. Lee reached over, rubbing his eyes, wondering if he was going crazy.

"You're not going crazy; You're just seeing how the girls look, With you fucking a succubus and being around me. You're what we should call it. Biology is transforming, and you can see under the veil. This place has quite a few gals running around, not

229

entirely human… Did you think Succubus were the only creatures running around our world?" Cain seemed to smirk while he took one of the beers and took a drink.

"Terrible stuff; now, if you ask me, the Romans, they knew how to make some great drinks. That stuff could nearly get me drunk." He put the beer down while staring at Lee, his eyes glowing as if he was trying to put Lee under some spell. Lee took a long deep breath, trying to calm himself down.

"What do you want… Cain?" He asked, raising his eyebrow while The man on the other side nodded.

"Yes, I am Cain, though I've been called other names."

"Listen, I don't have time to hear about every name you are called blah, blah. What do you want?" Lee asked as he found himself feeling angry, very angry, while looking at the man. He wanted to tell him to eat a dick and kick his ass while he gripped the table.

"Just to speak with you, maybe make a deal…. You want to make a deal, right?" Cain spoke, calm in his voice, making Lee very pissed while he held his tongue. His head felt like it was going to split apart. How he hadn't felt like throwing punches was beyond him.

"What kind of deal do you want? And why do I wanna beat the snot out of you right now?" Lee found himself asking, feeling his heart pounding.

"Relax, just my ability. See, I can bring sin out. All kinds, sexual, greed, and rage, are just a few that come to mind. Your sins are being amplified, a funny little curse the man upstairs put on me." Cain pointed over the scar on his face. One Lee wanted to stab with the beer bottle.

"Hmm, You are experiencing Rage, interesting. I figured with you fucking the succubus Whores, and you'd be more lustful, especially here. My own mistake." Cain said while he took another drink.

"Drink; it'll help you relax."

"I don't want the damn beer; tell me what you intend to do with my Fiancée and her sister?" Lee. Found himself banging the table, causing the drinks to bounce while Cain adjusted himself.

"Nothing too bad if you do as I say. Now cool yourself down and drink your beer. If I wanted to, I could have killed you at any second, and I'm good at that."

"Yeah, didn't you kill your brother fucker." Lee spoke while feeling himself see red, looking around. Something just kept pissing him off while Cain smacked his face.

"Hey, focus and listen to what I'm saying," Cain growled, looking more annoyed dealing with Lee being pissed off.

"So what's this deal you want?"

"I want you to surrender the Succubus you freed from that prison. Yeah, we know about it. Surrender her to me, and I'll take care of her. You can go back to your normal little life. You can get married, do whatever you want, white picket fence with your Succubus." Cain took another drink as he got comfortable. If Lee wasn't overwhelmed with being so pissed, he might have thought the guy was your everyday kind of person.

"You want me to see Lucy's sister, so we can have a normal life, right? What's the catch?"

"None, as I said, we— well, they want her back. I'm even willing to let go of what you did to Lucus. Now that pissed me off what you did to him. He was like a brother to me... or a son." He spoke as if he hit a sore spot, but Lee didn't have it.

"Yeah, and he was a sick little puppy, cut his balls off, and nearly killed Lucy and my friends," Lee growled, thinking about that night, as he was ready to just break the bottle over his head. Violent thoughts ran through his head while he looked back at Cain.

"Hey now, in the end, he became less stable; they fucked him up. But as I said, he was like a son of mine. Now I don't feel like killing. I want this over with; all I'll do is stick her back in the ring and put her back. Maybe drop it down in the ocean. But that's all. If I have to your fiancee, I'll put a bind on her so she can't kill someone by absorbing their life force." Cain was perfectly calm, which enraged Lee even more.

"You want me to starve my wife and just surrender her sister? How dare you." Lee reached over, grabbing Cain by the shirt. Moving in, ready to strike the man, but Cain caught his hand.

"I am being merciful, now, do not strike me. I'm patient, very, very patient. But you will speak to me with respect as I'm giving you." Cain growled, clearly showing the rage he held behind.

"Want to go? I'll take you on."

"Arrogant human, I've fought in more wars than you'll ever see. Do you think you'll be able to beat me? I could snap your neck like a twig." He growled and pushed his hand down.

He squeezed Lee's hand as the young man groaned; the shock caught him off as Cain looked at him.

"I will hand my number over to you when you have a few days to decide. Surrender the Succubus, and I'll be on my way.

Otherwise, I will be forced to end you and those two." He growled while looking at Lee as he added this.

"It'll be nice, especially returning what you did to Lucus." He growled while he let go of his hand. He reached down, dropping some cash and his card before he got up and walked away. Lee sat there feeling himself calming down, but his body felt wholly drained while he looked down at the card.

-000-

"What am I going to do?"

Lee found himself leaning down, thinking about what he could do. He was in trouble. "I've got to tell Lucy; I've got to tell them all." He groaned, taking a long deep breath, trying to understand how something like this could even go. He felt ashamed, his heart racing while he looked out the window. A part of him wanted to ask someone some questions as he groaned.

"So much for a fun night. But…" He went silent and decided he'd talk to Lucy tomorrow. However, he wasn't sure what was in store for him tomorrow. Lee could only hope that tomorrow would turn out well for him.

Such a thing made him worry. Lee let out a long groan as he headed upstairs, imagining that he would try and get some sleep.

He climbed the stairs, his heart pounding. Lee could feel himself ready to drop like a cinder block. He never realized how being angry wore him out. He listened to the squeaking of each step, somehow reminding him of more things. When he found himself stopped. Someone was standing at the edge of the stair. Lee let out a hard groan, his Leg hurting like hell when he looked up.

"Dad, what are you…" It took him a minute to realize just who it was. It wasn't his father.

"Lucifer?" He spoke carefully as he watched a small flame glowing, raising it to his face. There the handsome face showed itself as Lucifer, the fallen one, lit a cigar as he chuckled.

"You got it, kid; You needed some advice? I'm sure I can help my son-in-law. Sorry, I didn't make it to the party." He chuckled, stepping down. The silence as he descended the stairs met him halfway as he puffed the cigar with a wide toothy grin.

"Would you mind putting that out?" Lee asked, finding it somewhat funny he made this request to the Devil himself but stared at the fallen archangel. Lucifer looked down at it and rolled his eyes.

"Listen, I'll smoke one if I want." He blew another puff while he passed by Lee as they headed back down the stairs.

"You're kind of an asshole; what are you here for trying to save another one of your daughters?" he asked, remembering what happened last time.

"Oh no, We can do that later; you seem exhausted. I just figured you'd like my counseling." Lucifer chuckled while he plopped down on the couch, a foot on the coffee table.

"Not sure it's a good idea. Lee said while sitting on one of the recliners, while Lucifer laughed.

"Yeah, well, trust me, I'm great at giving advice hell, I've given God some wonderful advice. The Flood. I talked him into doing Noah's arc. He just planned on… well, rebooting humanity. I thought that was boring." He chuckled while he leaned back. "Rainbow thing was my idea." He snorted as he got comfortable.

"Um, thanks, Though. Why are you here?"

"As I said, you seemed troubled and needed advice, and my inferno wisdom thought you might need some help. After all, you are going to be my son-in-law soon." Lucifer chuckled as he got comfortable.

"I've been talking to Cain… he wants to get ahold of Betsy to lock her back into the ring."

Lucifer stopped there for a second. The cigar in his mouth when he looked back to Lee for a second.

"Cain, as in the son of my wife's Ex and Eve. That Cain?" Lee nodded while Lucifer let out a hard sigh.

"Great, it had to be him. So what kind of deal did he want to make?" Lucifer leaned in, his black angel wings appearing out of his back while he seemed ready to listen to the mortal.

"Well, he wants to capture Betsy and put that spell on Lucy, which prevents them from consuming too much energy. He says it's that, or he might kill them both." Lee found himself slouching over while Lucifer nodded.

"Hmm, interesting, Well, I'm sure you'll reject his offer… right?" Lucifer said, watching Lee, his eyes glowing while he examined him.

"I don't know, I mean… Alice said she stabbed him, and he just came back. This isn't going to be that Lucus guy…. This guy is on another level."

"Please, he's just as human as you, sure he's more resistant, but he's still mortal. Just tougher because God, might I add, has no imagination. Seriously. If I were making you creatures, I'd have given you four arms." He snorted while he took another puff.

"So what do you think I should do? I mean, I'm just human? Not blessed with Supernatural powers or an angel. I'm just a man."

"Which is why I got my money on you, kid. Cain is unimaginable, not creative. He has his tricks, sure bringing out a person's sin and killing, heck he only survived as long as he has because of the old man's mark. But that's all he's got. You, on the other hand. What do you have?" Lucifer said, leaning forward and poking Lee in the chest.

"I've got…." He stopped for a minute, thinking about what he had that Cain didn't while looking at Lucifer.

Lucifer smacked him upside the head.

"Use your bloody monkey brain! You have imagination. That guy relies on his abilities. Use it against him!" Lucifer rolled his head. "Sometimes you humans can be dumber than squirrels outside a nut house." Lucifer gave Lee a wack upside the head causing Lee to move his head forward.

"Hey!" He spoke up, ready to throw a punch, but Lucifer dodged.

"Trust me; you want to be my son-in-law, grow a pair, and Show me you are worthy. If Cain's coming out, smart him." Lucifer said while he puffed his cigar. The smell of it pierced Lee's nostrils while Lucifer chuckled.

"I have faith in you. Ironic, the Devil believes in you." He chuckles while leaning back. "So, I'm curious, what will you do with Cain's healing ability? The mark protects him from wombs, magical and physical. It's one of Heaven's strongest protections." Lucifer moved around his finger, playing with the cigar. At the same time, he watched Lee—the Devil, curious about what he might do in this situation.

"I'm willing to do anything to stop Cain and protect Lucy…." Lucifer raised his eye and looked at him, that smile on his face while he looked at Lee.

"Oh really, and what might you do… Would you be willing to surrender your soul to me? Hand it over, and I can give you the power to fight Cain. What an interesting idea." He crushed the cigar out on the coffee table. Lee could smell the sulfur scent while he shuddered.

"I don't think I'd be willing to do that… I mean an eternity in hell, or whatever you might do…." He also imagined how Lucy might act if he did that; she might be disappointed in him.

"Hey, I'm sure I could pull some strings, and you only got tortured on Tuesdays." Lucifer chuckled while he leaned back.

"So, do you plan to sell your soul to me? I find that interesting. Surrender the thing that keeps you human?" his eyes glowed bright red while he looked at Lee.

"Let me think about it, alright," Lee muttered, feeling inadequate in his gut.

"Well, you change your mind, kid. Let me know. I'm just dying to see what you do." Lucifer chuckled while he vanished in a puff of cigar smoke. It was as though he hadn't been here. Even the burn mark on the coffee table had disappeared.

"Well, at least the Devil knows how to clean up after himself. I guess that's a positive thing."

CHAPTER 15

It was late when Lee dragged himself back to his parent's house. Rufus helps him up with one arm and Beth with the other. They opened the door letting out a cheerful tone. Lee, however, remained silent. At the same time, he let out a hard groan. The door closed behind them while They stumbled in.

Lucy was sitting in the living room, wearing a white robe over her. In contrast, she looked at the two of them, smiling.

"Finally, I was kind of worried for you guys." She muttered while she went over, seeing Lee slumped over.

"Lee, are you ok?" she asked, noticing how quiet he was.

"Oh, he's fine. Just had a little too much to drink. It was a great night." Rufus let out a severe hiccup while he swayed. He was helping Lee get onto the couch. Lucy sat next to him for a minute while he took a long deep breath, feeling himself relax. But if anyone looked at his hands, they might have seen him shaking.

His Dad would head upstairs, a spring in his step, while Beth looked back,

"Hey, I'll head over to my Hotel. I'll check on you guy's later." She spoke up while looking at him. Her face was concerned as if she hadn't seen Lee so quietly. But she wasn't entirely sure what was going on. She hadn't drunk as much as the two guys had. Yet she was sure she could trust Lucy to get it from him. She had ways Beth wasn't quite sure about as she headed back out the door.

So there it was, Lee and Lucy sitting there for a good minute while Lucy wrapped an arm around him.

"Is everything alright?" she asked while rubbing his shoulder; Lee sat there for a good minute while he responded.

"I'm fine for the most part, but I ran into someone…." His mind drifted off, thinking about what happened a few hours ago.

"Do you wanna talk about it… I'm here." The Succubus said while looking over at Lee, her heart fluttering while she felt worried for him. What happened that left him so quiet as she leaned into him?

"Do you wanna see my tits that usually cheer you up?" She asked, a small smile on her face as she was about to open the robe for him, but Lee shook his head.

"Not tonight, no offense, it was a great night… I need a moment to think about some things." He muttered, his voice sounding monotoned while Lucy looked at him. I was feeling worried about her husband-to-be.

"Alright, but I'm here to talk, Don't forget about it. I'll be heading up to bed… If you want to come. Betsy decided to sleep outside after the party we had… I think she and Alice left with one of the strippers. I don't know what happened to Dawn; she passed out somewhere." She muttered while feeling more concerned.

"I'll be up. I need some time to think about a few things." Lee muttered while he looked off into the distance. Lucy looked at him for a hot second before nodding. She leaned in, kissing his cheek. She imagined his skin felt cold for a second, but she kept it to herself. Soon the Succubus headed upstairs and off to bed. She didn't bother if his mother said anything when waiting for him. Lucy knew she needed to be there for him and have him in her arms.

Lee would sit looking off into nothingness, remembering what happened a few hours ago.

-000-

He had come out of the back room, as he was adjusting himself and going back for a beer, when without warning, Cain. The man who was coming after they arrived grabbed his shoulders.

The man looked at him, that broad smile on his face. If anything Lee could describe, he looked like John Wick, though browner, as he gripped Lee's shoulder. While he spoke up, simply saying.

"Hello Lee, mind if I call you that? Let's sit down, and I'll buy you a beer." He squeezed his hands to empathize as he walked to one of the tables. Rufus and Beth not even noticing this happening as they were busy talking about something. What It might have been, he wasn't entirely sure. But right then, it was clear he had bigger fish to deal with.

The Waitress came, and Lee started to notice she had one eye and handing over a couple of beers. Lee reached over, rubbing his eyes, wondering if he was going crazy.

"You're not going crazy; You're just seeing how the girls look, With you fucking a succubus and being around me. You're what we should call it. Biology is transforming, and you can see under the veil. This place has quite a few gals running around, not entirely human… Did you think Succubus were the only creatures running around our world?" Cain seemed to smirk while he took one of the beers and took a drink.

"Terrible stuff; now, if you ask me, the Romans, they knew how to make some great drinks. That stuff could nearly get me drunk." He put the beer down while staring at Lee, his eyes glowing brightly as if he was trying to put Lee under some spell. Lee took a long deep breath, trying to calm himself down.

"What do you want… Cain?" He asked, raising his eyebrow while The man on the other side nodded.

"I am Cain, though I've been called other names."

"Listen, I don't have time to hear about every name you are called blah, blah. What do you want?" Lee asked as he found himself feeling angry, very angry, while looking at the man. He wanted to tell him to eat a dick and kick his ass while he gripped the table.

"Just to speak with you, maybe make a deal…. You want to make a deal, right?" Cain spoke, calm in his voice, making Lee very pissed while he held his tongue. His head felt like it was going to split apart. How he hadn't felt like throwing punches was beyond him.

"What kind of deal do you want? And why do I wanna beat the snot out of you right now?" Lee found himself asking, feeling his heart pounding.

"Relax, just my ability. See, I can bring sin out. All kinds, sexual, greed, and rage, are just a few that come to mind. Your sins are being amplified, a funny little curse the man upstairs put on me." Cain pointed over the scar on his face. One Lee wanted to stab with the beer bottle.

"Hmm, You are experiencing Rage, interesting. I figured with you fucking the succubus Whores, and you'd be more lustful, especially here. My own mistake." Cain said while he took another drink.

"Drink; it'll help you relax."

"I don't want the damn beer; tell me what you intend to do with my Fiancée and her sister?" Lee. Found himself banging the table, causing the drinks to bounce while Cain adjusted himself.

"Nothing too bad if you do as I say. Now cool yourself down and drink your beer. If I wanted to, I could have killed you at any second, and I'm good at that."

"Yeah, didn't you kill your brother fucker." Lee spoke while feeling himself see red, looking around. Something just kept pissing him off while Cain smacked his face.

"Hey, focus and listen to what I'm saying," Cain growled, looking more annoyed dealing with Lee being pissed off.

"So what's this deal you want?"

"I want you to surrender the Succubus you freed from that prison. Yeah, we know about it. Surrender her to me, and I'll take care of her. You can go back to your normal little life. You can get married, do whatever you want, white picket fence with your Succubus." Cain took another drink as he got comfortable. If Lee wasn't overwhelmed with being so pissed, he might have thought the guy was your everyday kind of person.

"You want me to see Lucy's sister, so we can have a normal life, right? What's the catch?"

"None, as I said, we— well, they want her back. I'm even willing to let go of what you did to Lucus. Now that pissed me off what you did to him. He was like a brother to me… or a son." He spoke as if he hit a sore spot, but Lee didn't have it.

"Yeah, and he was a sick little puppy, cut his balls off, and nearly killed Lucy and my friends," Lee growled, thinking about that night, as he was ready to just break the bottle over his head. Violent thoughts ran through his head while he looked back at Cain.

"Hey now, in the end, he became less stable; they fucked him up. But as I said, he was like a son of mine. Now I don't feel like killing. I want this over with; all I'll do is stick her back in the ring and put her back. Maybe drop it down in the ocean. But that's all. If I have to your fiancee, I'll put a bind on her so she can't kill someone by absorbing their life force." Cain was perfectly calm, which enraged Lee even more.

"You want me to starve my wife and just surrender her sister? How dare you." Lee reached over, grabbing Cain by the shirt. Moving in, ready to strike the man, but Cain caught his hand.

"I am being merciful, now, do not strike me. I'm patient, very, very patient. But you will speak to me with respect as I'm giving you." Cain growled, clearly showing the rage he held behind.

"Want to go? I'll take you on."

"Arrogant human, I've fought in more wars than you'll ever see. Do you think you'll be able to beat me? I could snap your neck like a twig." He growled and pushed his hand down.

He squeezed Lee's hand as the young man groaned; the shock caught him off as Cain looked at him.

"I will hand my number over to you when you have a few days to decide. Surrender the Succubus, and I'll be on my way. Otherwise, I will be forced to end you and those two." He growled while looking at Lee as he added this.

"It'll be nice, especially returning what you did to Lucus." He growled while he let go of his hand. He reached down, dropping some cash and his card before he got up and walked away. Lee sat there feeling himself calming down, but his body felt drained entirely while he looked down at the card.

-000-

"What am I going to do?"

Lee found himself leaning down, thinking about what he could do. He was in trouble. "I've got to tell Lucy; I've got to tell them all." He groaned, taking a long deep breath, trying to understand how something like this could even go. He felt ashamed, his heart racing while he looked out the window. A part of him wanted to ask someone some questions as he groaned.

"So much for a fun night. But…" He went silent and decided he'd talk to Lucy tomorrow. However, he wasn't sure what was in store for him tomorrow. Lee could only hope that tomorrow would turn out well for him.

Such a thing made him worry. Lee let out a long groan as he headed upstairs, imagining that he would try and get some sleep.

He climbed the stairs, his heart pounding. Lee could feel himself ready to drop like a cinder block. He never realized how being angry wore him out. Lee listened to the squeaking of each step, somehow reminding him of more things. When he found himself stopped. Someone was standing at the edge of the stair.

Lee let out a hard groan, his Leg hurting like hell when he looked up.

"Dad, what are you…" It took him a minute to realize just who it was. It wasn't his father.

"Lucifer?" He spoke carefully as he watched a small flame glowing, raising it to his face. There the handsome face showed itself as Lucifer, the fallen one, lit a cigar as he chuckled.

"You got it, kid; You needed some advice? I'm sure I can help my son-in-law. Sorry, I didn't make it to the party." He chuckled, stepping down. The silence as he descended the stairs met him halfway as he puffed the cigar with a wide toothy grin.

"Would you mind putting that out?" Lee asked, finding it somewhat funny he made this request to the Devil himself but stared at the fallen archangel. Lucifer looked down at it and rolled his eyes.

"Listen, I'll smoke one if I want." He blew another puff while he passed by Lee as they headed back down the stairs.

"You're kind of an asshole; what are you here for trying to save another one of your daughters?" he asked, remembering what happened last time.

"Oh no, We can do that later; you seem exhausted. I just figured you'd like my counseling." Lucifer chuckled while he plopped down on the couch, a foot on the coffee table.

"Not sure it's a good idea. Lee said while sitting on one of the recliners, while Lucifer laughed.

"Yeah, well, trust me, I'm great at giving advice hell, I've given God some wonderful advice. The Flood. I talked him into doing Noah's arc. He just planned on… well, rebooting humanity.

I thought that was boring." He chuckled while he leaned back. "Rainbow thing was my idea." He snorted as he got comfortable.

"Um, thanks, Though. Why are you here?"

"As I said, you seemed troubled and needed advice, and my inferno wisdom thought you might need some help. After all, you are going to be my son-in-law soon." Lucifer chuckled as he got comfortable.

"I've been talking to Cain... he wants to get ahold of Betsy to lock her back into the ring."

Lucifer stopped there for a second. The cigar in his mouth when he looked back to Lee for a second.

"Cain, as in the son of my wife's Ex and Eve. That Cain?" Lee nodded while Lucifer let out a hard sigh.

"Great, it had to be him. So what kind of deal did he want to make?" Lucifer leaned in, his black angel wings appearing out of his back while he seemed ready to listen to the mortal.

"Well, he wants to capture Betsy and put that spell on Lucy, which prevents them from consuming too much energy. He says it's that, or he might kill them both." Lee found himself slouching over while Lucifer nodded.

"Hmm, interesting, Well, I'm sure you'll reject his offer... right?" Lucifer said, watching Lee, his eyes glowing while he examined him.

"I don't know, I mean... Alice said she stabbed him, and he just came back. This isn't going to be that Lucus guy.... This guy is on another level."

"Please, he's just as human as you, sure he's more resistant, but he's still mortal. Just tougher because God, might I add, has no imagination. Seriously. If I were making you creatures, I'd have given you four arms." He snorted while he took another puff.

"So what do you think I should do? I mean, I'm just human? Not blessed with Supernatural powers or an angel. I'm just a man."

"Which is why I got my money on you, kid. Cain is unimaginable, not creative. He has his tricks, sure bringing out a person's sin and killing, heck he only survived as long as he has because of the old man's mark. But that's all he's got. You, on the other hand. What do you have?" Lucifer said, leaning forward and poking Lee in the chest.

"I've got…." He stopped for a minute, thinking about what he had that Cain didn't while looking at Lucifer.

Lucifer smacked him upside the head.

"Use your bloody monkey brain! You have imagination. That guy relies on his abilities. Use it against him!" Lucifer rolled his head. "Sometimes you humans can be dumber than squirrels outside a nut house." Lucifer gave Lee a wack upside the head causing Lee to move his head forward.

"Hey!" He spoke up, ready to throw a punch, but Lucifer dodged.

"Trust me; you want to be my son-in-law, grow a pair, and Show me you are worthy. If Cain's coming out, smart him." Lucifer said while he puffed his cigar. The smell of it pierced Lee's nostrils while Lucifer chuckled.

"I have faith in you. Ironic, the Devil believes in you." He chuckles while leaning back. "So, I'm curious, what will you do with Cain's healing ability? The mark protects him from wombs, magical and physical. It's one of Heaven's strongest protections." Lucifer moved around his finger, playing with the cigar. At the same time, he watched Lee—the Devil, curious about what he might do in this situation.

"I'm willing to do anything to stop Cain and protect Lucy…." Lucifer raised his eye and looked at him, that smile on his face while he looked at Lee.

"Oh really, and what might you do… Would you be willing to surrender your soul to me? Hand it over, and I can give you the power to fight Cain. What an interesting idea." He crushed the cigar out on the coffee table. Lee could smell the sulfur scent while he shuddered.

"I don't think I'd be willing to do that… I mean an eternity in hell, or whatever you might do…." He also imagined how Lucy might act if he did that; she might be disappointed in him.

"Hey, I'm sure I could pull some strings, and you only got tortured on Tuesdays." Lucifer chuckled while he leaned back.

"So, do you plan to sell your soul to me? I find that interesting. Surrender the thing that keeps you human?" his eyes glowed bright red while he looked at Lee.

"Let me think about it, alright," Lee muttered, feeling inadequate in his gut.

"Well, you change your mind, kid. Let me know. I'm just dying to see what you do." Lucifer chuckled while he vanished in a puff of cigar smoke. It was as though he hadn't been here. Even the burn mark on the coffee table had disappeared.

"Well, at least the Devil knows how to clean up after himself. I guess that's a positive thing."

CHAPTER 16

It was the day of the wedding. It was a beautiful day; the weather was warm, with no chance of chilling, while Lee woke up in bed. Lucy was gone, and he let out a long sigh.

"Today is the day." He muttered as he found himself getting up and getting dressed. He didn't know what he was going to do now. At the same time, he took a deep breath and headed over to the bathroom. The house felt quiet as he took a warm bath. The warm water soothed him. It was such a feeling. He didn't want to leave, though when the water got cool enough, he pulled out of the claw foot tub and turned to clean himself up. He took the razor. He was giving himself an excellent shave and even trimming his hair.

Lee looked at himself in the mirror, freshly shaved, his hair trimmed up; he looked almost like a new man. At the same time, he brushed his teeth and muttered to himself.

"It's a new day; our life will be different." The idea that he was about to marry Lucy had caused his heart to skip a beat feeling like he was on top of the world. He didn't even think about Cain.

He ignored that funny feeling while he dried his hair up.

There was a knocking on the bathroom door while Lee moved over, answering the door. His father is standing there with a smirk.

"Morning there, I'm gonna need to take a shower." He moved around, pulling Lee out as he closed the door behind him. Lee looked over when he heard the loudest rip he could imagine. Lee groaned while he felt himself bouncing back.

"Hey, open a window while you're in there!" he called out, unsure how to feel; he turned around and decided to get dressed.

-000-

Lee went on a quick run as he found himself moving. His heart was racing while he continued. Given that there was at least another ten hours before the wedding would start. He moved down the street. Lucy hadn't answered when he imagined she was getting her final touches before the wedding. He figured it would be good to get himself moving. That was when his phone rang, and Lee stopped and pulled it out. The number came as unknown. Lee was tempted to ignore it till an icey feeling ran down his spine, and he quickly answered it.

"Hello?"

"Hello Lee, I'd like to know if you decided?" Cain spoke that calm voice as Lee found his fingers shaking, as he felt overwhelmed with something but took up stealing his nerves.

"Yeah, I thought about it and slept on it… you know what I decided." Lee spoke carefully, trying not to show any fear that he might have hidden.

"Yeah, and what might that be?" Cain spoke, sounding

more casual than he really should have been.

"We have a saying down here in the south of Ohio; it's don't fuck with us, we're crazy as Floridians, and I say back off. Betsy's not for trade and keeps away from Lucy." Lee spoke up while taking a deep breath and holding it in while waiting for Cain's response.

"… So this is your final choice, then?" He asked with a steady voice.

"Yeah, it is. It's over." so how about you go home and leave us be? Lee muttered, knowing that this wouldn't stop him, but he took a moment feeling more courageous than he might have imagined.

"So you have made your decision?" Cain asked while Lee nodded, he knew the man couldn't see him, but he nodded.

"Yeah, so take this as a note don't come to my wedding. Otherwise, there will be hell to pay." Lee said while he heard Cain instantly laughing. He wasn't sure what was so funny, but the phone went dead. Lee looked back at the phone before he turned and stuffed it into his pocket.

"It's going to be a long day." Lee would return to his run before heading back to the house. He had to get ready for his wedding, after all.

-000-

Cain sat in his hotel room, taking a long drink. The phone was on the counter while he rubbed his temple.

"It could have been simple, but he leaves me no choice," Cain growled while he could almost hear Abel speaking up but tuned him out.

"I'm going to take the succubus and take them out." He growled while he reached the edge of the bed and pulled out a duffle bag, weapons filling it while he examined it. Lee West wanted a war for that Succubus; then, by the will of God himself, he was going to have one. Though he imagined he was going to be making a good few calls.

"Brother, don't do this. You can redeem yourself. Just trust me." Abel spoke, his form looking more like a shadow than a natural person. Cain ignored the ghost of his brother—the spirit of his past.

He picked up the phone, making a few calls and connections. He wasn't going to take a risk and imagine that the mortal might have something up his sleeves while he prepared himself.

-ooo-

It was nearly time for the wedding, and Lee found himself pulling the suit on, a hard grunt while he felt the tie wrapping around his neck. It might have just been a noose if he had to describe the thing.

"I swear whoever invented the tie needs an ass-kicking." He complained while his dad moved in.

"Oh, relax, it ain't going to be long. Just get this thing tied up and there." Rufus patted his shoulder.

"Congrats, kid; I never thought I'd see you getting married." He spoke with a light smile. Lee nodded,

"Thanks, Dad; I'm glad to have you here." There was a knocking on the door when Lee turned.

"So, who's going to be here?"

"Well, your mom invited a few people from the family, plus your little lady said she brought a few people." Rufus moved over, opening the door, and the first ones standing there were none other than Lucifer and Lilith. Lucifer is wearing a delicate pinstriped suit with sunglasses over his eyes. It almost made him look like a Dom in the mafia. In contrast, Lilith wore a red dress that dominated everyone as it screamed. *I'm here to be seen and desired.* She was showing plenty of cleavage as she gave a warm smile. She looked at Lee and gave him a wink. She was turning Lee red as a redwood.

"Ahh, well, I'm guessing you're here for the wedding; you with the bride?" Rufus said while he brought his hand out to Lucifer, smiling at an excellent ol' boy while he didn't realize he was looking at the devil himself at this very moment. Lucifer reached over and shook his hand.

"Yes, I am, Rufus and my name is Lou Cypher. I'm the bride's father, and this is my lovely wife, Lilith." He chuckled while looking over to Rufus.

Rufus nodded and said, "Well, Lucifer, come on in; get comfortable; Lucy upstairs is getting ready if you wanna see them here." Lee wanted to laugh his butt off when he saw Lucifer's face fall when Rufus called him his actual name.

"It's Lou Cypher, sir, not Lucifer." He tried correcting, but Rufus nodded.

"Yeah, that's what I said, Lucifer." He spoke up, his southern accent growing, while Lucifer sighed, heading on in. Lilith seemed amused by how her husband's ploy didn't work as he expected.

"You know what? I'm going to see Lucy. Lilith, if you will." Lucifer spoke up, heading up the stairs, while Lilith smirked,

"Why yes, my dear husband." She spoke with that sultry voice as she ran. To the back While Lee and Rufus sat there for a minute, watching as Satan himself walked up the stairs. Rufus looked back at Lee, giving a good minute, ensuring Lucifer couldn't hear him.

"I don't know about that guy. Seems a bit narcissist, I mean, naming his daughter after himself." Lee shook his head while he fought back the urge to laugh at this point.

"You wouldn't believe me if I told you. We should finish a few more things before the rest arrive." Lee chuckled while Rufus nodded. He turned around when he stopped for a second.

"Give me a second. I wanted to give you this," Rufus smirked as he reached around, pulling out a large box. It was simple and brown, but when he brought it out. It revealed a Stetson hat on there.

"I say wear it. It's a small gift from me." Rufus chuckled while Lee grabbed it and looked at it. The thing had seen a better day. Lee recognized it as it was Rufus's. He couldn't help but smile as he placed it on his head. It didn't go with the suit as well. However, to Lee, it was perfect.

"Come on, let's get this thing set up," Rufus smirked, patting Lee's side, giving a broad smile, and showing some of his missing teeth. They would get this redneck wedding under wraps while heading out to make some finishing touches. Hopefully, Lee's mother didn't blow a gasket out there while ensuring everything was perfect for Lee and Lucy.

-oOo-

Lucifer walked through the bedroom door, as he found himself standing in Lee's childhood room, and found himself shaking his head.

"I will say, your fiancée has no taste." He could see through and feel the room. While he couldn't help but chuckle.

"Oh, Dad, let it be; you can't stop me," Lucy said while standing on the end of the bed. Betsy with some other girl. He wasn't sure who but knew that she was a succubus. It wasn't one of his daughters when he moved over.

"I'm just saying; he seems a bit tacky." Lucifer poked the punching back, letting It sway around.

"Well, you are not the one marrying him," Lucy said with a sly smirk as she felt Betsy pulling the corset strings and causing her body to squeeze up, making her look more busty.

"My dear, why are you doing that? You can transform your body to look any way you want?" Lucifer said as he made an example of turning into a woman and showing off a full figure before returning to his original form.

"I just want to be beside. I don't want people suspecting anything." She muttered while putting on the rest of her dress as she stood there. She was wearing all white, Looking like the sun had kissed her skin. The elegance of her as she smiled at her father. "How do I look, Dad?"

"You look as beautiful as your mother was when we took our vows of eternal darkness." Lucifer smiles while Lucy. She couldn't help but return it. While she walked over, she hugged and kissed her father on the cheek. The dress was a bit older; it belonged to Lee's mother. So something borrowed and something old. However, it fits the succubus perfectly.

"Dad, don't be mad, but I managed to get a hold of Grandpa. He'll be coming to the wedding." Lucifer stopped right there as his hand dropped.

"What do you mean you invited your grandfather."

"Well, I managed to contact him and asked if he would come down, and he said he would. Didn't want to miss his granddaughter's wedding."

"Oh, my father…." Lucifer muttered, looking like he was about to shit bricks. He was not expecting the great Almighty to come to a wedding. He wasn't sure what madness would come from that. "I am going to have to do something, fuck nuggets!"

"Dad, I talked to Grandpa; he said he'd be on his best behavior. No smiting or turning people into pillars of salt."

Lucifer's eyes twitched while he wasn't sure what to say to his daughter—just knowing that the big man upstairs would be here. It almost made the devil want to blow a blood vessel, but he took a deep breath keeping his cool.

"Very well, though if he causes trouble, I better not get the blame." Lucifer turned around and left the room, knowing that this would turn into something entertaining or apocalyptic. He leaned back and smiled at her.

"I'm glad your happy, hun." Lucifer looked at his daughter. While Lucy smiled as she nodded,

"Thanks, Daddy." She spoke up. And as soon as Lucifer left the room. Betsy tightened the corset a bit more as Lucy let out a hard grunt.

"You know, Dad, forgot to even say Hi to me… typical," Betsy said, seeming more annoyed, as she groaned, adjusting to her dress and not liking it.

"Can I at least wear my hat?"

"No, you can not wear your Confederate soldier hat. People might talk about it."

"I don't see the problem; it's a part of my uniform. I like my hat." She grumbled before she got up.

"There, you should be ready for your wedding." Betsy was about to leave when Lucy pulled her in for a hug.

"Thanks, sis, and even if Dad doesn't pay much attention to you, I know he loves you as much as I do." Lucy couldn't help giving that infectious smile to her sister, who nodded but added in this quip.

"Love me enough to let me wear my hat."

"I love you, but the answer is still no." Betsy cursed under her breath. In comparison, they would move to get their hair worked on. They didn't have long before the wedding would begin.

-000-

People were coming to the wedding as they started to arrive. Lee found himself sweating like a pig while he rubbed his forehead with a napkin while Rufus walked over.

"Not getting cold feet, are you bub?"

"No, more like sweating my socks off. Why is it hot as hell here?" Lucifer popping over. "Don't blame me. It wasn't my idea."

He walked around while Lee took a deep breath, trying to keep his cool. His heart was racing like a locomotive when he saw her. Samantha over to the side. She was holding her son. Lee found himself confused, looking over at his dad.

"Why is Samantha here?"

"Think your mother invited her, trying to be nice. Don't ask me." Rufus said, just noticing her. While Lee nodded, he figured it would be better not to try and talk to his Ex, especially if it came down to the little boy who looked just like him.

Lee walked over to see Samantha as she turned to see him.

"Oh, Hi Lee, how's the groom doing?" she teased while she adjusted her little boy. Lee smiled, rubbing the back of his head.

"Yeah, just excited. I wasn't expecting to see you come to my wedding. But glad you came." He looked over at Al for a second when he steeled his nerves.

"I'm always here if you need help with Al." He gave the small boy a wave. Al waved back while looking back at his mom.

"He's funny, Mommy; what's he talking about?" Samantha raised an eyebrow while she put Al down.

"I don't know. Go and play Al; try and keep your clothes clean." She spoke while Looking over at Lee, her head tilting.

"Ok, Mommy," Al said while he ran off, clearly ready to get into trouble while the warden was out doing adult stuff.

"Lee, what is that all about?" Samantha asked quickly, not beating around the bush.

"Alright, I have to ask… Is Al my kid?" He found himself wincing while Samantha watched him. Her face turned from confusion. To annoyance, back to chaos. It was nearly comedic.

"No, he's not your son. Why would you even be asking this?" Samantha muttered while she finally realized what Lee was talking about.

"I mean, it makes sense; he looked like me when I was that

age, then the timeline from when we, well, you know… did it. I just assumed." Lee found himself saying though Samantha raised an eyebrow.

"Lee, listen… If you were the father, do you think I wouldn't have told your Momma, and she wouldn't have dragged your ass back here? If Al was your child."

Lee paused, realizing what she said made sense as he raised his hand.

"Alright, fair enough, I didn't think about that… But who is Al's father?" he looked over, watching the little boy chase a pair of dogs barking away.

"I'll be honest, Lee, I don't remember, it was after you left, and I went to the bar and got drunk. The guy looked like you, and it was a one-night stand. I don't regret it. I got Al as a result. So not going to look back. Sorry, you assumed you were a dad… If it is any consolation. I think you would have made a great dad for Al. At the very least."

"Thanks, I appreciate it." Lee smiled while the two shared a tender hug for a minute. When without warning, Maddy came out of nowhere and gave them a firm hug.

"I'm glad to hear you two talking, but it's almost time for the wedding. Alright, talk more after the ceremony. Lee, get you but up to the front. Father, Simon is up, ready to officiate it." She pointed over to the end of the aisle. Lee saw the rest of his family sitting on Lucy's side. Well, one thing is for sure. It was a sight.

The priest stood there, and he was not what Lee expected. The man looked ready to head off to a metal band audition and not perform a marriage ceremony. That's for sure. Lee walked over there nonetheless. While the man raised his hand, shaking his hand.

"Now, brother, my name is Father Zacharia; it's nice to meet you. Now are you ready to bathe in the Lord's light as he blesses your marriage?" Zacharia said the way he spoke sounded like a hippy, though Lee nodded.

"Not a problem; I guess we're about to start." He chuckled while the priest nodded as he cupped his hand. Lee saw the cross rings on his fingers, finding them rather strange but got into position. Though one thing is sure, it wasn't like his dream, which relieved him greatly. While he stood there, he saw Maddy over to the side.

She was holding a camera, taking plenty of pictures. While Rufus walked over, grabbing her by the shoulder as he dragged her off to her seat up front while she was smiling away.

She watched from afar as the music began playing. It was a soft tune, not a piano but more of a guitar playing. The gentle melody as the strings were played as Lucy started walking down. Followed behind were little Al and another girl. Lee wasn't sure who that might have been. However, he was focused more on Lucy. The woman looked stunning.

Lee's jaw dropped as she walked the aisle. She was the most beautiful being in the world. As Lee could barely look away, his heart skipped a beat at such a beautiful sight. She stopped standing before him. That caring smile while. It was just him and the world. The only thing in the world that mattered to him. While the priest, who looked like a hippy, started to give the opening ceremony. Such a thing was interesting. But Lee wasn't paying much attention to it. In contrast, he looked into Lucy's eyes.

"Now, do you, Lee West, take this bride to love and to hold? In sickness and in health, till death do you part?"

Lee was shaking as he realized he was asked the vital question. Startled up, he nodded, "I do." He smiled at Lucy for a good second. Then, Zacharia looked to Lucy, asking her the same question.

"I do," Lucy said, looking back at Lee. Her Ruby red lips spread into a smile. Zacharia smiled as he raised his hands.

"By the power vested in me. I now pronounce you man and wife! You may kiss the bride." With that, Lucy moved into Lee. While Lee wrapped his arm, kissing the succubus with such passion. The crowd cheered while Lee and Lucy pulled back the smile on their face as they looked at everyone cheering.

-000-

Everyone had gotten comfortable as they congratulated the new bride and groom. Some are drinking beer, toasting, and simply enjoying their time. Lucifer walked past a few of Lee's cousins while smiling at them.

Lee's cousin, known mainly as Cousin Jim, looked at his brother.

"You know, brother, I think that guy might be the devil." He said, pointing over to Lucifer.

"Nah, He's just one of those fancy new yorkers. The devil." He spoke in a more hick accent while they looked back at Lucifer.

"Besides, Cousin Johnny talked about meeting the devil when he went to Georgia, winning a fiddle from him."

"Don't be a full there, Jimmy. That's just painted no one stupid enough to wager a golden fiddle."

Lucifer found himself groaning in annoyance. Since it was

clear that he was somehow part of a family of people who realized he was the devil. Yet at the same time didn't know he was the devil. It confused the prince of darkness to no end. Lilith moved in, giving her husband a smirk.

"Oh, Darling, it's alright. I can pretend your Lou Cypher." She teased the devil, who smiled as he wrapped his arms around her. "You're the best, Lilith." He chuckled, kissing her.

Lee and Lucy cut the cake with a slight smirk as they placed it on the plate. Everything seemed perfect. A small smile while they had the usual pictures taken. At the same time, Lucy moved over and began checking some of the food. Lee couldn't help admiring it as he saw a cupcake and grabbed it, about to take a bite, when Lucifer came over.

"Oh, See, you've taken a liking to them. I had one of Hell's best chiefs make these. Her name is Lizzie Borden, and these are some of her famous Mary cupcakes." Lee's eyes widened as he looked down at the one in his hand. He slowly moved, putting them down and pushing them away from him. Lucifer watched, almost resisting a cackle, while he took one of the cupcakes eating them.

"Hmm, those look good; I might have to try one later."

"Very; I think she added something else, jelly, maybe," Lucifer said while looking over at Lee, who looked pale as a ghost.

"Um… I'm fine, just… Don't let my family have any of the cupcakes." He looked at it briefly as he thought about it being Lizzie Borden. While he shuddered in fright. Lucifer nodded with an evil smile.

"I'm sure I can keep them away from this, besides more for me." He proceeded to take another bite. Lee resisted feeling sick as he went to take a bite out of something else.

Everything about the wedding went well. As The sounds of the music started, Lucy grabbed Lee's arm.

"Time for the Bride and Groom, so share the first dance." Lucy smiled while she reached around, grabbing his arm and dragging him off.

One thing for a backyard wedding, it was a bit more relaxing as they didn't have to go too far for many things. Plus, the moonshine that Lee's cousins brought in. Betsy was already on her third drink as she was holding her own. However, Lee imagined the Succubus had gotten drunk on the honey shine. His cousin Sires brought in. Betsy's pure joy was on her face as she swayed with the cousins and called out to the heavens.

"I love redneck weddings!" she spoke with a heavy, slurred voice. Betsy might have just brought her tits out for everyone to watch if she had one more shot.

"You know, Lee, I think that's the happiest I've seen her in a long time," Lucy said, almost snorting as they began to dance to the rhythm of the music. Moving together as they looked into each other eyes.

"I'll tell you what, I don't blame her; today is going to be one of my better days," The two laughed while they continued dancing when Lucy brought something up.

"Lee, That little boy, Al. Who helped in the wedding a bit."

"What, what is it?" Lee asked, somewhat curious, while they continued swaying and moving around the dance floor.

"He's an incubus, well, a fledgling one. Does his mother know? I mean, he's half, but it's obvious he is one. Just too young to access his powers." Lucy found herself saying more over while Lee shook his head.

"I don't think so. I mean... should we tell her or?" Lee asked while Lucy shook her head,

"Probably not. He might go on to live a normal life, and if he knows well... It's hard to tell how it would affect them." There was a pause as Lee nodded, agreeing with her. Maybe if the time came, they could tell her. For now, however, it would be better to leave it as it was.

"Thank you, Lucy." Lee smiled while he spun her around a little. The music seemed to move faster as they followed on.

"For what?"

"Marrying me. Finding that ring was the best thing to ever happen to me."

Lee spoke with such tenderness as he leaned in softly, ready to kiss her as they held each other close.

Suddenly without warning, The sound of an engine coming at them. Flashes of bright lights shoot out at them. Lee, on instinct, grabbed Lucy and pushed Lucy out of the way as the car came at him. The dodge dart struck Lee. Lee let out a fierce yell as he landed on the hood. He barely had time to think when he rolled off the car.

The car crashed right into the power line as flashes of light bursts into the air.

"What the hell was that!" Someone in the crowd screamed. Lucy and Betsy ran over to Lee. The way he lay there, grabbing his leg hissing in pain.

"Fuck, why is it always my goddamn leg!" As Lucy looked, Lee held onto his bad leg, seeing that the bone was sticking out.

"Um, Lee... Your leg."

"I know, fuck! I need the hospital. Who in their fucking mind!" He called out, cursing his ass off, not caring who was in front of him; all he knew was he had a bone sticking out and poorly broken.

Rufus and Lucifer walk to the door. Rufus's eyes looked like they were in a blaze at the moron who just hit his son with their car. Lucifer followed, wondering how the situation was going to go. When Rufus grabbed the door, ready to pull the car door off its hinges. Lucifer uses some of his more demonic powers to keep the car in place. The tires squealed as if it was trying to back up, but there was nothing they could do. It was trapped while Rufus pulled the door open. There sitting behind the wheel, was none other than Jack Winslow. His head was bleeding as he tried pulling back. Yet there was nothing Jack could do. Rufus wasn't having any of it as he grabbed Jack by the seams of his jacket and dragged him right out of the car.

"What the Hell are you drunk? Cause if you aren't, I'm going to make this far more worst than possible." Rufus said the, anger in his voice. The control Rufus usually had in him was holding on by threads, and they were already at their limit while Jack spat at Rufus.

"Go to hell, besides. I'm getting paid big money. Going to get me out of this shitty town and factory." You could almost hear the strings snapping as Rufus started to throw punches just going at Jack as he smashed his face into the door. Jack barely held back as he tried fighting away when Lucifer grabbed Rufus's shoulder.

"Now, while I am enjoying, you are bringing justice out on this little shit. I do think you should calm it down. No reason to go to jail for this. I know a few people." Lucifer gave a broad smile while he was looking at the man.

Jack Winslow felt a chill run down his spine, one he had never felt before in his life. The kind of fear that screamed he had made a mistake, all while looking into the eyes of the man standing before him.

"So, tell me, what were you thinking? Where are you just going to drive off after trying to kill My son in law?" Lucifer kept a calm voice. The horror on Jack's face. As he could feel something not right about the man before him.

"I— I got paid to do this… I just."

"Oh, don't do the paid-for-me stunt. Tell me what you are hiding." The Charm in his voice as he leaned in closer. "Tell us what you were really planning?" Lucifer reached over, caressing the man's cheek as his eyes went blank.

"I was paid too. I would have done it for free if I knew I could get away with it. But the money just added the temptation. I hate Lee. He's gotten everything while I had to do everything to make it while he got a better life. The girl, a great job." There was anger on everyone's face as they looked at Jack. Lee was being brought over to a seat as he sat, trying to hold back the pain. Lee felt like he was going to pass out. Jack just simply continued talking. The blank look on his face continued. "I have nothing, and back in school, he was a better boxer. I took him out to take his spot. To try and make it out of this shit town."

Lucifer nodded while patting his head.

"Good boy. Now, stay here while we tie you up. Rufus. I'm

sure you've got some rope and can call the authorities. Don't kill him, and I really don't want to deal with paperwork." Lucifer smiled while he turned around and checked on Lee.

Lee sat back, taking long deep breaths while he tried not to let out a harrowing scream. Lucy grabbed his shoulder.

"Lee, just hang in there. We'll get you some help." Lucy muttered while she looked back to her husband. Lee is just gasping. He felt like he was close to passing out.

"Could you possibly get me some moonshine? Seriously I need something." He groaned, raising his hand when Lucifer walked over. He passed Lee a flask of Moonshine. Lee just downed it rocking his head back as he drank as much as he could. He groaned when looking over. Towards Lucifer, the blank expression on his face as he let out a hard grunt.

"Do you mind fixing it, or is that beyond your range of power?"

"Sadly, not one of my abilities, more so bringing the pain than giving it sorry," Lucifer said though he looked over to Lucy.

"Didn't you say you invited the old man? Where the hell is he?" Lucifer said while seeming more confused than anything. "Like, I know he prefers to make a grand entrance, but this is ridiculous." Lucy looked back to her father and raised an eyebrow.

"You know that is weird. He should have been here. He said he would."

"Typical, that old bastard always late when we need him."

There was a loud boom when they turned around. A man in white robes standing behind them Looked towards Lucifer and the others—the stone expression, as white wings expanded out.

Lucifer looked over at the being and rolled his eyes.

"Micheal, what are you doing here? Aren't you supposed to be more subtle than that? Where's dad?"

"He wasn't able to make it. Something had come up that distracted him." Micheal said when he looked at the others standing around. He shrugged his shoulder while Lucifer looked back at the other Archangel.

"Really, that's a load of bullshit. The guy can snap his fingers and fix everything in an instant. He doesn't just get distracted. Well, good, glad he didn't come to his granddaughter's wedding." Lucifer said, looking annoyed but a bit disappointed on his face asked, while Lee let out a hard grunt.

"What the?" he let out a hard groan as he leaned back, closing his eyes while he took another drink of the moonshine. He imagined he was going to need to get drunk after all of this.

"Lee, sweetie? Who are these two." Maddy came up, looking at her son/ Who was clearly drinking away the pain in his leg. In contrast, Lucy looked over at her new mother-in-law.

"Um… Maddy, there's something we didn't tell you." She spoke, looking a bit nervous, not sure how to really say this to Lee's mom.

"Please, we're family, so call me Mom, and what are you not telling us?"

Lucy turned to look at her father and uncle and shook her head.

"Well, it's a long story." It was then she proceeded to tell Rufus and Maddy the whole story, the real story. They listened to everything. At the same time, Lucy left out some of the more steamy parts. But they revealed that Lucy was, in fact, a succubus.

CHAPTER 17

"And that's everything," Lucy said while Lee let out a hard grunt, and Lucifer moved over and set the leg in place. Micheal is standing there watching as the Devil looks at his brother.

"Hey, mind helping out, asshole. Mortal here got hurt. I'm the devil and helping." Lucifer snarked while Micheal looked over. The mortal shook his head.

"You know the rules, brother. I can't interfere with mortals," Micheal stated while seeing Lucifer returning Lee's leg to normal.

"And they claim I'm the bad guy in that special book." Lucifer spat out while he turned and looked at Lee.

"I can probably get a few demons to heal you if you want?" Lucifer watched as he seemed to give a slight smirk, showing his more devilish action.

"Though might be more expensive than a mortal hospital." He chuckled when Lilith came over, smacking the devil upside the head.

"Ouch, come on, Lilith, I was just joking."

Maddy found herself shocked. Her mouth dropped while she looked at Lucy.

"So let me get this straight: you're a succubus trapped in a ring for nearly a hundred years, and your sister was a Confederate soldier, and your father is Satan himself," Lucifer called out.

"Me and Satan are different people, for crying out loud; he's a demon. I'm an archangel!" Maddy ignored him for a moment as she looked back at the others.

"You're the devil, and My son is married to your daughter and Cain. From Cain and Abel wants them dead."

"Yeah, for the most part, that's everything." Lucy found herself winching as she saw the face on Maddy's face and the way it sunk down. "I hope you're not mad at us; we were trying to protect you."

"You could have told us. I mean…" Maddy wasn't sure how to say it as she tried to find the words while looking back at her son.

"I wouldn't have judged, but you didn't trust us; we're your family." She looked back at Rufus, who nodded for a minute. He gave a smile.

"I mean, I'm not going to mind much. This is neat; good for you, son." Giving him a thumbs-up shows how much he approves of his son's marriage. "It's one of those things we should know just in case we do something stupid." There was a moment as Lee nodded.

"Maybe we should have, but we didn't think you'd believe us, that's," Lee said while Lucy leaned over him, kissing him on the cheek.

"So what now? I mean, what are we supposed to do?"

"We have to stop Cain; if he keeps coming after us, eventually he's going to kill one of us," Lee muttered, grunting as he tried moving his leg, as pain shot through him like buckshot.

"Careful there, kid, that leg will need a cast. You're out of commission till we can get it healed." Lucifer said while he summoned a cigar, he looked to Rufus and called another one. He offered it over to Rufus, who shook his head, more worried about his son than anything else.

"I just can't sit down and let him come after us. I've got to protect Lucy." He groaned while he found himself hissing in pain. He wasn't going to be getting up for a while.

Lucy gave him a smile pushing him down as he looked at him.

"You're my husband, and I'm glad you want to protect me but remember, I'm your wife, so it goes both ways. I protect you, and you protect me. That's the deal, remember." She leaned in and kissed his cheek, her crown of thorns twisting on her head as it began setting itself ablaze. At the same time, she looked at him with glowing red eyes.

It was clear about one thing. Lucy has pissed off someone who hurt her husband, and she was about to rip someone's dick off for it.

"Fine, but we've got to find Cain first. I'm sure he's heading back or doing something." Lee said while looking back at his leg. He is annoyed that there isn't anything he can do.

Micheal watched for a second, tapping his foot. Like he was trying to hide something, the archangel was standing around, not leaving.

"Micheal, why are you still here?" Lucifer spoke, annoyed by his brother being here. He was not doing anything to help and just observing while the archangel let out a long sigh.

"I didn't come here empty-handed. Father wanted me to bring a gift. But, I'm not sure If I should."

"Well, what is it? It can't be that bad. Besides, if the old man is going to drop something off, might as well give it out and get out of here." Lucifer said, adjusting the tie on his suit while Micheal rubbed the bridge of his nose.

"Well, fathers gift is a miracle. But it shouldn't be used lightly."

"You're telling me, Dad, is giving us a basic Deus Ex Machina, and you were going not to tell us that. Give it to them; we can blow Cain off the face of the earth."

"That's not going to work. Besides, Cain's curse would rebel against any damage; Dad made it strong even if he couldn't kill Cain. He wanted to make sure Cain was punished."

Lucifer groaned, annoyed by the situation. In comparison, Lucy and Lee looked back at each other.

"So this miracle, what can it do?" Lee found himself more curious about the situation. A gift from Lucifer's father… God himself that has to be something. But he wasn't sure how it would even go. But Lucifer looked back at Lee while Micheal seemed to be holding back.

"It depends on what he wants, but trust me, those things can go from summoning a sandwich to Noah needing a boat."

Micheal nodded, "The power of the lord is unbreakable. He can do anything he desires. So long as it does not contradict his past words. Nor can it break the natural order of things. So you can't bring someone back from the dead." Micheal added while looking towards them.

Lee nodded some while Lucifer looked at him.

"So, what's your plan? I might suggest using this miracle for something vital." Lee found himself agreeing with the devil. He was tempted to ask his leg be repaired. But this might be the only chance they had against this killer.

"If we need it, we'll let you know, Uncle Micheal," Lucy said, annoyed by everything happening. Micheal was close to leaving when he stopped. His wings spread out, showing the eight golden wings, almost matching Lucifer's own.

"You know, I didn't give you a gift, niece. So maybe I can bend the rules just once." He raised his hand, and they glowed a heavenly gold as he looked at Lee.

Lee found himself arching in pain. His leg shot with fire as he wanted to scream. Lee moved a bit on his arm and muffled loudly in them. He was trying to curse so many obscenities. It wasn't funny. Then without warning, the pain was gone. Everything turned back to normal when Lee looked down. His entire leg was back to normal.

Lee turned, looking over to see Micheal, only to see that the angel had gone. Golden feathers ruffled the ground. At the same time, it was just Lee and his family there.

"Well... Thanks." Lee Muttered, unsure how to react, while looking down at his leg as he tried standing up. Lucy tried pushing him down, not wanting him to get up, but Lee shook his head, standing up.

His leg felt good, really good, as he moved it around a little more while he let out a sigh, then his leg popped as he groaned.

"Alright, gonna say this Angel magic seems pretty good." Lee smiled before falling right over and passing out.

Maddy and Rufus ran over while Lucy tried helping Lee up, who was out like a light.

"Dumbass," Lucifer muttered as he looked over. All his brother Micheal had done was accelerated the healing process, but doing something like that took a lot of energy out on the person it was using.

"Relax, guy, he'll be fine in a few hours. He's just worn out." The devil said while Lilith rubbed his shoulder.

"Why don't you help the young man, darling."

"I'm the devil. I don't help humans. That's my deal," Lucifer smirked while he looked over to Lilith, imagining his job was done for now.

Betsy stumbled around as she swayed more.

"What did I miss?" The succubus muttered, rubbing her head, as she nodded and saw the passed-out Lee being picked up by the others.

"I think I'm gonna…." Before finishing that sentence, she ran to the bushes and began puking her guts all over the brush.

The whole situation had been wile. When the police finally came, the people that could give their statements gave them. And Jack Winslow was taken off to be booked. To say that much of the family stayed for the rest of the night was an understatement as they headed off. The wedding was over, and Lee and Lucy were finally married.

-000-

Lee let out a hard groan as he found himself moving his head around as he got up. He felt like shit. The kind of shit feeling, as Lee slept longer than was needed. Lee tried getting up. When he felt himself being held down, Lucy was next to him. Her slender arms were over his chest as she held onto him momentarily.

"What happened last night?" He muttered, trying to remember what had happened. However, his head hurt as he rubbed it.

"I know I didn't drink that much at my wedding." He muttered while relaxing with Lucy, who snored gently while he lay there. It was a nice feeling. At the same time, he felt many of his worries going away.

Lee felt tempted to go back to sleep and get comfortable when the door to his childhood bedroom opened. A loud thump as it caused both Lucy and Lee to jump in the air. While looking over, seeing Betsy standing there. Her hand rubbed her head as she groaned.

"Ok, I regret doing that… how is this even possible. I didn't even know Succubus could get hangovers, damn it." She groaned while Lee, Looked back, his head hurting as he complained.

"Betsy, it's…." He glanced at the alarm clock and saw it was around noon when he groaned.

"Fuck when did we head to bed."

"You went to bed early after Micheal fixed your leg. Partner passed out like a baby. We had to drag your butt back up here." Betsy groaned while she looked back at her sister.

"Mind putting on clothes? We've got to talk about a few

things."

"What about?" Lee groaned as he stood up, seeing he still had his dress pants on, as Lucy pulled herself up. She was wearing one of his regular shirts while Betsy watched them.

"We've got to talk about Cain; come before your parent's way up. I think they were kind of shocked about a few things. Especially after finding out who Dad is." She muttered, looking over to Lucy, who nodded. She remembered what happened last night. Lee groaned, knowing it was slowly coming back.

"Anyone else?" Lee found himself asking.

"There's also Alice and Dawn. They decided to stay as well. Slept on the floor instead of heading back to their hotel."

"Well, I guess it's something. Well, let us get dressed, and we'll head downstairs." Lee said while he looked back at Lucy. Who stood there for a second? None of them acknowledged as Betsy gave them a nod.

"I'll see you down there." Betsy walked out of the room, closing it right behind her. Lee and Lucy looked back at each other. For a good minute, they gave each other a small smile.

"Well, I never expected our marriage to begin with fighting an immortal being." Lee chuckled. Lucy snorted at that.

"I know, I was just going to say we try some anal play, but this is not what I was thinking."

The two would eventually get dressed and head right downstairs.

Betsy, Alice, and Dawn sat at the kitchen table for the longest time as they waited for Lucy and Lee. The silence between them was strange. The tension was in the air while Lee sat back down.

"So, we have to do something about Cain," Lee muttered while sitting there. "Do we have anything planned or any idea we can do to put him down?" He looked over at each of them, While Alice looked at Dawn.

"You've heard stories. Is there anything that we could do to deal with this guy? Any rumors of people that survived?" There was pure curiosity in her voice while Dawn shook her head.

"Not much. The nuns didn't like us talking about Cain since he is considered one of the first sinners. But when some of us girls would hear them talk about Cain. They claim he is immune to all weapons, magical and mortal." Dawn paused for a second, her foot stammering while Lee looked over.

"Is there something else? What you're not talking about." Lee asked while reaching over and rubbing Dawn's hand.

"There are rumors that he once got put out of commission. Vanishing for about ten years. But I'm not even sure it's true." Dawn said while watching the others.

"What is it? If there's anything we can do to take him down. You're the only one we know of who even knows much about this stuff. You were a part of his world."

"Fine, but I don't fully believe the rumor. But apparently, Cain was sent to go after someone. Please don't ask me who. The nuns never spoke the guy's name. Yet, he got the best of Cain and managed to knock him out. They tied him up, cut him into dozens of pieces, and spread them out. To different places."

There was a moment of silence while they heard that. Lee found himself almost curious yet remained silent.

"What happened to the guy?" Lee asked, wondering if there was anything else about it.

"Not sure; he might have still gotten killed by Cain when he put himself back together. That's the issue with rumors. It's impossible to prove unless you've got proof."

"It's the best we can go by. We've got to figure something out. We also have that miracle that the big guy upstairs has. But what can we use it for? I don't know." He thought about it. But the fact that things could give them an advantage. But could it even help them with the requirement?

Betsy pushed her hat back while she kicked her feet up.

"That's the thing. It's our best plan, either cutting him up into small bits and putting them around till he can put himself together. Or use the power of God. We got some options." She reached over, grabbed a beer hanging on the table, and took a drink. It didn't help much with her head. But she was trying to focus on something.

"It's just the thing; how are we even going to get Cain into a situation where we could cut him up into little bits of pieces? He might expect us to think this plan." They looked around at each other.

"What if we put up some bait?" Betsy asked while she looked back at her sister.

"What are you talking about?" Lucy found herself asking.

"I mean is… Cain is after us. What if one of us puts themselves up for bait, and the rest of you jump them when he comes after it? Knock him out, and we take a chainsaw on him." She spoke through. Lee could hear the shaking in her voice. It was clear she was nervous about this.

"No, I won't let that happen," Lee stood up. "I can't let one of you guy's just become bait for this guy. Especially if what Dawn said is true, he might still kill one of you." He found the courage growing in him like embers in a fire, finding dry grass.

"Lee, what can we do? I mean… I could be the bait." Lucy said when Lee interrupted her.

"No, I— I can't lose you. I don't want him hurting any one of you." He muttered while he felt his heart race. But Lucy grabbed his hands.

"I'm not asking. I'm saying one of us does. We can't just sit around and act like nothing will happen. He tried to kill you." Lucy said her eyes were glowing red while she was angry. Lee could feel the rage behind her and nodded.

"Well, we just have to figure out something."

It was as though speaking to the devil when without warning, Lee's phone started ringing. Lee looked over at it. The number was none other than Cain's. He could recognize it from the last time as he looked at the others.

They knew who it was as they each went silent while Lee answered the phone.

"Hello…" Lee said, his voice drawing out, careful not to give anything away.

"Lee, it's so good to hear from you. Now then, how was your wedding? I heard someone crashed the fire." Lucy's face turned bright red at that, like she was about to scream something, when Betsy grabbed her shoulder, reassuring her as she held her tongue for the time being.

"Well. I can say that you didn't get the results you wanted. I'm very much alright. Now what do you want?"

"I was wondering if you were ready to come to a deal. I thought about it and imagined it wasn't fair to you. So how about it? We meet up and talk. Human to... well, I'm formally human. But it's close enough."

Lee found himself looking at the girls while he tapped the table.

"Well, that depends on what you want to talk about. Cause, as I said, I won't surrender my wife or her sister to you."

"Well, that's for us to discuss. Now how about it? We can meet where ever you want. You and I and we can talk things out. But you come alone." Cain spoke. There was a confidence in his voice that made Lee clench his fist while trying to hold back a snarky remark.

"You know what, I think it should be fair. How about we meet at the library, we can talk and see if we can come up with some deal." At that moment, Lee wasn't sure if it would be the best place to be. It was the first thing to pop into his head beside one of the local taverns.

"Sounds fair. We can discuss our terms there. Also, Lee, I know your girls are listening. So don't try any funny business while we're there." Cain smirked as he remained on the line.

"You got it, just you and me at the library. About an hour, I'll get up there."

"Oh, there's no rush. Make it two hours. I'm just going to enjoy my coffee." Cain hung up at that point while Lee sat there looking at the thing—his eyes on it for the longest time. In contrast, Lucy looked back at him.

"We should jump him." The Succubus queen said while she cracked her knuckles.

"I think I should go on my own," Lee said while looking down at the phone. He held back his tongue for a minute while Lucy looked at him, more shocked. The other succubus was the same, while Alice exclaimed.

"Lee, don't you dare. You're being an idiot."

"I know I am, but if he sniffs one of you guy's out, he might do something drastic besides… He does stuff. He… when I met him at one point. I was so angry I wanted to hurt something hurt someone. I just can't risk if my temper was shot. So… Let me do this. If I'm in danger, I'll call you." Lee stated while he looked at the girls for a minute.

"Lee, what if he kills you or…"

"Lucy, I'd rather it be me than you besides if anything happened to me. I want you to run, run hard, run fast, and find a place to hide. Heck, go to your fathers for all I care. I don't care much about myself. So long as your safe." Lee smiled while he leaned back.

"Beside… I don't think Cain's going to attack me. He would have done it himself if he wanted to. I mean, besides the fact he hired someone to run me over with a car." Lee found himself more curious about that; why would Cain hire someone else to try and kill them? Why not do it himself? This was the big question. It's something that got on his nerves.

"Lee— If you want, go for it. But you're being an idiot… But I won't stop you, but I want to be there."

"How? What are you going to do that won't let him notice you? It'll be obvious if he sees you." Lee said while trying to think of what they could do to get their plan to work out.

"I can do a few tricks." Lucy smiled as she gave off a devilish smile, the same kind she inherited from her dad, while Lee nodded.

-000-

Cain hung the phone up, taking a long deep breath and rolling his neck.

"Now then, what shall I do next." He took another drink of his coffee. The long silence as he saw Abel on the other side of the table, a ghost of his past. Still there for the longest time.

"We should stop. Go on with your life. Besides, what could the silver cross do that could harm you? Just walk away."

"Yet they have something I want. A way to finally leave this world." Cain spoke while he looked over at his ghostly brother. On days like this, he wondered if he was real or if Cain had finally snapped and was seeing things on his own. It wouldn't have surprised him. He was old, after all. Old enough to go truly mad.

"What if they're lying? You know that they will do anything to get what they want." Abel said while he looked at his brother.

"Besides, you've looked for as long as you had that mark and never found anything, and they just happened to have found something you didn't." Abel pointed out while Cain nodded; the apparition had a good point. Such a thought came to him because most humans lied to get what they wanted.

"You have a point, but I'm also a killer. It's what I'm good at." Cain pointed out while he moved and took a bite from the burger the waitress had brought him.

"I'm like the scorpion. It's in my nature," Cain muttered while he looked down.

"Yes, you are a killer, You invented it, but you don't have to be. You can be far more than who you were. We've watched humans change. We've seen the best and worst. You can be one of them."

"I'm not sure," Cain muttered while he took another bite. The tired look on his face. A man who thought he was a monster but felt more tired than anything else. Like he just wanted to have a good night's sleep.

Cain somewhat wondered what he was going to do next. But he had to decide soon if he was going to do what he wanted or what was actually right.

-000-

Lee looked back at the girls as they nodded. Lucy was wearing black hoody sunglasses over her face as she tried to hide herself a bit more. In contrast, Lee looked over at Lucy.

"Alright, you get to the library and talk to Samantha. Maybe try and convince her to leave early and take on her form. Do what you have to. I'll head there soon. So that he doesn't suspect anything." Lee said. It was the first part of their plan, as they hoped that if they caught him off guard, they could probably knock him out or do something.

"Sounds like a plan... But I don't like this plan." Lucy said while she looked over at her sister for a second. She was watching while loading her pistols up as she put them away.

"Well, it's the only plan we've got, so we have to go with it. If not, well, There's always plan B."

CHAPTER 18

Lucy arrived at the library, her face looking down. Doing everything she could to try and not look noticed while she prepared herself to deal with Cain. Lucy found herself moving past the bookshelves as she attempted to find Samantha. She would make it simple. Use a bit of her Succubus magic and convince her to go home. Lucy imagined a lot of things she might do. To get the women out of here. Lucy looked down at her feet.

"Lee, I hope you know what you're doing." Lucy looked down at her wedding ring. They were already married for a day, but she never felt more alive as her heart skipped a beat just thinking of Lee. While Lucy looked at it, she couldn't help thinking about the ring, the way it looked like the one she had been trapped in for years. Somehow it didn't bother her as much as when she saw it; all she could think about was that Lee gave it to her and their promise to each other.

Samantha walked towards Lucy, a slight look on her face as the young librarian looked at the Succubus.

"Hey Lucy, how was the rest of the wedding? Sorry, I had to leave early, but Al had to be in bed; otherwise, he would have been up all night." Samantha said that calmness on her face while Lucy came in closer.

"It's alright; thank you for coming along; it cleared a few things out." Lucy smiled as she moved in, her eyes beginning to glow at this point as she caressed Samantha's cheek. Samantha watched as her pupils dilated, a slight moan escaping her lips. As the young librarian was feeling a fire grow in her stomach.

"I—It's alright. I'm just glad to see Lee, and he's happy," Samantha said as she started to turn red in the face like she was trying to hold back something. Yet Lucy knew what the main problem was. The woman was getting horny, and Samantha didn't understand why she felt this way.

"Sorry, I just feel a little hot." Samantha tried saying while she rubbed her forehead, though it wasn't her head burning as she could feel a fire grow between her loins.

"You don't look so well, and maybe you should head home a bit early," Lucy said, smiling at her, adding a bit of power as she looked into her eyes, licking her lips. She could smell the sexual want on her face while Samantha felt herself squirming, her legs rubbing against each other as something about Lee's wife was igniting something inside her, yet she found that she couldn't fight it as she could feel her panties dampening.

"M-maybe your right. I should let my boss know. I— I." She found her stomach tightening as she looked into those eyes while Lucy reached down, cupping her breasts. It didn't even register in her mind as the succubus licked her lips.

"You might have to head home and take care of that. I'm sure they won't notice you're gone." Lucy spoke in a seductive tone as she licked her lips. Samantha groaned hard as she started to think about it more; when was the last time she had taken care of herself? Probably a good while, while she felt images of someone on top of her fucking her. She tried shaking her head.

"I really shouldn't. I mean, I have to pick Al up after my shift."

"Trust me. You've got plenty of time; I won't tell anyone." Lucy moaned softly, blowing hot ear into Samantha's ear, as the librarian shuddered, feeling as though she had a mini orgasm already nodded.

"Fine, I should go and get myself checked out quickly. It might be a stomach bug." She lied, but Lucy nodded, knowing the truth as the young woman found herself running out of the building like it was nothing.

Lucy giggled, "Have fun there, Samantha; I hope you have a perfect time." She took in the scent Samantha left, a sweet honeydew smell. As she started to spread her arm out and transform, she appeared with rearranged breasts shrinking her hair, growing out, as she allowed her clothes to turn, becoming sexier as she looked like the sexy Librarians teenagers always wished they could see but never could find in their local ones.

"Hmm, I should lighten it up and make sure no one notices me." She wiggled her tush and changed them to become modest as she summoned a pair of glasses. She was placing them around her face. She puffed her hair up and began doing Samantha's work.

She would bring out the classic fake it till you make it, while she started putting random books up. She was still trying to figure out where they were going but looked busy waiting for Cain to arrive.

She imagined taking on Cain herself. She didn't want him harming her husband. Lucy growled, feeling the fire in her stomach, a rage she had never felt before. She rolled her neck and hoped their plan might work.

-000-

Cain walked through the doors of the library. It wasn't what he expected. He imagined they would be somewhere a bit more public. He could influence the people around him with his ability. Sure, a few were walking around checking out books, but it wasn't what he hoped it would be. Yet at the same time, it will do.

"Brother, are you sure you want to do this? You can walk away and just let them live. Lie to the church. They won't find out." Abel said as Cain walked past him. He didn't say a word to Abel. He was done talking; it was time for him to work. It was what he did best. He was the first killer; It was all he was meant to do.

Cain moved down, sitting at one of the tables, relaxing; he leaned back. Taking a deep breath as he awaited for Lee West to come over. If he came alone, it would be good if the succubus came just as good. It would save him time; that's how Cain imagined it.

He took long, drawn-out breaths as he listened for Lee to come in. He just knew that sooner or later, this might be over with. He didn't have much to worry about.

-000-

Lee walked in, his heart pounding as he tried keeping a cool head. At the same time, he took his hands and rubbed them.

"Just relax, Lee, it'll be alright… it'll be alright." Lee found himself repeating himself. It was like a prayer, as he hoped it would go as planned. He also began thinking about what Lucifer said to him.

You have imagination. That guy relies on his abilities. Lee found himself thinking about it and then adding what Dawn said about the guy having a possible weakness. He hoped it would work. He would need a miracle that this would work. Lee took a long deep breath looking at the library door, soon pushing it in.

Lee looked around and saw Cain sitting there—his calm expression. Lee found himself more irritated when the guy just rested his head back. The man sent a car out to hit Lee, and he just wanted to take a damn nap. Lee growled but stopped thinking about Lucy, Her in his head, while he heard his old man say.

When something gets you mad or upset, think of some titties that'll smile at you. He wasn't sure how it made him feel, but he took the advice as he took in long deep breaths as he groaned. It helped him feel calmer, yet he could still feel his anger boiling over while he walked toward the first killer.

Lee sat down, scooting in a while, watching Cain. Cain finally took notice of Lee while he smiled.

"So you finally arrived. Are you ready to make a deal?" Cain asked while looking over at Lee; he saw the anger in his eyes and could feel the rage going into the young man's veins.

"What's the deal this time?" Lee asked, taking a long, drawn-out breath.

"It's simple, give me the succubus, and I will leave. You'll never see me again, and I'll convince the organization that I killed you. They shouldn't bother you guys again." Cain smirked while raising his hands.

"I give you my word."

"Yet how do I know I can even trust you? You sent someone to try and run me and my wife over?" Lee said, his voice staying steady as he balled his fists.

"Because when I make a promise, I keep it. I don't break my promises." Cain said, his voice turning mellow. "Heck, I'll even forget about the traitor Dawn. Besides, the church doesn't care about the half-breed. She won't kill someone like the rest of her kind accidentally." Cain spoke while watching Lee. Lee, though felt angry.

"She's still family, as far as I'm concerned."

"She's an abomination, born from Lucus and a succubus after it forced herself on him."

"And that was wrong, but Dawn is innocent; she wasn't a part of this."

"It drove my boy insane to cut his nuts off and damn him."

"From what I heard, he was a sick little puppy, which shows how you raised him," Lee said. While he tried not to spit, Cain slammed his fist into the ground.

"I did not make him that way they did. I was doing my job, and If the succubus didn't fuck him up, he might have been better." Cain said as Lee noticed he touched a nerve.

"Getting angry there. Were you like this when you killed your brother?" Lee added while Cain moved in closer, grabbing him by the collar.

"I did what I had to do! Do not judge me for what I did in my past; God willed it."

"How about you take some damn responsibilities, Cain. Walk away from this. Let me and my family be." Lee returned the statement as he stood up. Looking into Cain's eyes as he felt himself overwhelmed with bloodthirsty rage. He was shaking.

"I am doing my job, and I think we're not going to come to an understanding. I might let you run so that I can enjoy the hunt. But there is no place on earth you can ever hide from me." Cain said while he let Lee go. Watching him more, Lee nodded when he turned around.

"Oh, Cain, I've got to ask you something?" Lee turned back at him, overseeing the first killer.

"What might that be?" Cain asked while he stood there, willing to let his prey ask a final question.

"How good is your healing factor?" Lee moved over to the side. Cain looked more confused when he looked down. He saw a rope tied around his leg. How he hadn't noticed that.

"How in the?" But before he could finish his question, the rope was being pulled as He was knocked on his back being dragged away. Cain didn't even have time to react as he was pulled out of the library.

Outside the library, and in a Dodge pickup truck from around nineteen-eighty, Betsy, Alice, and Dawn were sitting in it, pushing the car at high speed as Alice called.

"Let's hope this works!" She muttered, looking back. Cain was being dragged all over the road. Dawn watched as Cain was getting run over by another car. The fact no one seemed to notice this was an understatement.

"How is it no one noticing they're running Cain over."

"Succubus Illusions while he's attacked to the rope, he looks invisible to some humans. Not going to last long!" Alice explained as she made a quick turn. Cain slammed against a pole. Betsy grunted as he watched how Cain back bent even though she thought that hurt.

Cain felt pain all over his body as he kept slamming into various things. The ground pealing his skin as he tried figuring out how fast he was going as. Cain grunted; if Cain had to guess, they were going at least forty-five miles an hour. When he felt himself bouncing in the air, he hit the pole with a hard grunt, his back snapping in response before it was repaired.

"Oh, I am going to fucking!" He screamed as he found himself turned around, his face rubbing on the Asphalt road, his voice quiet as he continued being pulled. Cain did have to admit the rope was very sturdy. He imagined he might use it on the succubus and Lee for cruel things when he got out of this.

He a massive grunt as he felt a KIA run over his neck, as it cracked. His body continuously healed itself with every bit of damage it took as Cain let out a fierce yell. His skin smelled like roasted pork.

Alice, Dawn, and Betsy stopped in a parking lot. As they turned around, seeing Cain lying there. It looked like he was a complete splatter all over the road, but they kept an eye on him. Lee, driving up along with Lucy, stopped next to the girls as they exited the car, looking back at Cain's body.

"Do you think it worked?" Lee asked while they looked at the motionless body. He didn't want to touch it. The way it looked, he wanted to gag more than anything.

"Grab the ropes… we should tie him up while he's out cold," Lee muttered, holding back his stomach. He wasn't going to brag or make a quip. He felt disgusted, never imagining he would do this to a fellow human. But it had to be done. It was him or his family. So Lee chose his family.

The succubus nodded as they untied the end of the truck as headed over to Cain, cautious about what might happen next when

Lee moved over, pushing Lee around. The way Cain's face was ripped off. He didn't even see his skull. While Lee, Imagined that he saw Cains' brains. He wasn't sure if Cain would wake up from that, not for a while.

"Lee, are you ok?" Lucy asked while he looked back. The worried look on Lucy's face as he shook his head.

"It's alright. Just… Disgusting, that's all." He muttered while he tightened his stomach and was ready to put the rope around Cain. Then without warning, Cain's hand reached up, grabbing Lee by the wrist. Lee's eyes widened in horror as Cain pulled himself up. There was a gurgling sound as Lee watched Cain's face begin to rebuild itself. Muscles regrowing around his face as he pulled himself up using Lee Like it was nothing.

"Yooou," Cain growled out, as his mouth formed as he returned to his usual self. Lee tried pulling back. Cain stood there, his clothes ripped apart as his skin healed over, and he returned to looking like his usual self and gagged out.

"Did you just try and kill me using… Looney tune logic!" He called out the rage in his voice while Lee stepped back. He could feel his anger building up faster than it had before. It was like a loop building up between them.

"I mean, I'm impressed that you were even able to do that. So how's this? I'll make your death quick because it was just that amusing!" Cain said as he slammed Lee down into the ground. His strength was inhuman, and Lee groaned, feeling the wind knocked out of him. While looking up, Cain fully healed as he looked at him with burning red eyes and kicked him.

"I was trying to be a nice guy! I didn't want to kill you if you just handed me the damn succubus. I would have been on my way, and you could have lived happily ever after or whatever shit you believe in!" He gave Lee a hard kick, sending Lee off to the side as he felt himself grunting.

"So what? I would rather die than let you hurt Lucy or Betsy." Lee groaned as he tried pulling himself up. Cain grabbed his neck, tightening his fingers around him. Lee is trying his best to gasp for air.

"Well, congrats, you'll die, and I still win," Cain growled as he planned on strangling Lee. He didn't care right then. The immortal was pissed, not even Abel screaming for his brother to stop.

Cain growled, "Not this time. I am sick of you trying to influence me!" Lee gasped, feeling like he was about to black out when There was a cracking sound without warning. Lee dropped to the ground as he took deep breaths and pulled himself up, looking over.

Samantha was standing there with a baseball bat as she had cracked over Cain's head. Though Samantha looked at Lee, she transformed into Lucy as she looked at him.

"Lee, are you alright?" She looked at him, the worry on her face. Lee gave him a thumbs up.

"Where did you get the bat from?" Lee groaned, standing up, his legs wobbling while he groaned.

"From the truck, it was in the bed." She pointed over. At the same time, Lee grunted as Cain snapped up. As he looked over at the succubus, the annoyance on his face as he rolled his neck. Lucy instantly turned into her Succubus queen form as she took another crack at Cain.

Cain was prepared for this as he caught the bat in midair, snapping it with strength. Lucy watched in shock as she pulled back, trying to stab the immortal killer.

"Come on now, that's not impressive at all!" Cain muttered as he looked at Lee. The anger is boiling over.

"I thought you'd do something more interesting but try to kill me! I invented the game of murder!" He called out while he was focused on Lee. He'd take care of Lucy later.

Lee brought his fists up and started throwing fists. He brought a right hook over at Cain, who moved out of the way as Lee, made a turn bringing his elbow off as he hit Cain in the chest. Cain took it with strive as he threw his punch. Lee groaned, feeling his jaw crack as he got knocked back. His back is going against the truck.

"Well, that didn't work." He looked back to the girls as they jumped out of the truck. The succubus transformed fire engulfing their bodies as they began running at Cain as he watched them, his eyes turning demonic, while Lucy turned and stabbed him with the splintered end of the back as he groaned.

"What a backstabber," Cain grunted while he turned around, backhanding Lucy and spinning her into the air. Her Raven wings came out as she used them to break her fall.

Betsy brought out her Colt revolver and started firing at Cain, getting nice and close, but Cain managed to dodge it, moving his body around as he grabbed the gun. He tried spinning her around using the weapon against the other, but Betsy dropped one of them as she turned into his arm, slamming her head into his. The two stumbled back in shock. Betsy rubbed her head while Cain smirked.

"Nice try, there!" He cackled, feeling alive as he watched Alice running at him. She bit into his neck, trying to rip a chunk of it out as he flung her around. Cain didn't look amused while Dawn watched in horror. He looked at her for a second, a smirk on his face.

"What's the problem, Dawn... too afraid? Your father was a killer; he was like a son to me. Now he knew how to fight!" He growled while Dawn's anger overwhelmed her when she ran at him. She screamed out.

"I'm nothing like Lucus! You sick, demented fuck!" she moved, tackling him. This managed to get Cain. As he pushed back onto the ground, she slammed her claws into him, dragging them out as she looked at him with hatred. The rage is overwhelming. The thought of Lucus. The idea of Cain, the fact she's reminded of who she was, and the death she helped in.

"I'll kill you! I'm nothing like him! I'm nothing like him!" she called out, not caring who watched as she clawed at him. Her body was overwhelmed with adrenaline as she felt rage running through her while Cain smirked as he threw a punch right into her stomach.

Dawn's eyes went blank as she felt him ripping right through her gut as she fell over.

"That was Lucus, you traitorous bitch!" He growled while he looked to see Abel, the sad expression on his face. He was shaking his head.

"What are you looking at? Go, I don't need you! I don't need anyone!" Cain said as he growled, annoyed that the ghost of his past kept coming at him. He wanted this to be over with. The father of Murder is sick of it. When he felt a punch going in his jaw, he turned to see Lee. This annoying little human had attacked him again.

298

"Why won't you stay down, you little shit!" He growled, his hair turning disheveled while Lee kept throwing punches. It didn't impress the immortal. If he had to describe it, he'd been hit by people stronger than him at this point in his life. It was like just being punched by a kid.

"Because I have to keep going! You wouldn't understand!" Lee shouted as he kept throwing punches, Cain taking them unimpressed as he was ready to end this man's life.

Cain was ready to snap Lee's neck when a gun was shot without warning, and everything went dark.

Lee stood there looking at the bullet size hole that went through Cain's head. A hard groan while Cain collapsed. There was a moment of shock as Lee was covered in the immortal being's blood.

"Is that it?" he huffed. His muscles burned while watching Cain lay there. He was looking at Betsy.

"Don't stand around and ask questions. Get the damn rope! Before he wakes up!"

It seemed like the girls were ahead of this as they started pulling the rope, tying Cain up, and ensuring it was nice and tight. He was moving over his body and knotting them so Cain couldn't break out. His arms were tied up. His legs bound up.

"Good thing I learned Shibari." Lucy panted as they tightened the last rope. Betsy looked over, more confused.

"The Hell is Shibari?"

"Rope plays… don't worry about it, come on. Let's finish this." Lucy panted while they watched Cain's head regenerating. Lee had to describe whatever happened as a miracle, but Cain seemed cold as they stuck him in the back of the truck and covered him with a tarp as they drove off. They had much to do.

Lee groaned as the girls drove. They looked worn out. Lucy looked the worst for wear as her wing bent from landing on them the wrong way.

"How's your wing, Lucy?"

"It's fine… it should heal in time." All she could say as they drove back to Lee's house.

-000-

Cain found himself waking with a hard groan as his head hurt. He tried rubbing his head when he came to realize something. He couldn't move his hand.

"What in the… What's going on." He tried moving around but couldn't see that he was in a garage. All Cain knew as he looked over, seeing the American flag. That was all he could notice.

"What is going on? Release me!" he shouted, almost demanding when Lee moved over.

"I don't think so, Cain." He came in, his body looking more bloody than needed.

"What did you do?" Cain demanded while he began to realize something. He saw bits and pieces of his body, the shock on his expression as he looked over at his arms, his fingers tied together being placed in metal boxes.

"We heard a rumor about how it takes a while to put yourself together. You can thank Dawn for that. So we decided to go with that plan. It took a while to separate. Your body kept trying to come back together. But with some torches and a bit of luck. We got you separated."

"I'll come back; I always do. I am forever."

"I believe you… why we'll make sure it takes a while before you can put yourself together." He grabbed Cain's head. Lee screamed internally as he wanted to throw the talking head but was nervous.

"I will kill you all and make sure you suffer." He growled while Lee put him in the lock box and added some duct tape, wrapping it around his mouth.

"We'll have a rain check on that." He shuddered while the girls were putting parts of his body in boxes. Nothing like the lock box, not enough that the pieces couldn't fully get out. He imagined Cain would get out, but they would be ready. But at the same time. Lee imagined they might cash in that miracle that Cain didn't escape in their lifetime.

"So where should we take this… I mean, not like we can dump it in the trash; they might hear him muffle." Lucy said while she looked exhausted, they never imagined she would cut someone open. The long motion as Betsy shook her head.

"I've dealt with worst. But we do need to find a place to hide these body parts."

The muffling from Cain's box continued while Lee shook his head.

"I have an idea, the forest; we'll bury boxes in different parts of the woods. As for the head… we'll keep it with us. Better to have it around us. So no one can find them."

They would do just that, heading out in the middle of the

night and taking boxes around the woods just outside of town where they would bury parts of Cain's body, putting them down as deep as possible. The group could only pray that no one would find these parts of Cain's body. Such a feeling while Lee looked up at the full moon. It would be a night they wouldn't soon forget.

-000-

"Are you sure you guys have to go so soon? It feels like you guy's just got here," Maddy said, hugging Lucy; The two shared a moment while Lee put their bags in the back of their truck.

"Yeah, we've got to get back to work. But it was good seeing you guys." Lee muttered while he moved, hugging his mom. Maddy nodding,

"Well, I'm glad to have you guys come over... even if it wasn't something I would expect." She said, smiling at the others. It seemed she had gotten used to the knowledge that Lucy was a succubus. It was awkward, but she accepted it.

"It was good to see you also. I'll make sure to call you guy's more often." The soft smile on his face as he tossed the muffling safe into the bed, as it let out a hard grunt.

"You better, and I want to see any grandkids you might have." Maddy teased as she moved over, kissing his cheek. Lee snorted, feeling embarrassed.

"We'll see. I'm unsure if kids will be in the future so quickly." He looked to Lucy, who smiled more, the way she watched him. It made Lee curious, but he ignored it.

"Well, don't keep me waiting, alright, bud? I wanna be a grandma." She snorted while Rufus walked over.

"Maddy, let the boy be. It'll happen when it happens."

Rufus shook Lee's hand before pulling him in for a big old bear hug. The two held it for a second, as Rufus said.

"You've become a good man Lee; I'm proud of you." The moment was soft before they separated

"Thanks, Dad; well, we better get going."

Lee and Lucy got into the truck, Betsy sitting inside, and they soon drove off, heading home. A moment of silence as they listened to the radio. They could only hope that everything would go back to average, at least as usual, for someone married to a Succubus.

EPILOGUE

Lee and the girls made it back to the apartment. Lucy is resting up in the seat next to him. Her head rested against him while Lee smiled; Betsy looked out the window. It was clear that the drive had taken a bit out of them. Even Cain had eventually stopped making noise at this point. Lee imagined it didn't help with how many bumps they took. But he chose to ignore that.

"Well, we're here." He smiled, looking back to Lucy as he nudged her awake. Lucy looked around with a small smile.

"Finally, home. Glad to be home." Lucy muttered while she stretched out her body, popping and looking at Lee.

"Hmm, you know, with Cain and all that, we didn't get to celebrate our Honeymoon." She smiled, leaning in and kissing his cheek. All while, Lee laughed as they got out of the car.

"Well, I'm sure that we can come up with something. But it'll come back later." He remembered that card the succubus Mirage had given him, and it made him wonder if he would bring it up to her. Before deciding to leave it be for the moment.

"I'm sure you will. Though one thing we need to do." She leaned in closer. Her succubus form was still in place as her crown of thorns glowed gently. She gave him a seductive smirk.

"Hmm, you have a point there. Yet your sister is still here, and

I wanna make this night special." He chuckled while he wrapped his arms around her, his fingers brushing against her wings, which had slowly healed up during the drive.

"Go one; I'm going to deal with the head. Besides, I don't wanna listen to my sister and her husband fucking." The southern cowgirl said as she jumped into the truck bed, her arm resting on the safe as Lee nodded.

"Hey, thanks for that."

"Don't thank me. Get going and let me know when you're done," Betsy said as she reached around, polishing her gun. While she got comfortable imagining that it might be a while before she would head inside. Besides, it was a beautiful night. The stars are sparkling at night, and the moon is packed like a dinner plate. Betsy imagined she could sleep under the stars. Remind her of those simple nights back in the South.

Lee looked over to his wife and gave a nod, a light smirk.

"So how about it, want to consummate the marriage?" he said in a cheesy tone while Lucy found herself giggling at the reaction.

"Oh, I suppose, but never do it in that tone again." She smirked, flicking his nose as they headed up the stairs. Lee ran behind her. Betsy could watch their stuff. For the time being. As they headed up the stairs to their apartment building. Lucy standing there as he took the final step up. She looked beyond beautiful. Those sultry red eyes, the light smile on her dark skin. She showed her succubus form, not caring if someone caught them. The fact it was just the two of them. Lee found himself tempted to take her right now in the hallway.

It took every ounce of willpower for him not to do that as he looked at her, unlocked the door, and opened it.

"Ladies first." He chuckled, but Lucy shook her head as she expanded her wings, jumping into his arms.

"You know the rules carry me in there." She winked, her arms wrapping around his neck as he steadied himself.

"Oh, how could I have forgotten." Lee snorted while walking through the door, helping her right inside while he let out a few grunts.

"Grr, gru grunt!" Lee said to her while she returned it.

"Urrg urr hurrg!" They laughed at the primate noises as Lee kicked the door behind him closed and put Lucy down. She smirked while the two ran to the bedroom, removing their clothes as much as they could as they tossed them where ever they landed. Lucy enticed him to the bedroom door as she opened the door, covering her naked frame as she stood there nearly naked.

"So, my sexy human, are you ready to ravage your Succubus wife?"

"Don't you know it?" He smirked, licking his lips as Lucy pulled her red silk down. She tossed it to him, and Lee caught it. The soft fabric in his hand as he chuckled,

"Well, Mrs. West, shall we begin?"

Lucy headed into the room while Lee closed the door behind him—the panties hanging from the knob.

It would be a night of lovemaking and the beginning of a new chapter in their life.

The End…

.

ABOUT THE AUTHOR

Dustin Midnight, the author of the first Bordello series and the book, married to a goddess and to buy a succubus works on them in his home up north of Ohio. When he's not writing his stories he works off in a factory, or reading a good book, if you wish to support him check out his patreon and Discord.

Patreon/ https://www.patreon.com/Mrmidnightwolf
Discord/ https://discord.gg/AeZBhyR
Scribblehub/ https://www.scribblehub.com/profile/77594/mr.midnight/

Made in the USA
Coppell, TX
11 July 2023